"I've really enjoyed happenstancing with you, Miz Renzetti," said McGee.

"Always before I felt squeamish about big tall men," said Annie.

"And little dark women have not exactly figured large in my erotic fantasies, kid."

"They might from now on?"

"Front and center."

"You said enjoyed?"

"I did."

"Past tense?"

"My dear lady, it is quarter past three in the morning."

"So?"

"My ramparts are breached, my legions scattered, my empire burned to the ground, my fleet at the bottom of the sea. And you would—"

"Hush," she said softly.

Fawcett Gold Medal Books
in the Travis McGee Series
by John D. MacDonald

FREE FALL IN CRIMSON

John D. MacDonald

FAWCETT GOLD MEDAL • NEW YORK

A Fawcett Gold Medal Book
Published by Ballantine Books
Copyright © 1981 John D. MacDonald Publishing, Inc.

ISBN 0-449-12378-2

Manufactured in the United States of America

First Fawcett Gold Medal Edition: December 1981
First Ballantine Books Edition: June 1982

For Dorothy again

I had so often in the past seen dumb domestic animals in Africa so aware of the secret intent of the people who had bred and reared them and earned their trust that they could hardly walk, knowing they were being led to a distant place of slaughter.

Laurens Van Der Post,
The Night of the New Moon

He will wonder whether he should have told these young, handsome and clever people the few truths that sing in his bones.

These are:

(1) Nobody can ever get too much approval.
(2) No matter how much you want or need, *they*, whoever *they* are, don't want to let you get away with *it*, whatever *it* is.
(3) Sometimes you get away with it.

John Leonard,
Private Lives in the Imperial City

1

We talked past midnight, sat in the deck chairs on the sun deck of the *Busted Flush* with the starry April sky overhead, talked quietly, and listened to the night. Creak and sigh of hulls, slap of small waves against pilings, muted motor noises of the fans and generators and pumps aboard the work boats and the play toys.

"I don't really know how the law works," Ron Esterland said. "But I would think that if you arranged someone's death, even if he were dying already, you shouldn't inherit."

"Where do you come in?" Meyer asked.

Esterland took a long time answering. "All right. If some money came to me, I wouldn't turn it down. Maybe to that extent I've grown up a little. But I can get along without it. Years ago I would have turned down anything my father wanted to give me or leave me. If, Travis, as a result of your efforts, anything *does* come to me, the deal is that you get half. But the chance is so remote, I pay expenses."

I got up and stretched, went to the rail, and did some push-offs against it and some deep knee bends. The night was chill for April, and after my heavy morning workout, sitting so long had made me stiffen up.

I turned and asked Ron to straighten out the chronology of the Esterland wives for me. "I guess it is confusing," he said. "My mother, Connie, was wife number one. She died when I was eleven. Dad married Judy Prisco when I was twelve. She was a dancer. They had no children. They were divorced in six months. It was quick and ugly, and she accepted a sizable settlement. When I was thirteen he married Josephine Laurant, the actress. She and I got along well. I was sent away to school when I was sixteen. Romola, their daughter, was almost three then. I never really went home again. There were some big scenes. My father didn't like to be crossed by anybody, for any reason. He and Josie got a legal separation after ten years of marriage. Romola was nine. A nice little kid. Josie went out to the West Coast to live. It was what they called a friendly separation."

"When did they find out your father had cancer?" I asked.

"A little over three years ago. He spent the first few months liquidating his holdings. That is, when he got out of the hospital after the exploratory, and when the radiology and the chemotherapy didn't leave him too debilitated. Then he began to feel better. He had a remission. That's when he moved down here to Fort Lauderdale and bought the motor sailer and moved aboard with the woman who had been working for him for several years. Anne Renzetti. As part of putting his affairs in order, he made a new will. As I remember, his previous one left me ten dollars. So he could mention my name, I guess. The new will set up some bequests for Josie and Anne and left the bulk of the estate to Romola. Then there was a paragraph about what should happen if Romola predeceased him, which nobody really expected her to do at that time. If that happened, then the money she would have gotten would go to the setting up of an Esterland Foundation, to make grants for research into neutralizing dangerous chemical wastes before disposal by industry. He thought that's where he got his cancer, from working with plastics and reagents, chemicals of all kinds. That portion of the will, that contingency portion, left me a hundred thousand dollars. Which of course I didn't get. But it was nice to know my stock had risen that much in his estimation."

"And then Romola had her accident?" Meyer asked.

"Yes. Two years ago next month. May tenth. There was a severe skull fracture, and she never came out of the anesthetic. She was plugged into a life-support system. The brain waves were increasingly flat. Josie kept trying to believe there was hope. She died finally on August tenth. She had turned twenty. But by then my father was dead. He was beaten to death near Citrus City on the twenty-fourth of July. So Romola was his heir."

"How much did the girl inherit?" Meyer asked.

"Three and a half million after taxes, but then of course when Josie inherited from Romola, the government took a large slice. A little more than a million dollars."

I went back and sat down. Ronald Esterland sighed audibly. He was a blond man, going bald at thirty-four, with big hands and thick shoulders, a bland face, a good smile.

"I think what is bothering me," Meyer said, "and

Travis too, is why you waited a year and a half to look into this whole thing."

"I can't give a good answer to that. I'm sorry. I was in London, and I had a chance to exhibit in the Sloane Gallery. I had enough work on hand for about half the space they were ready to let me have. And it was a chance to work in some bigger pieces. I kept telling myself I didn't care what had happened to my father. He was a brutal man. He said brutal things. He tried to destroy the people around him. And somebody had the good judgment to beat him to death. I worked like hell, and I filled the good spaces in that gallery. The show was a success. The reviews were better than any of my group expected. Eight paintings were sold at the opening, and by the end of the first week there were only four left unsold, and three of those were huge. I went back one afternoon. Very few people there. I roamed the show, seeing all the little red stars they stuck on the paintings to indicate they were sold. I had a feeling of pride and satisfaction, but at the same time I felt a kind of desolation. A kind of bleakness. I realized then that my father had been dead a year and I hadn't really understood what it meant to me. A lot of my motivation had been to *show* him that I had value, that I was valued by the world, and so I was worthy of his love and his respect. He had never shown me love or respect. I know how deeply I had wanted those things. I had wanted to make him come around. And I couldn't. He was gone. He had somehow escaped, and I felt frustrated. When the show came down, I closed the studio and moved back to New York. Back home. I found that I could work, after a fashion, but not as well as I wanted to work. I kept thinking about my father and Romola and the ugly fact of the murder of a dying man. So I came down here because this is where he had lived, aboard his boat, for the months before he died. That's how come I ran into Sarah Issom. I hadn't seen her for years, since I lived in Greenwich Village. She's doing damned fine work, and she said you bought one of her paintings."

"A little seascape. An aerial view. Lots of blue in it. I am a junky for blue."

"She has a lot of skill. She told me you did a favor for her a few years ago, and you might be the one to do a favor for me."

"I'm not a private detective."

"You said that before. I know."

"I have no official standing. I don't want to get into anything where I attract too much attention from the law, because I have no status. They don't like people meddling. They don't like amateurs."

"I've put ten thousand dollars aside for expenses."

"I want to think about it," I told him. "I'll be in touch one way or the other."

So we shook hands around and he went down the ladderway and back to the stern and down the little gangway to the dock. I heard his heels on the cement as I watched him walk off, passing under the dock lights, his long shadow moving and changing with each light.

I went back and sat by Meyer.

"So?" he said.

"So. So I know now that I can't make it doing odd jobs here and there, and if I want to make it, I will have to seek honest work, like in Rob Brown's Boat Yard. Or with Acme Diving and Salvage. Or working for a yacht broker. Travis McGee, your friendly boat salesman. With a salary, bonuses, and a retirement plan."

"And," said Meyer, "on your days off you can sit around here on the houseboat and whine and whinny about how jaded life has become."

I stared over at him in the darkness. "I have been doing that quite a lot, haven't I?"

"Not more than I can stand. But enough."

"What can I tell you? I swam for three hours yesterday, some of it as hard as I could go. I woke up this morning feeling great. Absolutely great. Busting with energy. Know something? I *want* to get involved in the life and times of Esterland and son. I want to go out and con the people. I want to have to bust a couple of heads here and there and have somebody try to bust mine for me. Why should I feel a little bit guilty about feeling like that, Meyer?"

"Maybe you got so you were enjoying the ennui."

"The what?"

"Ennui, you illiterate. That is the restless need for some kind of action without having the outlet for any action at all. It is like *weltschmerz*."

"Which, as you have so often told me, is homesickness for a place you have never seen. I miss Gretel, Meyer. God, how I miss her! But she is dead and gone, and the stars are bright and the night wind blows, and the universe is slowly unfolding, revealing its wonders. What was your impression of Ellis Esterland?"

"I did spend a couple of evenings with him. And Miss Renzetti. Not actually out of choice. He wanted to pick my brain, and I his. He wanted to know some of the banking practices in Grand Cayman, and I wanted to know which plastics companies were going to lead the pack in the future, based on new discoveries. What was he like? He tried to give the impression of being bluff and hearty and homespun. But he was a shrewd and subtle man. A good watcher. A good listener. I had no idea he was as sick as they say he was because that had to be—let me think back—two years ago in May, two months before he died."

"What happened to his lady? Do you know?"

"Anne Renzetti? She stood up to him pretty well. I think he had a habit of bullying his women. I heard that she's over in Naples, Florida, working in a resort hotel. Mmmm. Eden Beach! Correct."

"She was in the will?"

"I don't know, but I would think she was. She had been an employee. When he sold out his plastics company years ago, he set himself up as a management consultant, specializing in chemical and plastics companies, and from what he said I think he must have had a staff of a dozen or so. The offices were in Stamford, Connecticut. When he got sick he sold out and kept the Renzetti woman as a private secretary to help him put his affairs in order. After he was killed, the executor let her live aboard the boat until it was sold."

I went back to the rail, snuffed the night. No traffic sounds. No surf sounds. Fifty boats away a night woman gave a maniacal cry of laughter, as abrupt and meaningless as the honk of a night-flying bird. I did not trust the rising sense of anticipation I felt. I had tried to fit myself to somberness, to a life of reserve. I had located a couple of boats for people, for a finder's fee. I had ferried a couple of big ones—a Hatteras over to Mobile, a Pacemaker up to Maryland—and flown back. I'd done some work for one of the brokers, putting bargain boats through their paces for people who wanted to believe how easy it was before making the down payment.

I told myself I had lived in a house of many rooms, but there had been a fire, and it was all charred to hell except for a small attic bedroom. A bed, a chair, a table, and a window. And if anybody wanted to take a shot, I would happily stand in the window.

But you can't cut your life back like some kind of ornamental shrub. I couldn't put the old white horse out to pasture, hock the tin armor, stand the lance in a corner of the barn. For a little while, yes. For the healing time.

It was more than economics. I could tell myself I needed the money. And I did. More than the money, I needed the sense of being myself, full size, undwarfed by my disasters.

I turned to Meyer and said, "I think I could find something where the chance of some kind of recovery would be better."

"Maybe."

"Ron Esterland is a little paranoid about the whole situation. He's got a hang-up about his father. He isn't thinking clearly."

"Probably he isn't."

"I don't see what Anne Renzetti would be able to tell me that would be any help at all."

"Neither do I."

"Want to ride over to Naples with me?"

"I would enjoy that. Yes."

"Thanks for talking me into it, Meyer."

"For a little while I didn't think I could do it."

2

Meyer waited in my old blue Rolls pickup while I talked money and time with Ron Esterland. Then in midmorning on a fine April Saturday, I drove over to Alligator Alley and we went humming westward past the wetlands, the scrub palmetto, the dwarf cypress. Traffic was heavy. Each year the gringos stay down longer. Each year too many of them come down to stay forever. Once the entire state becomes asphalt, high rises, malls, highway, fast food, and littered beaches, they will probably still keep coming.

The computer in one of the basements inside Meyer's skull predicts an eventual Florida population of thirty-two million folk, and by that time it will level off because it will not be any more desirable to live in Florida than it is to live in Rhode Island or West Virginia.

"What can you remember about Ellis Esterland's murder?" I asked Meyer. He walked back into his computer room and checked out the right floppy disc and played it back for me.

"On a very hot day Esterland drove up to Citrus City, in River County. That is about a hundred and twenty miles from Fort Lauderdale. Miss Renzetti offered to drive him, but he said he would go alone. She said he was feeling much better that month, even though he was depressed by his daughter's condition. He did not tell Miss Renzetti why he was going to Citrus City. And nobody ever found out. He was driving a dark gray Lincoln Continental. He had lunch alone at the Palmer Hotel, in the center of the city, and sat in the lobby for a time reading the *Wall Street Journal*. No one noticed his departure. Apparently he drove his car back over to the Florida Turnpike and stopped at a rest area six miles south of the interchange for Citrus City. A trucker found the body and reported it on CB radio. He was face down on the floor in front of the rear seat with his legs doubled under him. His wallet was on the front seat. His money was gone. Miss Renzetti said he probably had about two hundred dollars with him. He had been severely beaten. Blood beside the car and spattered against it indicated that he had probably been tossed into the back after the beating. Skull fractures, jaw fracture, broken facial bones, broken ribs. Nobody saw anything. No witness ever came forth. There were no clues."

"I think I was out of town at the time."

"You were. It was an overnight sensation. DYING MILLIONAIRE SLAIN. KILLED IN HIGHWAY ASSAULT. But it soon became yesterday's news. Oh, as I remember there was a second little flurry when the terms of his will became known. GIRL IN COMA INHERITS FORTUNE. That sort of thing. I think the headlines called him the Plastics King."

"And if you had to guess?"

"Ellis Esterland was a very abrasive man. He was

cordially disliked by a great many people. I think that if he felt unwell, he would have stopped where they found him. And if anyone had tried to talk to him, he would probably have said something ugly to them. I would guess there was only one person involved."

"Why do you say that?"

"The money was taken, but not the expensive car. It was a new car. If two people had arrived in one vehicle, one of them could have taken the car. If there was only one person, their identity could have been traced through the vehicle they would have left behind."

"Meyer, there is a difference between logic and implausibility."

"I've never noticed that logic needs be plausible."

He retreated into silence. I knew that he was back there in one of his thinking rooms, working things out. Staring into the fire. Patting the cat.

I noticed a marsh hawk on a dead branch and pointed it out. "*Circus cyaneus hudsonius,*" Meyer said. I turned and stared at him. He coughed and said, "Sorry about that. It's a twitch. Like hiccups. Compulsive classification. I try not to do it. Can't help observations. Such as what you do when you get annoyed. You go ten miles an hour faster."

I dropped the speed back where it belonged.

We got off the Alley and took 858 into downtown Naples and out to the beach, turned right, and drove along hotel row until we came to the Eden Beach. I drove the long curve of sleek asphalt past the portico and on over into their parking area. A man tending the plantings stopped and stared slack-jawed at the Rolls pickup. It has that effect. The conversion was done clumsily during the Great Depression. Four fat women in shorts were on the big putting green, grimly improving their game. Through big-leafed tropic growth I could see the blue slosh of the swimming pool, and I heard somebody body-smack into it off the rumbling board. I saw a slice of Gulf horizon, complete with distant schooner. We went up three broad white steps and through a revolving door into the cool shadows of the lobby. A very pretty lady behind the reception desk smiled at us, frowned at her watch, picked up a phone, punched out two numbers, then spoke in a low voice.

"She'll be right out," the nice lady said.

"What kind of work does she do here?"

"Oh, she's our manager! She's the *boss*."

Anne Renzetti appeared a few minutes later, looking unlike a boss. I had forgotten what a vivid little woman she was. Black black hair, dark eyes, black brows, a slash of red mouth. She wore a beige suit, white crisp shirt, green silk scarf knotted at her throat, very high heels. She walked trimly, swiftly, toward us, giving Meyer a smile of genuine pleasure at seeing him again, holding her cheek up for a kiss, favoring me with a quick handshake and a dubious look.

"McGee?" I said. "Travis McGee?"

"I think I remember you.... Meyer, how *are* you? You look absolutely wonderful. Gentlemen, perhaps you will join me for a drink? I was getting ready to leave. Marie? I'll be at my place if anything comes up."

We followed her out the west doors, through the pool area past a thatched outdoor beach bar, and down to the farthest cabana. It was on pilings six feet high. We went up the stairs to a shallow porch with a broad overhang. A nice breeze was coming off the Gulf. The tubular chairs were comfortable. We approved her suggestion of vodka and grapefruit juice, and she declined any help. When she came back with the drinks on a small tray, she had changed to white shorts and a pink gauze top.

Meyer said, "Congratulations on your exalted position, Anne."

She made a face. "It was sort of an accident, actually. First, I was secretary to Mr. Luddwick and then the company moved him to Hawaii, to a bigger hotel. His replacement was driving from Baltimore, and he got into a really bad accident. He was alone and fell asleep and went off the road. They thought he might be laid up for six weeks to two months, and they asked me if I could carry on alone here—with a small raise in pay, of course. I said sure. They had to pin the man's broken hip, and he got an infection, and finally, when he was ready to report, somebody had the good sense to look at the results for the three months I had been running it, and they decided they shouldn't change a thing. I owe getting the top job to Ellis Esterland."

"You do?" Meyer said, astonished.

"I cover every inch of this place at least once a month. I know what every employee is doing and what they are supposed to be doing. I know where every penny of expense goes. I listen personally to every gripe. Ellis taught me that there are people who try to look as if they are doing a good and thorough job, and then there are the people who actually damn well do it, for its own sake. I'm proud of myself, damn it. And I *love* being the boss. I really love it! Everything you do in life is worth infinite care and infinite effort, Ellis said. He said that in a half-ass world the real achiever is king. He used to make me do things over if I made the tiniest mistake. He used to make me cry. But, wow, I really owe him."

"Nice-looking place," I said.

"Why have you looked me up?" she asked.

Meyer left it up to me. "We were talking with Ronald Esterland yesterday night in Lauderdale, Miss Renzetti."

"With Ron! You were? How is he? What is he doing?"

"Fine, apparently. He had a big show of his work in London and he sold most of it. He is beginning to get a lot of attention."

"I'm so *glad!* You know, I thought Ellis had really gutted him. I really thought Ron would never amount to anything. His father thought Ron's ambition to be a painter was absurd. He thought it was a cop-out, an excuse for not working. I tried in little ways to get Ellis to get in touch with Ron. But he wouldn't. I felt ...maternal about Ron, which is strange because he's a little older than I am. I think Josie felt that way, or feels that way, about him too, and though she is older than he is, she certainly isn't old enough to be his mother. It really crushed Josie, losing Romola the way she did.... What does Ron have to do with your looking me up?"

"His attitude toward his father has mellowed, Miss Renzetti."

"Please call me Anne."

"Thank you, Anne. Ron realized that he lost some of the fun of success because his father wasn't alive to see it happen."

"Ellis would have been totally astonished. He used to say to people, 'I've got a middle-aged son living abroad making funny daubs on canvas, trying to live in the wrong century.'"

"He isn't satisfied with the story of his father's death."

"Who is? They never found out a thing. Not a single thing. And it happened in such a public place. It doesn't seem possible they couldn't find out *something*."

"So I'm poking around."

"Are you some sort of police officer?"

Meyer answered, "No, he's just a private citizen. But he's had a lot of luck finding things for people, answering questions people have had. You can trust him, Anne."

"With what? I don't know anything I haven't told the police long ago. It wasn't too pleasant, you know. I was a single woman living aboard a fancy boat with a rich old dying man. They were less than polite. They wanted to know what boyfriends I had on the side. They wanted to know, if Ellis was so sick, why I hadn't driven him up there. Was he getting a divorce from Josephine? Did I plan to marry him if he got a divorce? Had we quarreled before he drove up there? Finally I had enough and I told them I wasn't answering any more questions. They tried to bully me, but I had been bullied by one of the world's greatest, so it didn't work. Look, tell Ron I'm so glad he's making it. And tell him I feel quite certain Ellis would have come around and been proud of him too. Will you do that?"

"Of course we will," Meyer said. "Did Ellis go off on trips like that often, without telling you why?"

"Never! Here's all I know about that trip. He was feeling better. He'd been—regaining lost ground for a month. He had picked up some of the weight he had lost, and his color was better. He was talking about being strong enough to fly out to Los Angeles to see Romola and talk to Josie and the doctors. He wanted to see Romola, but at the same time he dreaded it. He had talked to the doctors on the phone. They said there was no hope at all for her. It was a terrible thing for him. I think he really loved Romola. I don't think there was ever any other person in his life he had loved. Not me. Not anyone. So, okay, when I came back from shopping on Monday, the day before he was killed, he was talking on the phone. Mostly he was just saying 'Okay, okay, okay.' I had the feeling it was a long-distance call. They checked the phone records afterward, and if it was long distance, it wasn't an outgoing call. He seemed thoughtful that afternoon and evening, and before we went to bed he told me he was going up to Citrus City the next day. He said he would go alone. He wouldn't tell me why he was going. He told me to stop asking questions."

"Do you have any idea why he didn't want to tell you?"

"It wasn't like him not to. Not that he was so very open with me. It was just that he didn't care what I knew about him. I wasn't in any position to disapprove of anything he might do. I don't know why I didn't walk out. It just didn't occur to me that I could. Does that make any sense? I was in a cage with the door open, and I never even noticed the door. Now here is the only dumb guess I could come up with. He had a scientific mind. He started as a research chemist, you know. The one thing he hated above all else was doing something ridiculous and being found out. He knew how sick he was. We told each other that the remission was holding, and maybe he had licked the cancer. But he knew better than that. It had metastasized before it was first diagnosed. Chemotherapy had knocked it down for a little while, long enough for him to recover from most of the effects of the therapy, but when the remission ended, the next series of chemotherapy treatments would, if they suppressed the cancer at all, knock him back further than the previous set. And the pain would be back too. The only thing I can think of that would make him keep a secret from me was the idea I might ridicule him. Hope can be a dreadful thing, I guess. If he was going off to track down some sort of a quack cure, I don't think he would have told me."

"Is there some kind of miracle cure available in Citrus City?"

"I never tried to find out. But I would think that if there was, the police up there would have checked to see if he made contact, once they knew of his condition."

Meyer cleared his throat and looked uncomfortable. We looked at him and he said, "There's always the remote possibility that he didn't tell you because he thought you would try any means of stopping him if you knew."

"Knew what?"

"That he knew exactly what was in store for him with what was left of his life, and he had been arranging to get himself killed."

She stared at him wide-eyed. "No," she said firmly. "No, Meyer. Not Ellis. Not like that. This might sound sick, but I think he was enjoying the battle too much. He was a very gutsy man. All man. Cancer was challenging him. It pushed and he pushed back. He would delay taking pain pills, and keep track of how bad the pain was. No. To him it would have been like some kind of dirty surrender. He was building himself up to give it another battle."

"Suggestion withdrawn," Meyer said.

"Would it have had anything to do with Romola?" I asked.

"If that was so, he would have told me."

"Could he have been going to buy a present of some kind?"

"He wasn't much for presents and surprises. On my birthdays he would give me money to go out and shop for myself."

"Was there any clue as to what he was going to do in what he picked to wear?" I asked.

"Not really. He wore gray slacks and a pale blue knit sports shirt with short sleeves. He took a seersucker jacket along to wear if he was in very cold air conditioning. I think he wore it in that hotel, from what the police said. But he wasn't wearing it when he...when they killed him."

She hitched her chair forward and hooked her bare heels over the porch railing. Her legs were well-formed and slender. The skin, moderately tan, looked flawless as plastic.

"I've been over it ten thousand times. It seems so pointless, dying like that. I wouldn't admit it to myself at the time, but I did later: I was relieved. I'd been bracing myself to go all the way with him. Through all the pain. Caring for him when he became helpless. I was getting myself charged up to really do a job. But at the same time I dreaded it. Which is natural. He didn't love me. He sort of *liked* me. I had good lines and I was obedient, like a show dog. And I sort of loved him.

"There can be a habit of love, I think. You justify the way you are living by telling yourself that love leaves you no other choice. And so you are into love. Women stay with dreadful men. You see it all the time. You wonder why. You know they are wasting their lives. You know they are worth far more than what they have. But they stay on and on. They grow old staying on and on. They say it is love so often to themselves, it does become love. I can't understand the Anne Renzetti I was then. I look back and I don't understand her at all. We're all lots of people, I guess. We become different people in response to different times and places, different duties. Maybe in a lifetime we become a very limited bunch of people when, in fact, we could become many many more—if life moved us around more.

"Well, it moved me here and I know who I am now, and I will stay with this life for as long as I can. I never even suspected who I might really be. If it hadn't been for that new manager falling asleep at the wheel, I might never have known about this Anne. You can't miss what you don't know, can you? Maybe that's why we all have that funny little streak of sadness from time to time. We are missing something and don't even know what it is, or whether it will ever be revealed to us."

Meyer looked approvingly at her. "When you know who you really are, you fit more comfortably into your skin. You give less of a damn what kind of impression you make on people. My friend McGee here has never been at all certain of his identity."

She gave me a quick, tilt-eyed, searching glance. It had an unexpected impact. "Thinking of himself as some kind of rebel?" she asked.

"Something like that," Meyer agreed. "A reluctance to expend emotion, and a necessity to experience it. Cool and hot. Hard and soft. Rattling around in his life, bouncing off the walls."

"Would it make you two any more comfortable if I went for a walk?" I asked. "Then you can really dig into my psyche. Meyer, for God's sake, what kind of friendship and loyalty are you showing me?"

"Sorry," he said. "I keep thinking of Anne as an old friend of both of us. As a matter of fact, we only really talked one time, didn't we?"

"For a couple of hours one night, aboard the *Caper*, after Ellis went to bed. But it made me feel as if I'd always known you. All the way back to childhood."

"The way he can do that," I said, "could have made him one of the world's greatest con men. But he has scruples. And they get in the way of the con."

"So you are sort of a team of con men, conning me?" she asked.

"Let's say we share your interest in finding out more about how Ellis Esterland died," I told her.

"Perhaps I haven't got a hell of a lot of real interest left? No. That's unfair. He was an important part of my life. I worked for him for six years. I can say I never really understood the man."

"Did any of his wives?" I asked her.

"I don't know about the first one, Ron's mother. Her name was Connie, and I've heard she was a real beauty. I've never seen a picture of her. Ellis didn't keep pictures of people around. Of course Judy Prisco and Josie Laurant were—are—both handsome. He liked to be seen in the company of women who make heads turn. I would suspect I was low on the list. But in the right light I've had my moments. Whenever we went out together he would look me over first. Very critical of the color and design of clothes, the shape of a hairdo, the right jewelry. The marriage to Judy ended very quickly. And she did very well; she walked away with a bundle. Of course, at his death, he was still married to Josie, even though they were legally separated. Maybe she understood him, I don't really know. I like her."

"You've met her?" Meyer asked.

"Oh, yes. When Ellis went downhill so fast, in the beginning, she flew out. I don't really know if it was genuine concern or a feeling of obligation. He was sending her almost five thousand a month as support. She spent a lot of time with him during the ten days she was in Stamford. She and I talked a lot, after visiting hours were over. That was after the exploratory. We were wary with each other at first. You can understand that. After all, she was still married to him, and I was the quote other woman close quote. She's an unusual person. She's very emotional. I don't think she knows what she's going to do or say next. And I will tell you, she at that time was just about the best-looking mother of a twenty-year-old I have ever seen. Wow. Fantastic. And she used to be such a marvelous actress."

"She gave it up?" I asked.

"Or it gave her up. Ellis talked about it a few times. Too much temperament. Or temper. Too hard to handle."

"Have you seen her since?" I asked.

"No. But we talked, after Romola was hurt. She would call me up and we would talk. It seemed to help her to talk to me. It seemed to settle her down. She'd be practically hysterical when she would place the call."

"Did Ellis know how bad off he was?" Meyer asked. "Did the doctors level with him?"

"Oh, yes. They had to. He was quick to detect any kind of evasion. It was almost impossible to lie to him. He had an excellent specialist. Dr. Prescott Mullen. Prescott flew down several times to check him over when we were living on the *Caper*. We became very good friends, actually. He's a fine man." There had been a subtle stress on the qualifying word "very." "As a matter of fact," she continued, "I'm expecting him here tomorrow, to stay for a week. He said on the phone he's been working too hard and needs a break."

"I wonder if he could add anything," Meyer said.

"Like what?" Anne asked.

"Well, if Esterland was facing a very untidy end, a highly unpleasant finale to his life, he might not have told you, Anne. I still wonder about his arranging his own death. Was there insurance?"

"Yes. Quite a large policy. But it would have been good even if he had killed himself with a gun. He'd had it a long time."

"You knew his personal financial affairs?"

"I was his secretary, Meyer. I kept the books, balanced the checkbooks, dealt with the brokers and the lawyers. That was my job. There was a lot to do because he changed his legal residence to Florida and established new banking and trust department connections in Fort Lauderdale. The bank and I were co-executors of his will, so I got a fee for that as well as the money he left me. I can see you both wondering. Was it very much? I'll tell you. It was twenty thousand dollars. It fooled me. I guessed it would be lots or nothing. I thought it would be nothing because I wasn't in the will. It was a codicil he'd added a month before he was killed. But to repeat myself, Ellis would never never arrange his own death."

"The point Ron was making," I told her, "was that anybody who arranged the death of a dying man shouldn't inherit. So what we are talking about is the way Josephine Laurant Esterland inherited the bulk of the estate."

It startled her. She swung her feet down from the railing and turned to face me more directly. "Ron is thinking that? It seems sort of sick. I mean, it seems so...cumbersome. A public place like that. Witnesses. So much could go wrong. I see what he means, of course: that if Romola died in that coma, which she so apparently was going to do and finally did, then Josie would get only a small bequest. The support stopped when Ellis died. We—Ellis and I—we were taking it for granted that he was going to outlive his daughter. And we were talking about the foundation. And he had appointments with the lawyers and trust people and his CPA to work out the final details. He died before he could keep those final appointments. He hadn't really put much thought into the foundation until Romola had that terrible accident. And we knew she probably would die. And yes, it did make a difference of an awful lot of money to Josie to have Romola outlive her dad. Josie would make such a terrible conspirator. She babbles. She can't keep secrets."

"Are you in touch with her?" I asked.

"I think I owe her a letter. We've been tapering off. After all, Ellis was all we had in common, and memories of Ellis aren't enough to keep a friendship going. In her last letter she said she was going back to work, that it wasn't really a very good part, but she was looking forward to it, to working again."

She sighed, looking downward into her glass. I liked the line of cheek and jaw, the gentle look of the long dark lashes, the breasts small under rosy gauze, the pronounced convexity of the top of the thigh. Except for small lines at the corners of her eyes, a puffiness under her chin, the years had left her unmarked. She checked the glasses, took them in to fix another drink.

When she came back out, she said, "I can understand why Ron is suspicious and upset. But I think it just happened. I don't think anybody planned it. What will you do next?"

"Go to Citrus City and see if the River County sheriff has anything at all," I said.

"If he had anything, wouldn't he have arrested somebody?"

"You have to have some pretty solid facts before you arrest anybody. He might have some suspicions he'd talk about."

"Let me buy you gentlemen some lunch, one of the Eden Beach's great luncheon taste treats."

"Why should you buy us lunch?" Meyer asked.

She patted his arm. "Promotion and advertising, dear Meyer. I have a nice expense account all my own and I hardly ever get a chance to use it. So humor me."

3

In the early afternoon I turned off Route 41 onto 846 and drove the small empty roads over past Corkscrew, Immokalee, Devil's Garden. The tourists were booming down the big roads, white-knuckled in the traffic, waiting for the warning signals from their Fuzzbusters, staring out at endless strips of junk stores, cypress knees, plaster herons, and instant greasy chicken. We rumbled gently along through the wild country, watching the birds, the dangle of Spanish moss, the old ranch houses set way back under the shade trees, the broad placid faces of the Brahma cattle.

I went up 27 past Sebring, Avon Park, and Frostproof, went over 630 through Indian Lake Estates, and came up on Citrus City from the west. The groves marched over the rolling land, neat as Prussians. Some rain guns were circling, the mist blowing across the ranks of trees.

We agreed on a motel west of the city limits at about six o'clock. Low white frame structure with a central office and restaurant portion looking like a piece of

Mount Vernon. Above five cars were lined up in front of their thirty units.

There was a thin, middle-aged, weather-worn woman behind the desk. She had tooth trouble and held her mouth funny when she talked, and quite often put her hand in front of her mouth, the gesture of a child hiding laughter.

Once we had signed in and paid in advance, I said to her, "Say, is Dave Banks still sheriff?"

She stared at me. "Lordie, no! Dave's dead six year anyway. Guess you *have* been gone a time. The sherf we got now, he's new last election. Milford Hampton. They call him Fish, but not to his face, on account he looks kind of like a fish, his mouth and the way his eyes are set. Maybe you heard of the family. His granddaddy had the big Star Bar ranch north of town. Still in the family, what's left of it after they sold off some for groves and some for town houses."

"I think I heard the name."

"He's trying to do a job, but this place is getting rougher every year. I don't know what's doing it. Floaters and drifters. Boozing and knifing folks. Used to be quiet and pretty and nice. Now a lady wouldn't want to go into town of a Saturday night at all. The good stores, they're all out in the Groveway Mall. Look, you men want a good honest dinner at an honest price, we're serving from six to eight thirty. Tonight is ribs and chicken."

The River County sheriff's office and jail were in a white modern building diagonally across the street from the ornate yellow turrets and minarets of the old county courthouse. County cars and patrol cars were parked in a wire enclosure beside the building. When we went in, I could hear the flat mechanical tone of voice of the female dispatcher somewhere out of sight. A fat girl in a pale blue uniform with arm patch sat behind a green desk, typing with two fingers.

She glared at us and said, "You want something?"

"Sure do," I said, "but if I asked you for it, you'd probably bust me alongside the head."

"Oh, *you!*" she said, with a chubby simper. "Who you wanna see?"

"Whoever is still assigned to the Ellis Esterland killing."

"Esterland. Esterland. Oh, the rich millionaire guy. That was a *long* time ago. Look, what we got around here, we got Sunday evening, which is supposed to be a big rest from Saturday night, but tonight it isn't, you know what I mean? I got to finish this dang thang. It has to go in. Couldn't you come back tomorrow, fellas?"

"Would it be assigned to anybody in particular?"

"I wouldn't rightly know myself. My guess is, it would just be an open file, you know. And in the monthly meeting, the sheriff, he goes over the open files with the officers, to kind of remind them to keep their eyes open and keep asking questions even when they're checking out other stuff. You fellas from another jurisdiction?"

At that moment a sallow man in baggy yellow slacks and a Polynesian shirt came out of one office, heading for another, a stack of papers in his hand.

"Oh, Barney! Look, can maybe you help these fellas? They want to know who's still working on that rich millionaire that got beat to death at that rest stop over on the turnpike a long time ago."

33 —

He stopped and stared at us, a slow and careful appraisal, and then managed to herd both of us over into a corner away from the girl typing. He smelled tartly of old sweat.

"My name is Odum," he said.

"Meyer. And Mr. McGee," Meyer said. There was no hand extended.

"What would be your interest in that case? We're short-handed here at the best of times. No time for book writers, newspaper people, or those who're just damn nosey."

As I hesitated, hunting the right approach, Meyer stepped in. With a flourish, he handed Odum one of his cards. I knew it was meaningless. But it is a thick card on cream-colored stock with raised lettering. There are a lot of initials after his name, all earned. In the bottom left corner is his adopted designation: Certified Guarantor. He had conducted some field surveys of his own and had weeded his options down to these two words. They sounded official and had the flavor of money and personal authority. People treat a Certified Guarantor with respect. If they asked what it meant, he told them in such a way that respect was increased.

"Mr. McGee is assisting me, sir," Meyer said. "The Esterland estate is a phased estate, in that certain incumbrances and stipulations have to fall into place in a time frame that takes heed of certain aspects of taxation on properties coexistent with the residual portions. So I'm sure you understand that just as a formality, sir, we have to go through the motions of testifying and certifying that yes, we did indeed proceed to Citrus City and review the status of the open case of murder and report back to the administrators and adjudicators, so that things can move ahead and not be tied up in jurisdictional red tape. Please believe me when I tell you that in return for your cooperation, we will take a minimum of time from busy officers of the law."

Odum's eyes looked slightly glazed. He shook himself like a damp dog and said, "You want to just...check out where we are on that thing?"

"On a totally confidential basis, of course."

"Sure. I realize that. Fine. Well, I guess Rick Tate, Deputy Rick Tate, would be the one who'd have it all clearest in mind. Where's Rick, Zelda?"

She stopped typing. "Rick? Oh, he's went up to Eustis with Debbie on account of her mom is bad off again. He'll be back on tomorrow on the four to midnight."

"You can get hold of him tomorrow," Odum said. "He'll come in about three thirty, around there. I won't be here."

"If we could have some kind of informal authorization?" Meyer asked. "Maybe you could just write it on the back of the card I gave you."

He went over to a corner of Zelda's desk and wrote on the card, *Rick, you can go ahead and tell these men everything we got to date on Esterland, which isn't much anyway. Barney Odum.*

When we walked back out into the warm evening, I said, "Certified Guarantor! You could write political speeches."

"Let me see. You are a Salvage Consultant. Anne called us a couple of con men. From now until tomorrow what do we do?"

"We can check out the Palmer Hotel. Where Esterland was last seen alive. You did nicely with Barney Odum, friend."

"Yes. I know."

Most of the old hotels in the central cities of Florida, in the cities of less than a hundred thousand, have gone downhill, decaying with the neighborhoods. Some of them have turned into office buildings, or parking lots, or low-cost storage bins for elderly indigents.

Though the neighborhood had evidently decayed, the Palmer was a pleasant surprise. A clean roomy lobby, pleasant lighting, trim and tidy ladies behind the desk and the newsstand. Walnut and polished brass.

The dark bar off the lobby was called The Office. Prism spots gleamed down on the bald pate of the bearded bartender, on shining glassware, on good brands on the back bar, on the padded bar rim, on black Naugahyde stools with brass nailheads. A young couple off in a corner held hands across the small table.

The bartender said, "Gentlemen," and put coasters in front of us. I ordered Boodles over ice with a twist, and Meyer selected a white wine. After serving us he moved off to that precise distance good bartenders maintain: far enough to give us privacy if we wanted it, close enough to join in should we speak to him.

"Good-looking place," I said to him.

"Thank you, sir."

"Do much business?"

"Not much on weekends. Big noon and cocktail-time business during the week."

"This is a very generous shot of gin."

"Thank you, sir. This is not really a commercial place, I mean in the sense that there is a lot of cost control. It's owned by National Citrus Associates. The cooperatives and some of the big growers maintain suites here. There's a lot of convention and meeting business, a lot of businessmen from overseas, a lot of government people, state and federal. It's something like a club. The number of available rooms is quite limited."

Meyer said, "A friend of ours from Fort Lauderdale had lunch here the day he was killed at a rest stop over on the turnpike. A year and nine months ago. Ellis Esterland."

"A tragic thing," the bartender said. "Beaten to death and robbed. There is so much mindless violence in the world. I've been here five years, and I can see the difference in just that short time. Mr. Esterland had a drink here at the bar before he went to the grill room for his lunch. He sat right where you are sitting, sir. He had a very dry vodka Gibson, straight up, and soon after he left there was an order for another one from the grill room. Of course, I did not know his name at that time. They showed me his Florida driver's license, the police did, and I recognized the little color photograph as the man who was in here."

"What did they ask you about him?" I asked.

He shrugged. "If we had any conversation beyond his ordering his drink, and I said we didn't. I had a dozen customers at the bar, and I was quite busy. I had no chance to notice him, really, to guess at his state of mind. That's what they asked. Was he nervous? Was he elated? I just couldn't help them at all. From his manner I judged him to be a businessman of some importance, used to good service. He spoke to no one else, and no one joined him. They questioned his waitress and the people at the desk and the girl at the newsstand. I don't think they learned anything useful. At least they've never arrested anyone."

"It's puzzling," I said. "Why would a man pull into a rest stop on the turnpike after he had been driving only six miles?"

"Car trouble?" the bartender said.

"He had a new Lincoln Continental with just over two thousand miles on it," Meyer said.

"Perhaps he felt unwell," the bartender said. "He didn't look like a really healthy person. His color was bad."

Three new customers arrived, laughing and hearty, dressed like Dallas businessmen, ranch hats and stitched boots. Juice moguls, maybe. They called the bartender Harry, and he greeted them by name. Two bourbons and a scotch.

We had a second drink and then went to the dining room for better than adequate steaks, green salad, and baked potatoes, served efficiently by a glum heavy woman who knew nothing about anybody who'd been a customer over a year ago, because she had not been there a year.

Back at the motel, Meyer went to bed with a book called *Contrary Investment Strategy*. I told him to be sure to let me know how it came out. I tried to think about Esterland's misfortune, but my mind kept veering into trivia, to a memory of the fine matte finish on the slender Renzetti legs, and the tiny beads of sweat along her forehead at the dark hairline as she sat in silhouette against the white glare of beach. Meyer, in bright yellow pajamas, frowned into his strategy book.

I slipped away into nightmare. I was running after a comedy airplane. Gretel was the pilot, very dashing in her Red Baron helmet, goggles, white silk scarf, white smile as she turned to look back at me. The little biplane bounded over the lumps in the broad pasture. I was trying to warn her. If she took off, she would fly into the trees. She couldn't hear me because of the noise of the engine. She thought I was making jokes, chasing her. I could not catch her. The engine sound grew louder and the tail skid lifted and she took off toward the pines.

As I ran, still yelling, I saw her tilt the plane to try to slide through a gap in the trees, saw the wings come off, heard the long grinding, sliding, clattering crash into the stones. I climbed down the slope. The whole gully was cluttered with large pieces of airplane, but strangely old, stained by time and weather, grass growing up through rents in the aluminum. I couldn't understand. I kept hunting for her. I flipped over what seemed to be a small piece of wing, big as the top of a card table, and there was a skull in the skull-sized stones, helmet in place, the goggle lenses starred by old fractures, a bundle of soiled gray silk bunched under the bones of the jaw.

Meyer shook me out of it, and I came up gasping, sweat-soaked.

"Okay?" he asked.

"Thanks."

"A lot of moaning and twitching going on."

I wiped my face on a corner of the sheet. "Gretel again. She doesn't seem to want to stay dead."

He went back over to his bed and covered himself and picked up his book. He looked over at me, thoughtful and concerned.

"How is the book coming?" I asked.

"The bad guys are winning, I think."

"Sometimes they do. Sometimes you can't tell the bad guys unless you buy a program at the door."

And when my heart slowed back to normal, I was able to go back to sleep.

At breakfast Meyer said, "I'd hoped to be back by early evening. In fact I would very much like to be back."

It took me a few moments to understand the urgency. Then I remembered that Aggie Sloane was due in on her big Trumpy again, called the *Byline*. Aggie, an ex-news hen who had married a publisher and assumed the management of the chain of papers when he died, had first come to Meyer as the friend of a friend, with a delicate international money problem. Their friendship had blossomed during and after Meyer's deft solution to her problem.

Though Meyer loves to look upon the lively young beach girls and is often surrounded by little chittering platoons of them, running errands for him and laughing at his wise jokes, when it comes to any kind of personal involvement, Meyer feels most at ease with—and is usually attracted to—mature capable independent women, the sort who run magazines, newspapers, art galleries, travel agencies, and branch banks. For them, Meyer is a sometime interlude, reassuring, undemanding, supportive, and gentle. They return, refreshed, to their spheres of combat. They are women who take great good care of themselves and are not inclined toward any permanent attachment. Meyer smiles a lot.

Aggie Sloane makes an annual pilgrimage. She flies

down and boards her big Trumpy in Miami, cruises up to Lauderdale to pick up Meyer, and takes him along on the one-week vacation she allows herself every spring.

"Aggie arrives today?"

"I suppose there'd be pretty good air service back."

"Would you mind driving Miss Agnes?"

"Not at all. Of course, when I drive that thing, I always feel as if I'm hurrying to catch up with the antique classic car parade. But why?"

"I think a nice inconspicuous rental would be more useful somehow. And—I might go back to Naples and have a chat with that doctor."

"Just for the hell of it?"

"I'll give your regards to Anne."

"I think she might be too involved with that doctor to hear much of what you say. She had that look when she brought him up."

"I didn't notice."

"I think you'd better get back in the habit of noticing everything, Travis. That trait has kept you alive up until now."

"I've noticed one thing I should mention. Whenever you feel a bit guilty about anything, you give these little stern warnings to people, usually me."

His bright blue eyes looked quite fierce for a few moments. Then he smiled. "All right. The guilt isn't about Aggie, of course. It's about leaving you alone with this Esterland thing."

"I managed everything alone for quite a few years, professor."

"Always happy to leave you to your own resources. The things you get into make me highly nervous."

"I didn't mean that the way it sounded. Give my love and admiration to the lady Sloane. I might be back late tomorrow or the day after. But you won't be there, will you?"

His smile spread wide under the potato nose, wide and fatuous and tenderly reminiscent. "With any luck, I won't."

4

Rick Tate was a lean, dusty, bitter-looking man with eyes deep set under shaggy brows, narrow nose, heavy jaw—a slow, lazy-moving man who looked competent in his pale blue cotton, black leather, and departmental hardware. I guessed his age at forty.

He took the card and held it by one corner, looking at it with suspicion and distaste as he read it. "Says men," he said.

"My boss had to get back."

"Why you got to know this stuff?"

"My boss explained it to Barney Odum. It's a legal and tax thing."

He slammed the door of his gray steel locker and twirled the combination dial. We went out the back door into the lot and stood in the shade of the building waiting for the cars to come back in from their shifts. There were only three out, he told me.

"Look," he said, "instead of your riding around with me, the best way is I give you the file so you read it and then we talk, but I don't damn well know you at all, McGee, and I don't feel right about not being with anybody when they are reading a file I put together."

"Dave Banks could have told you I was all right."

He shoved his hat back off his forehead and stared at me. "Hell, I married Dave's middle girl."

"That would be Debbie?"

"Sure would."

"How's Mrs. Banks these days?"

"Not good. Not good at all. She's up in Eustis, living with her sister. We was up to see her yesterday. Looking terrible. It cut Debbie all up to see her mom looking so poorly. What she's got is kidney trouble, and they put her on a machine up there once a week. They drive her over to Orlando. Costly."

"Social Security paying for it? With the Medicare?"

"They pay shit. They pay eighty percent of what it used to cost to have it done eight years ago. With the four kids, we can't help out as much as Debbie thinks we should. The oldest girl, Debbie's sister Karen, lives in Atlanta, and she sends what she can. Now they say she should have it twice a week instead of once, and that's how come she looks so bad. I don't see how the hell we're going to swing it. I really don't."

"I'm sorry to hear about it."

"Well, come on in and I'll get you the file, and you can set and go through it in one of the interrogation rooms. Then when you get done with it, take it back to Records and ask them to ask Dispatch to tell me to come in and pick you up."

The file was thick. There was a sheaf of glossy black-and-white photographs of the body still in the car, and the body on the stretcher. Closeups of left profile, right profile, and full face. Sickening brutality. To hit a man once that hard is brutal. To keep hitting him is sickness.

Fingerprinting got nothing, as usual. There were lab reports on blood samples. Trace of alcohol. Contents of stomach. Decedent had eaten approximately two hours before death, give or take a half hour. There was a long technical report on the physical findings dictated during the autopsy procedure. Cause of death was massive trauma to the brain causing a pressure from internal bleeding that suppressed the functions of breathing and heartbeat. Five broken ribs, all on the left side, indicating a right-handed assailant. Incisions from operations noted. Decedent had multiple areas of evident malignancy affecting the liver, spleen, lymph glands, and soft tissue areas, adjudged terminal.

All the local newspaper coverage had been Xeroxed and put in the file. The *Citrus Banner* had given it a pretty good play. The rest of the file was taken up with signed statements, depositions, and reports made by the officers assigned. Rick Tate had signed most of the reports.

I read the reports and interviews and statements with care and I made notes of the things I had not known before.

————"I would guess he sat there in the chair in the lobby for nearly three quarters of an hour, reading that newspaper. I did notice that every little once in a while he would look at his watch, as if he was waiting for somebody or had to be somewhere at a certain time. I didn't see him leave. I guess I was busy when he left."

————"It was one hot day in July, and I remember I was hoping it would rain some. But it didn't. That

Lincoln car was parked right out in the sun all closed up tight and locked, and I saw the man come from the hotel, shucking his coat off as he walked. I was just standing in the store, over here by the window, looking out, wishing somebody would come the hell in and buy something. He was parked in that space second from the corner. The second meter. And I saw the red flag was up in the meter, but they don't check it real careful in the summertime like they do in the tourist season. He unlocked the driver's side and he pushed on something in there, and all those windows all went down like at once, and I thought how handy that was. He threw his coat into the back, and he got in and started it up, but he yanked his hands back when he touched that wheel. So he got out again and stood around, and I guess what he was doing was letting the air conditioning cool it off in there for him. I'm always watching people, trying to figure out what they are doing and why they do it. Pretty soon he got in and all those four windows came sliding up, nice as you please, and then he turned out of the parking place and headed east on Central. I guess from what I read, he went all the way out Central to where it becomes Seven Sixty-five and takes you right to the interchange. Got on it and went six mile south to get beat to death. Wouldn't have had an inkling any nasty thing was going to happen to him. Comes to dying, money don't help you a damn."

———"What I do when I start getting the nods, I pull off soon as I can, make sure I'm locked in good, and I climb into the bunk behind the seat and set this little alarm for twenty minutes and put on my sleep mask and put everything out of my mind. Then when I wake up I get out of the cab and walk around for ten minutes or so to get the blood stirred up, and I'm good for another five or six hours. So yes, I noticed, or half noticed, that Continental when I first stopped. It was parked a hundred feet in front of me, angled in toward those logs they've got that mark the edge. I remember wondering what kind of gas mileage they get on those things now with that automatic shift-overdrive deal. There was a big orange moving van parked behind me. I had passed him and pulled into a parking area ahead of him. I think there was maybe a camper van pulled in way beyond the Continental. So I corked off and the alarm went off and I climbed down out of the cab and stretched and started walking around. The Continental was still there, and it seemed strange because that sun was coming down hot, and it wasn't in any shade. I couldn't see anybody in it. First I thought maybe some-body had gone off sick into the bushes. They don't do much business at that rest area. There's no shade where you have to park, and no crapper. There are bushes and trees between it and the turnpike so it's quieter than most, a good place to nap. I walked on over to it and looked in and seen him on the floor in the back, kind of kneeling and slumped, blood on the side of his face and neck. I ran back to my rig and got onto Channel 9 and told my story and waited until the patrol car came screaming in."

———"He ordered a drink and I went out to the bar and Harry made it right away and I took it back. He was very careful about what he wanted to eat. A green salad with our creamy Italian dressing, and the baby lamb chops, asparagus, boiled potatoes, iced tea, no dessert. It's not hard to remember about yesterday, because we had a slow day. And he was the kind of man you remember. How do we make our house dressing, and exactly how big are the lamb chops, and is it canned or fresh asparagus. Like I said, he was very careful and serious about ordering. It came to six something and he left me a dollar tip along with the dime and some pennies that was in his change. He seemed, you know, cold. Knew what he wanted and was used to getting it. He certainly didn't look like any happy kind of person. He wasn't somebody you'd kid around with when you're taking their order or anything. He was real tan, but he didn't have good color under the tan. Yellowish, kinda. What I keep thinking, he wasn't the sort of person you hit. Not for any reason at all. I know that doesn't make sense, but I can't help it. I just can't imagine somebody hitting that man in the face. It's a terrible thing to happen. But lots of terrible things are happening everywhere, I guess. Why is everybody getting so angry?"

———"I'd say he pulled up to the pump about eleven thirty or quarter to noon. You can see from the ticket he took six and four-tenths gallons of unleaded, which come to eight sixty-four. I did his windshield and he asked me was there a good place to eat and I told him the fast food places were further along, and he said he meant a real good place and I told him to go on into town to the Palmer Hotel, that I couldn't afford to eat there but it was supposed to be the best. I said it got awards every year for being good. He showed me a bug smear on the windshield I'd missed. Then he signed, and I gave him back his card and his copy, and away he went."

* * *

When I'd finished the whole file, I took it back to Records. Dispatch called Rick Tate, and he told them to tell me he would pick me up out in front of the building in five or six minutes. It was almost six thirty. He came ghosting up to the curb and I got in. Daylight was dying, and I had heard distant booms of thunder as I waited.

"Like the file?" he asked.

"You sort of took it right out to a dead end."

"What do you make of it, McGee?"

"He got a long-distance call in Fort Lauderdale, aboard his motor sailer, telling him to meet somebody at that specific rest stop on the turnpike six miles south-bound out of Citrus City, at a specific time. It was important to him to be there, and he either decided to be alone or it was requested that he be alone. It had to be in reference to something important to him: his illness, his money, his dying child, or the woman he was living with. So he drove on up in plenty of time, got gas, found a good place to eat, waited in the lobby out of the heat until it was time to go to the appointment. He kept it and they killed him."

"Anything else?"

"It isn't as bad a place for a killing as I thought. I'm going down the road and take a look at it tomorrow. Apparently, it is screened from the highway traffic. And it is not a high-use facility, especially in the heat of a late July afternoon. A planned killing taking place there would look unplanned, I think. Kind of coincidental. Spur-of-the-moment. And no problem getting away clean, back into traffic."

"Any more?"

"Not much. Vague stuff. Somebody had to decide on

the place. Why up here, all this way from Lauderdale? Did they come and scout it out first? Or is it just a kind of cleverness—that when a well-to-do traveler is killed far from home, it always sounds like a coincidental killing, a robbery with assault. Kill a man close to home and the choices are broader."

"Ever a lawman?"

"Not quite."

"I put it together pretty much the same. Except the appointment and the killing could be two different people. If he was early, he could have been killed, and then when the person who called him showed up, they took one look and took off like a rabbit. A few years back in Florida and Georgia we had an M.O. of somebody sneaking up on sleeping truck drivers, shooting them in the head with a twenty-two long-rifle hollow-point, and taking whatever money they had. A long-haul trucker tends to carry a fair piece of cash for emergencies, especially an independent owner. As I remember there were eight or ten incidents. Never solved. They just all of a sudden stopped. My guess is that whoever was working it got picked up for something else. Maybe he's in Raiford and it'll start again when he gets out. He had the truckers real jumpy all over the area, believe me."

"I remember reading about that."

He started up and cruised toward the center of the city, moving up and down the side streets, looking at the dark warehouses and old apartment buildings as he talked.

"That murderous little bastard had to have some kind of transportation. We gave a lot of thought to that. A report came back from south Georgia, where he killed a driver in a rest stop on Interstate Seventy-five, just up past Valdosta, that a driver turning in had seen a motorsickle taking off like a scalded bat, and the rider didn't hit the lights until he was back out onto the interstate. The way they think he worked it, he'd sneak in and trundle his machine back into the bushes and hide and keep watch on the night traffic in and out of the rest stop. He might have to wait two or three nights until he got the right setup, a single driver in a truck, the truck parked well away from any others, and enough waiting time to be sure the driver was sacked out. But the killings stopped soon after that, before they could set anything up to try to trap him."

"What are you getting at, Rick?"

"That old M.O. that never got proved out stuck in my mind, and I woke up before dawn the day after the Esterland killing and went on out there and looked around back in the bushes. You won't find this in the file because I didn't put it in the file. We were getting the July rains. The ground was pretty soft. I poked around until I found where somebody had run a real heavy machine back through the bushes and made a half circle and brought it back to the place where it had been driven in. Okay, so it was a brute. It made a deep track, so I'd guess about a five-hundred-pound bike, and where the tread was clear in one place in the mud I saw that funny Y. pattern of that rear K-One-twelve of a set of ContiTwins, like those BMW Nine-seventy-two cc come through with. You pay six or seven thousand for one of those, for just the bare-bones machine. I would like to think no biker had anything to do with it."

He parked in shadows and turned toward me.

"Listen, we got a group of nice people here. Maybe close to thirty couples in our club. The C.C. Roamers. Me and Debbie, we got a Suzuki GS-550-ET I bought used. We don't get a chance to go as much as we used to, but we still go when we can. We take tours. Guys and their wives or girl friends. There's real estate salesmen, and a dentist and his wife, store managers, computer programmers, a couple of builders, a guy in the landscaping business. People like that. It's great. We lay out a tour so we can take the back roads, ride along there in the wind. Have a picnic in a nice grove. You can hear the birds and all, those engines are so quieted down these days. I like it. So does Debbie. A lot. We've got our own special matching jackets and insignia. But the outlaw clubs give the whole thing a bad name. Like those damn Bandidos out west, and those Fantasies down in south Florida. Some of their officers are into every dirty thing going. Maybe, like they say, most of the troops are pretty much okay, just blue-collar guys from body shops and so on, who like to go roaring around with their women and drink a lot of beer and get tattooed and let all their hair grow and scare the civilians. Little recreation clubs like ours draw a lot of flack, McGee. And when there is biker violence, it reflects on us too, and people look at you funny and make smart remarks. That's why I hope whoever was on that machine, he just pulled off to adjust something, or get out of the sun, or eat his lunch, or some damn thing. But he could have been an outlaw biker riding alone, and he could have run short of cash money, and so he hid there behind the bushes waiting for somebody to stop who looked worth robbing."

"And if that's how it was?"

"He's away clean. No ID, no witnesses. I couldn't even get a mold of the tire track. The rain washed it out before I could get back with the kit."

"What do you really think?"

"I've got the gut feeling that whoever was on that machine beat Esterland to death. How long would it take him, a man powerful enough to hit that hard? You saw the autopsy report. They guessed he was hit six or seven times. Pull him out of the driver's seat, brace him against the car, bang him six times, open the rear door and tumble him in, and slam the door. Fifteen seconds? Twenty seconds? Take the wallet, take out the cash, toss the wallet into the car. Walk back into the brush, crank up, and roll away. Forty seconds?"

"Was it the person he had the appointment with?"

"I've got no gut feeling about that at all. Maybe yes, maybe no. When you try to figure out the odds on whether a man setting up a secret meet is going to get killed by somebody else who just happened to be there, you can tend to say it had to be the one he was meeting. On the other hand, it could be just another one of those damn coincidences that screw up the work I do forty times a year."

"I appreciate your cooperation. And when you see Mrs. Banks, you give her my best wishes."

"I surely will. Dallas McGee? Is that right?"

"Not quite. Travis. Tell her it's been ten or twelve years. I was at their house for supper. With them and those three pretty daughters."

"My Debbie was the middle one. Here, I'll drop you on back at your car. Seems like a quiet night around here, thank the good Lord. I better knock wood. Soon as I say quiet, those grove workers start sticking knives in each other. Or rolling their pickups over and over, dogs and shotguns flying every whichaway."

He drove me back to the jail. We shook hands. He went off down the dark streets, a man alone in a county car on an overcast evening, waiting for somebody to do some damn fool thing to himself or to somebody else, wondering, as he made his patrol, if he was going to have to peddle the Suzuki to be able to help out with his mother-in-law's new schedule of dialysis.

5

I checked out of the motel after breakfast and headed southwest in my little dark blue rental Dodge, a Mitsubishi, I think, with a VW engine and almost enough legroom. I took it over to Interstate 4 and made the mistake of staying on 4 all the way to the outskirts of Tampa before turning south on 301.

It had been a couple of years since I had driven that route, and I found all north-south highways clogged full of snorting, stinking, growling traffic, the trucks tailgating, the cowboys whipping around from lane to lane, and the Midwest geriatrics chugging slowly down the fast lanes, deaf to all honkings. Bradenton, Sarasota, Venice, Punta Gorda, Fort Myers—all the same. Smoggy vistas and chrome glitterings down the long alleyway between the fast food outlets, the sprawl of motels, car dealerships, shell factories, strip shopping centers, gas stations, and gigantic signboards. It is all that bustling steaming growth that turns the state tackier each year. Newcomers don't mind at all, because they think it has always been like this. But in two years, they all want to slam the door, pull up the ladder, and close the state off. Once in a great while, like once every fifty miles, I even got a look at a tiny slice of the Gulf of Mexico, way off to the right. And remembered bringing the *Flush* down this coast with Gretel aboard. And wished I could cry as easily as a child does.

I had phoned ahead to the Eden Beach, and they had a second-floor single for me, with the windows facing inland. After I put the duffelbag in the room, I went over to the lobby to find Anne Renzetti.

I saw her coming diagonally across the lobby, walking very swiftly, her expression anxious and intent. Today she wore an elegant little dress: a cotton dress in an unusual shade of orange coral, which fitted her so beautifully it underlined the lovely fashioning of hips, sweep of waist, straightness of her back and shoulders. The color was good for her too. A small lady, luxuriantly alive.

"Hey, Anne," I said.

She came to a quick stop and stared at me, an instant of puzzlement and then recognition. "Oh, hello there. Mr. McGraw."

"McGee. Travis McGee."

She was looking beyond me. "Yes, of course. I'm so sorry. Travis McGee. Is Meyer with you?"

"He had to get back."

She started to sidle away. "You will have to excuse me. I really have to—"

"I was hoping you would introduce me to Dr. Mullen. I want to ask him about Ellis Esterland's condition at the time he—"

Even the sound of his name made her glow. It seemed almost to take her breath away. Her smile was lovely.

"That's why I'm so busy at the moment. He didn't get in yesterday. He's due any minute. I just checked the room I set aside for him, and the damned shower keeps dripping and dripping. Excuse me just a moment, please."

I followed her to the desk. She told Marie about the leak, and Marie picked up the phone to get the maintenance man on it. Anne turned back to me and looked beyond me toward the entrance. Her smile went wider, and she flushed under her tan and slipped past me, quick and cute as a safety blitz. She half ran toward the entrance, arms outstretched, and I heard her glad cry of welcome.

The man was in his middle thirties, with a russet mustache, blow-dried hair, tinted glasses with little gold rims. He had a likable look about him. Strong irregular features, a good grin. And he wasn't very big. He was a dandy match for Anne Renzetti. Five foot two fits pretty well with five foot seven. He put his hands on Anne's shoulders, kissed her on the cheek, and then with a gesture very much like a magician's best trick, he reached behind him and pulled a large glowing blonde. She topped the good doctor by an inch or two. They both wore the same jack-o'-lantern toothy grin, and over the lobby sounds I heard a portion of his introduction of her: "...my wife, Marcie Jean..."

Anne's shoulders did not slump. I'll give her that much. And I think her smile stayed pretty much in place, because she was still wearing it when she turned around and came back, leading them toward the desk. I sensed that this was no time to ask for an introduction to the doctor and his bride. Anne kept smiling while the doctor registered. She pointed out the location of his room on a chart. A bellhop went with them to cart their luggage through the gardens to their room.

The two girls behind the desk had arranged to disappear. They recognized the storm warnings. Anne leaned back against the counter, her arms crossed, staring at me and through me, a glare that pierced me through and through, at chest level.

"Honeymoon!" she said in a half whisper. "Big dumb blond dumpling comes out of nowhere and nails him. And I put two bottles of chilled champagne up there in the room. Shit! Hope the shower never stops dripping."

"Pretty hard to stop a good drip in a shower."

She slowly came back to here-and-now and focused on me. She tilted her head a little bit to one side and looked me over with great care. She moistened her lips and swallowed. "What did you say your damn name is? McGee? You are a sizable son of a bitch, aren't you?"

"Wouldn't try to deny it."

She looked at me. She was all a-hum with ready. She was up to the splash rails with electric ready. Everything was working: all the blood and juices from eyeballs to polished toenails.

"You better comfort me with apples, fella. Or is it roses? And stay me with flagons, whatever that means. Always wondered. And for God's sake you better be discreet or it'll undermine any authority I have left around here."

"Appointing me an instrument of revenge?"

"Do you particularly mind?"

"I'm thinking it over."

"Thanks a lot! Take your time. Take four more seconds, damn it."

"Three. Two. One. Bingo."

"My place," she said. "Nineish."

"Try to remember my name."

She tried to smile but the smile turned upside down, the underlip poked out, the eyes filled, and she spun and darted away toward her office, the proud straight back finally curving in defeat.

I was on time, after wondering all the rest of the day whether to show up or not. It made me feel ridiculously girlish. Despite all the new freedoms everybody claims they have, I still feel strange when I am the aggressee. One wants to blush and simper. I was dubious about my own rationalization. She seemed a nice person, and her morale had taken one hell of a scruffing when the Doc had walked in with his surprise bride. What would be the further damage if even the casual semi-stranger didn't want her as a gift?

Anyway, it seemed to me that after a day of thinking about it, she would have cooled on the whole idea. It had been an abrupt self-destructive impulse that had made her proposition me so directly. She might not even be at her cabana on stilts. And if she was there, and if she said she had reconsidered and it was a dumb idea and all, then it would be time for both of us to disengage gracefully.

She was there. A thread of light shone out under her cabana door. When I knocked the light went out, and she came out onto the porch, shaded from the starlight, carrying two glasses and the ice bucket, and a towel with which to twist out the champagne cork. She wore dark slacks and a white turtleneck against the night breeze off the Gulf. She said, in too merry a voice,

"Champagne for you too, pal, so you shouldn't feel everything is a total loss."

"Second thoughts, eh?"

"Definitely. I don't know what the hell I was thinking of. I mean I do know what I was thinking of, and it wasn't my very best idea. I was wondering a little while ago, what if you arrived all eager and steamy? Would she or wouldn't she?"

"You'll never know. I guessed you'd have second thoughts."

"Thank you. Any friend of Meyer is a friend of mine. Meyer has pretty good taste in friends. Open that good stuff."

I unwound the wire and stood the glasses on the rail, where the starlit sand beyond gave enough light for me to fill them properly. Poured. We clinked glasses.

"To all the dumb dreams that never happen," she said. "And the dumb women who dream them."

"To all the dumb dreams that shouldn't happen, and don't," I said.

She sipped. "You are probably right. Ellis was dying. Prescott Mullen was an authority figure. He was comforting. When you lean on strength, I think you can get to read too much into it."

"I thought you seemed very very happy with your job here."

"Oh, I am! I wouldn't *think* of giving it up. He was going to come down and go into practice here. Another segment of the dumb dream."

We drank, chairs close together. Silences were comfortable. I told her portions of my life, listened to parts of hers. We had some weepy chapters and some glad ones. About five minutes after she had snugged her hand into mine, I leaned over into her chair and kissed lips ripe and hot as country plums, and when that was over she got up, tugged at my wrist, and said in a small voice, "I think I have been talked into it somehow."

We lay sprawled in the soft peach glow of a pink towel draped around the shade of her bedside lamp, sated and peaceful and somnolent. Big wooden blades of a ceiling fan turned slowly overhead, and I could smell the sea. A passel of marsh frogs were all yelling *gronk* in a garden pond, voices in contrapuntal chorus.

She propped herself on an elbow and ran her fingertips along the six-inch seam of scar tissue along my right side, halfway between armpit and waist.

"How many wars did you say you were in?"

"Only one, and that wasn't done there. That was an angry fellow with a sharp knife, and if I could have had it stitched right away, there wouldn't be hardly any scar."

"You should put out a pocket guidebook."

"Some day I'll arrange a guided tour. Meyer says there isn't enough unblemished hide left to make a decent lampshade."

"Are you accident-prone, darling?"

"I guess you could say that. I am prone to be where accidents are prone to happen."

"Why do you want to ask Prescott about Ellis?"

"I haven't really got anything specific to go on. It's what I do, the way I go about things. If I can get enough people talking, sooner or later something comes up that might fit with something somebody else has said. Sometimes it takes longer than other times, and sometimes it doesn't happen at all. Like finding out last night that whoever beat Esterland to death might have been a motorcyclist, a biker."

"Why would you think that? I don't understand."

So I went through it for her, editing it just enough to take out things that were obviously meaningless. Her arm got tired and she snugged her face into the corner of my throat, her breath warm against my chest. I slowly stroked her smooth and splendid back as I talked, all the way from coccyx to nape and back again.

When I finished, she said, "Well, I guess it is interesting, but I don't see what a motorcycle would have to do with anything, really. The only person I ever met who knew anything at all about motorcycles is Josie's weird friend Peter Kesner."

It startled me. "He rides them?"

"Oh, no! He's what they call out there a genius. He's a double hyphenate."

"A what?"

"No, darling, it is not some form of perversion. He made a couple of motion pictures where he was the writer-director-producer. He made them years ago on a very small budget, and they were what is called sleepers. They made a lot of money, considering what they cost. Maybe you heard of them. One was called *Chopper Heaven* and the other was *Bike Park Ramble*. It was all a kind of realism, you know. He used real tough bike people and hand-held cameras. And they were sort of tragic movies. The critics raved. I saw one of them, I can't really remember which. It was too loud and there were too many people getting hurt."

She sat straight up and combed her dark hair back with her fingers and smiled down at me.

"Dear, I'm getting chilled. Can you reach the fan

switch?" I turned it off. She reached down and got the end of the sheet and pulled it up over us when she stretched out again.

"You said Kesner is Josephine's weird friend."

"He came to Stamford with her when Ellis was in the hospital the first time. That's when I met him. He's big, maybe about your size, and from what I could gather from Josie, he's been on every kind of pill and powder and shot ever invented. He was treating Josie like dirt, and she didn't seem to mind a bit. It's hard to carry on a conversation with him. I can't describe it. It's just...frustrating. And he's weird-acting. Really weird."

She kicked at something, then ducked under the sheet and came up with her discarded briefs. She held them to the light and said, "One of my romantic little plans for the good doctor." They were white, with a regular pattern of bright red hearts the size of dimes.

"Glad he didn't get a chance to appreciate them."

"You didn't appreciate them. I got shuffled out of them too quickly."

"Protesting all the way?"

"Well—not really. Did you notice how fat her face is?"

"What?"

"The bride. A fat face and piggy little eyes."

"I didn't particularly notice because I was watching you, Annie. I lay there in my trundle bed in the Groveway Motel last night and thought about your pretty legs hiked up on that porch railing until I had to get up and take a cold shower. And then I came dashing down here in my domesticated Mitsubishi. Meyer had told me you had eyes for the doctor, but I didn't want to believe it."

"Come *on!* Really?"

"Cross my heart. Hope to spit."

"You know, that makes me feel a lot better about this whole—uh—happenstance."

"I've really enjoyed happenstancing with you, Miz Renzetti."

"Always before I felt squeamish about big tall men."

"And little dark women have not exactly figured large in my erotic fantasies, kid."

"They might from now on?"

"Front and center."

"You said enjoyed?"

"I did."

"Past tense?"

"My dear lady, it is quarter past three in the morning."

"So?"

"My ramparts are breached, my legions scattered, my empire burned to the ground, my fleet at the bottom of the sea. And you would—"

"Hush," she said softly.

And so in time the impossible became at first probable and finally inevitable. As before, I found that through her response she led us into the way she most enjoyed. She was not, as I would have guessed, one of the twitchy ones with tricky swiveling, kinky little tricks and games, contortionist experimentations. What she wanted, and got, was to be settled into the unlauded missionary position, legs well braced, arms hanging on tight, and there exercise a deep, strong, steady, elliptical rhythm.

She lay sweat-drenched and spent, small face bloated and blurred, mouth puffed and smiling. "There!" she said. She pulled my mouth down for a sisterly kiss. "Everybody to his own bed, darling. Be sneaky, huh?"

By the time I was dressed she was snoring softly. I pulled the sheet and the thin blanket over her and turned off the light. When I went out the door, I made certain it locked behind me. I walked out to the edge of the water, where the small waves lisped and slapped against the sand. A seabird flapped up, honking, startling me.

The hours before dawn are when the spirits are supposed to be lowest. That is when most hospital deaths occur. That is when the labored breathing stops, with a final rattle in the throat. I tried to heap ashes on my head. McGee, your handy neighborhood stud. Always on call. Will provide references. I tried to summon up a smidgin of postcoital depression. But all I could tell about myself, in spite of all introspection, was that I felt content. I felt happy, satisfied, relaxed—with an overlay of a kind of sweet sadness, the feeling you get when you look at a picture of yourself taken with someone long gone on a faraway shore long ago.

6

The dining room at Eden Beach had a wing like a small greenhouse, with an opaque roof. Broad-leafed plants in big cement pots provided the illusion of privacy for each table.

I arrived for brunch at one thirty, and while I was still examining the menu, a pair of unordered Bloody Marys arrived, complete with celery stalks for stirring. A few moments later the lady herself arrived and slid into the chair across from me. She looked shy and a bit worn. Her lips were puffy and there were bruised patches under her eyes.

We looked at each other in that moment which has to set the style for the whole relationship. I had guessed that perhaps we would have a bawdy little chat about how we had missed arranging a nooner, and how exhausted the male might be, and how badly lamed the female.

But from the look in her eyes I knew that was not the way to go, and knew that I would have relished that kind of talk as little as she. So I hoisted the glass. "To us."

"To us," she said, and we touched glasses. The drink was spice-hot and delicious.

"It's going to be kind of difficult and awkward, keeping control of my staff, Travis. I really want us to be very very discreet, very careful. This job does mean an awful lot to me."

I smiled at her and said, "You are implying, of course, that these fun and games are going to continue."

She flushed and said, "Don't you want to? I thought we were—"

"Hey! I was afraid you might have second thoughts. Remember, I was sent into the game as a substitute for the doctor."

"That's not fair!" she said angrily. I kept smiling. Anger faded. She laughed. "Well, maybe that was the way it started. Okay. Let's say I got lucky."

"We both got lucky. It has to happen like that sometimes."

She reached and touched my hand, her eyes glowing, then looked and saw a waitress coming and yanked her hand back.

"Look," she said in her business voice, "I have to finish this and run. I really do. I am getting some kind of a short count in supplies, and as it isn't my people, it has to be the wholesaler, and I had him hold the next truck. I have to go down there with my bookkeeper and prove to him he's got thieves in his warehouse. I talked to Prescott Mullen this morning—by the way, he looked kind of shrunken and uninteresting—and gave him your name and told him you were checking out how Ellis got killed and said you'd find him sometime today."

"Thank you."

"We always put a sprig of mint in the half grapefruit. All the time Prescott was talking to me, Marcie Jean stood there smiling, with a piece of mint leaf stuck on her front tooth."

"I've thought it over and decided she does have a fat face."

She patted my hand. "Thank you, dear. You know the old joke about the ideal wife?"

"Deaf and dumb and owns a liquor store?"

"Right. Well, you've got an old lady now that runs a hotel, and she's entitled to put dear friends on the cuff, so you better count on coming across the state at pretty regular intervals, hear?"

She got up, touched a fingertip to my lips, and hurried away.

I found Dr. Prescott Mullen on the beach, sitting in a sling chair under a big blue and white umbrella. The bride was face down in the shade beside him, a towel over her head, her legs and back pinked by fresh sunburn. Her new rings winked in reflected sunlight. I introduced myself and he told me to pull another chair over, but I sat on my heels, half facing him.

"I'm just doing a favor for a friend," I told him. "Ron Esterland is suspicious of the timing. If Ellis had outlived his daughter, a lot of money would have moved in a different direction."

"Some of it to him?" the doctor asked.

"Yes. But I don't think that's the primary motive."

"So what is?"

"Anxiety. Guilt. A sense of loss. He's sorry they didn't get along, and he's sorry his father didn't live to see him make it as a painter."

Prescott Mullen looked thoughtful. "I suppose in some sense it would be an easier murder to justify than if the man was healthy. How many months was he robbed of? If I had to guess, I'd say six at the outside. And the last six weeks would probably not have been what you'd call living."

"What was his attitude toward his illness?"

"He seemed to think of it as a challenge. To him the cancer was an entity, an enemy, a thing that had invaded him and plotted against his life. I was no fan of Ellis Esterland. He was a highly competitive organism. I used to wonder how Anne could put up with him, why she didn't just walk out."

"When did you last see Esterland?"

"Mid-June. About five weeks before he was killed. He looked better than I expected him to look. But he was in pain. He wouldn't admit it. I know he was in great pain."

"How could you tell?"

"Observation. You see a lot of pain, you know what it looks like. Sudden sweats. Quick little intakes of breath. A sudden pallor. I think he could probably handle more pain than most, just out of arrogance and pride. He was a stubborn old man. I knew there would be more coming, and it might get to the point where he couldn't handle it. I tried to get him to admit the pain, and I tried to tell him it would get worse. He told me not to worry about it. He said he was fine. I remember giving him a little lecture about the psychology of pain."

"Would he have arranged to get himself killed rather than admit he was hurting?"

He shook his head slowly. "No, I can't see Esterland

in that role. I gave him a lecture about the effects of the hallucinogens on pain. We know now that cannabis can quell the nausea some people feel during chemotherapy and radiology. Cannabis and hashish and LSD have an interesting effect on the subjective experiencing of pain. Intense and continuing pain seems to the patient to be a part of him, something swelling and burning inside of him, taking him over. The hallucinogens have the odd effect of making the pain seem aside and apart from the patient. The pain may be just as intense, but it is, subjectively, off to one side. Pain creates a terrible and consuming anxiety, on some very deep level of the brain. Pain is nature's warning that something is terribly wrong. If anxiety is quelled by any hallucinogen, then pain, though still as intense, becomes less frightening and consuming. That may be the answer. I thought Ellis was fighting the pain relievers because they would dull his wits, dull his perceptions of the world. He wanted to stay just a little brighter than anybody else he knew. I urged him to find a private source for hallucinogens and experiment with them. I explained that it would leave his mind unimpaired but would enable him to handle pain better. I told him that it was the best way for him to get any enjoyment out of the time he had left."

"Did you tell him how long he had left?"

"I told him my guess. That was our relationship from the start. Total candor."

"Maybe the pain got worse and he took your advice and went up there to make a buy. That's why he didn't take Anne or tell her why he was going."

"And somebody cheated him and killed him? Possible. I can tell you that if he did buy something, he would take it secretly, and if it helped, he would never have told Anne or me. It would have been his private solution. It would leave his macho image unimpaired."

"Lovely guy."

"Prince of a fellow," Mullen said, grinning. "McGee, I like your reconstruction. It seems to fit what I read about the circumstances of his death. The news accounts implied he was keeping some kind of appointment at a highway rest stop."

"Did you recommend any particular substance?"

"I think I told him that hashish would be easiest to manage, and probably reasonably available in the Miami area."

"Everything you ever heard of is available in Dade County. But he couldn't get much with two hundred dollars."

"That's all he had?"

"Anne gave out that figure, and she kept the accounts."

"I have the feeling that Ellis Esterland could put his hands on money in one form or another without Anne knowing about it."

"Okay, suppose he was carrying five thousand dollars. If Anne had known that and reported it, the local authorities would have been thinking about a buy that went wrong. There could have been contacts they could have developed. In his condition, at that point in the progression of the disease, how much pain do you think he should have been feeling?"

He thought it over. "Enough to send me running for the needle, whimpering all the way."

The big bride rolled over, clawing the towel off her head, looking blankly and stupidly at the two of us.

One nipple showed above the edge of her white bikini top. Prescott Mullen, smiling, reached down and tugged the fabric up to cover her. A few tendrils of russet hair curled out from under the bikini bottom.

"Whassa time, sweetie?" she asked in a small sweet voice.

"Three fifteen, lambikin. This is Travis McGee. My wife, Marcie Jean Mullen."

"Oh, hi," she said. She prodded her pink thigh with an index finger as she sat up, watching how long the white mark lasted. "Honeybun, I better get the hell off the beach. I think the sun kind of reflects in under the umbrella from the sand and sun and stuff." She stood up, yawned, swayed, and then lost her balance when she bent to pick up her towel. She yawned again. "Marcie Jean Mullen. Still sounds strange, huh?" She beamed sleepily at me. "Used to be Marcie Jean Sensabaugh. Hated every minute of it. Be a rotten world if you had to keep the name you were born with." She picked up her canvas bag and looked inside. "I got a key, honeybun. See ya in the room."

"Pretty lady," I said when she was out of earshot. "Congratulations."

"Thanks. She's a great girl. Absolutely perfect disposition. No neuroses. Healthy as the Green Bay Packers. And an absolutely fantastic pelvic structure. She was a delivery-room nurse."

"That's interesting."

"We've talked it over. We want as many kids as we can have. She's twenty-three and I'm thirty-six, and as near as we can tell, she's two months pregnant right now. We agreed not to get married until we were sure we could have kids. I don't want her to have them too close together. It wears a woman out too much. They should be two years apart. Okay, she'll be twenty-four when our first one is born. Her mother had her last baby when she was forty-four. So, with a two-year spacing, we could have nine or ten. Of course, her mother had one set of twins."

"It's nice to see people get their lives all worked out."

"I always wanted a big family. It was a case of finding the right girl before I got too old to enjoy the kids. As it is, if we stay on schedule, the last kid won't get out of college until I'm about seventy-eight."

"That's cutting it pretty close, doctor."

"I guess it is. But I come of long-lived stock. Both of my grandfathers and one of my grandmothers are still living. Late seventies and early eighties."

"It's something to look forward to, all right."

"I think of it as a very precious responsibility. It's really the only immortality we have. Did you ever think of that?"

"I guess I think of it all the time."

"Are you married?"

"No."

"Then you better find a healthy woman right away, Mr. McGee. Or you won't be young enough to enjoy your kids."

I stood up and shook hands with him. "Thanks a lot. That's probably a very good idea. Nice to have had this chat with you, doctor."

"If I can be of any help, please call on me. Funny thing. Ellis was dying and I didn't particularly like the man, but it made me furious that somebody had the gall to kill him. My patient!"

* * *

That night in Annie's cabana, she had thrown a pale green towel over the lampshade. It gave the room an underwater look.

The fan overhead made a small ticking sound. The waves were louder. A mockingbird tried silvery improvisations. She was saying, "And so, of course, Sam couldn't believe that any of his people were stealing. It had to be my people. He acted as if he was doing me a big favor, checking that big order item by item. But then the discrepancies began to show up. Short cases, opened and resealed. And his face sagged and his voice got tired. I felt so sorry for him. All his people have been with him for years and years, and he has been so good to them. And it did look as if one person couldn't have done it. It had to be two working together. I got credits on the other shortages we had picked up. He was really depressed when we left. I found myself wishing I wasn't a boss. But not for long. Not for long. You talked with Dr. Mullen, I hear."

"Had a nice chat. Have you got a fantastic pelvic structure?"

"My God! I don't know. You mean for babies. Well, I'd have a little problem, I guess. I always heard I would. My mother had two Cesarian deliveries. Why?"

"Would you be prepared to watch your final child graduate from college when you are sixty-five?"

"Hell, no! He can carry his diploma home to his poor old mom. What *is* this about, darling?"

So I told her the conversation with Prescott Mullen. At first she was incredulous. Was I sure he wasn't joshing? When I convinced her that he was totally serious, deadly serious, in fact, she went into something close to hysteria. That then subsided into a giggling fit, and that turned into hiccups.

"Poor big old brood mare—*hic*—can hear him saying—*hic*—roll over, Marcie Jean—*hic*—time to start number six—*hic*. And I wanted to get myself into a deal like *that?—hic*. Oh, God."

I poured her more wine, and she sat on the edge of the bed to drink it out of the far side of the glass, holding it in two hands like a child. There was a pale narrow stripe across her back matching the pallor of her buttocks.

She lay back again, saying, "All gone. Thanks."

"Were you there when he gave Ellis the argument about maybe he should try hash or LSD for pain?"

"Oh, yes. The last time he saw him. In June."

"Did you know Ellis was in pain?"

"I didn't know how much. He'd get up in the night and go up on deck. Sometimes he would get up from a meal and go walking. His face would twist. But he wouldn't let it twist if he knew you were watching. Prescott told me Ellis was probably in a lot of pain. After Prescott had gone back north, I tried to get Ellis to do what he had suggested. But he got angry with me. He wouldn't listen. He said he wasn't going to baby himself. He said he was not going to turn into a junky at the very end of his life. He said it was demeaning."

"After talking it over, both Dr. Mullen and I have the feeling he went up there to Citrus City to make a buy. We think that was what the long-distance phone call was about."

"But wouldn't it take more money than he had?"

"What makes you think he had only two hundred dollars, more or less?"

"But I took checks to the bank! I knew what we had and what we needed. I paid the bills. I made the deposits."

"Let me ask it another way, Annie."

"I've never let anybody else in my life call me Annie except you."

"After he was killed, it was up to you to go through everything on the boat. You and the man from the bank. Tell me this. Did you come across anything—anything at all—which led you to believe that maybe there were some money matters you didn't know about?"

"How did you know about *that?*"

"Know about what?"

"The Krugerrands. Those big gold coins from South Africa, guaranteed one ounce of pure gold in each one."

"I didn't know about them at all. I just had the idea that he was the kind of man who would have to keep secrets from everybody, even you."

"There were ten of them. Worth, I don't know, five or six hundred dollars each at that point. There was no clue as to when or where he got them, or at what price. They were way in the back of the hanging locker, in the pocket of one of his old tweed jackets that he never wore any more. When I lifted it out, it was so fantastically heavy. It made me *so* damn mad, him hiding something like that, like some sneaky little kid. But what has that got to do with anything, dear?"

"Where there were ten, there could have been twenty, or forty. The ten you found were worth from five to six thousand dollars. What if he took half of what he had stashed?"

"Could be. Yes. Yes, damn it! *Damn* him."

"So I'll go on from there, assuming he left half of them home and took half for the buy. And see what I can turn up. And I will look into the question of bikers, hard core."

"How?"

"I have a contact who has good reason to trust me."

"Who?"

"I am very glad you don't mind my calling you Annie."

"I see. Okay. When are you leaving, dearest?"

"Midmorning, I guess."

She dipped a finger in her remaining half inch of Moselle and drew a slow circle on my chest. "Hmmm," she said.

"Hmmm what?"

"I guess everybody has heard that ancient joke about how do porcupines make love."

"Very very carefully," I said.

She reached and set her empty glass aside. Her eyes danced. "So?"

I gathered her in. "Let me know if it gets to be not careful enough."

7

When I arrived back in Lauderdale the next morning at eleven o'clock I turned the little car in at the airport and taxied back to Bahia Mar. After I dumped the laundry in the hamper aboard the *Flush,* showered, and changed to a fresh white knit shirt and khaki slacks, I checked the houseboat over to see if the phone was dead, or the batteries, or the freezer. I was hungry, and I decided I'd go over to the Beef 'n' It for their big sirloin—decided to walk over, as the miles in the little car had made me feel cramped. I fixed a Boodles on ice in one of the heavier old-fashioned glasses and carried it up to the sun deck to stand and survey what I could see of the yacht-basin world.

I looked over toward the ships'-supplies place and was surprised to see the familiar lines and colors of Aggie Sloane's big Trumpy. I locked up and walked down there, glass in hand. There was a mild fresh breeze off the Atlantic that fluttered the canopy over the little topside area where Meyer and Aggie were hunched over a backgammon board.

I hailed them, and Aggie invited me aboard. I went

up and took a chair and said, "Go ahead. I don't want to interrupt the game."

She said, "It might just be over. Meyer, take a look at this." She picked up the big doubling cube from her side of the board and plunked it down on his side. The number on top was 16.

Meyer studied the board for a long time. He wore a sour expression. He sighed. "Too slim," he said. "No, thanks. Travis, if I take the double, she just might close her board on this roll."

"Class tells," said Aggie, marking the score pad.

"Aggie," I said, "you look fantastic."

In her husky baritone she said, "Just because I had a few more tucks taken in this sagging flesh? Just because I got back down to one thirty? Just because I do one solid hour of disco every morning, starko, behind locked doors? Just because my hair is longer, and this is the best tint I've had in years, and my new contacts are this nice lavender color, and I'm off the booze, and after three years of shame I've been able to get back to bikinis? Thank you, darling McGee. I think I do look rather fantastic, comparatively speaking. I went through all this hell as a special present for good old Meyer."

"Good old Meyer appreciates it, dear lady," he said. "It all fills me with awe. But I think you did it for the sake of your own morale."

"Why is he so often right?" she asked me.

"Because he is Meyer. It's a character flaw. What are you doing here anyway?"

She looked exasperated. "We are waiting for some kind of a turbo-seal whatsit that has to be flown down from Racine. It blew yesterday. Made a noise like a gigantic fart. My dear little captain will not proceed without it. Some sort of fetish, no doubt. It is going to shorten our little cruise, maybe down to no cruise at all. But what the hell. Lovely place here. Not a trace of mal de mer. Of course, it does work out a bit more pricey than a hotel suite. But the two dear little papers I added to the chain last year are churning out money you wouldn't believe. It's almost vulgar what you can make these days out of a monopoly morning paper in a city of forty thousand people, after you really get into automation and electronics and all."

"Jay Gould would have loved her," Meyer said.

"Foo," she said. "My taste would have run more to Diamond Jim Brady. Or John Ringling."

"How did you make out?" Meyer asked me.

"The doctor arrived," I said. "With new bride. Blond. With a fantastic pelvis."

Meyer looked startled and then amused. "Not according to Anne's plan at all. So you were the catcher in the awry."

"Please!" Aggie said. "Not when I'm thinking of eating. I'll go down and make sure they are fixing enough for three."

"I can't stay, Aggie. Really."

"Nonsense, dear boy. I would really resent it if you left. Today we are eating Greek. With the feta cheese, the moussaka, the grape leaves, and all. And they always fix tons, so there'll be enough for them too."

She went off belowdecks. I said, "That has really turned into some kind of special lady."

"Always was, had you but the eyes. How is Anne?"

"Recovering from the shock. She really runs one of the better places around. Anyway, I can give you a very quick rundown of the facts and hunches so far. Ellis was hurting badly, refused to admit it. The doctor tried to talk him into one of the hallucinogens to moderate pain. Good chance pain was getting worse. Ellis set up some kind of contact. They called back with a time and place for the meet. He went up there with a batch of Krugerrands to pay for his hash or fix or whatever. Traces found of a heavy motorcycle in the shrubbery. Possibility that the vendor, confronted with an elderly fellow, decided to keep the product and the money both. Or perhaps it was a scam from the beginning. Come to the place alone, Dads. Or no sale. Knowing there would be no sale anyway. Oh, one more thing, which may or may not fit: Josie's boyfriend, since the separation, is one Peter Kesner, weird cinematic genius who made two motorcycle movies on small budgets and got a big reputation. I mention it only because motorcycles have started cropping up. I thought I might go see my friend Blaylock about people who peddle from their bikes. I mean, if it's a common practice or what. I can see the advantages. Narcs can stake out street corners, but they can't stake out the countryside."

"Why so far upstate?" Meyer asked.

"That's a question for Blaylock. It might be a territorial thing."

Aggie came back up and said it would be twenty minutes. We fixed another drink from the little rolling bar. It was nice under the awning, watching the pedestrian traffic, laughing at bad puns. We went below and ate in the alcove off the main lounge, served there by a very skilled Cuban lad. A slightly resinous wine went beautifully with the mountains of Greek groceries. I left in good season, full of resolve. But once I was aboard my houseboat, my knees began to buckle. I nearly dislocated my jaw yawning. I stripped down and fell into my gigantic bed.

The rattlesnake buzz of the bedside phone awakened me and I groped for the phone in the dark, wondering how it had gotten to be night.

"Uh?" I said.

"Well, hi! Were you asleep?"

"Certainly was. What time is it?"

"Little after nine. Missed you, love."

"Me too."

"Wondered if you made it back okay. Tell you the truth, I found time for a little nap today myself."

"Good for you."

"I know you will be as upset as I am to know that the bride picked up another dreadful sunburn this morning and is in bed with chills. And terrible little runny blisters all over her big meaty thighs."

"You are a mean one, aren't you?"

"Not really. I feel sorry for both of them. As a doctor, he should have seen what was happening to her and gotten her out of the sun."

"Interrupted honeymoon."

"I had a drink with him before dinner. She was sleeping, finally. I really looked at him and listened to him. You know, he is a very good-natured, sweet, earnest, solemn, dull little fellow. He chuckles a lot, but he hasn't any sense of humor. He laughs in the wrong places. Really, he's a *very* good doctor. Practically any cancer clinic in the world, you go in and mention Dr. Prescott Mullen...Travis, I just don't know how there got to be such a difference between what I thought he was and what he really is."

"Myths. Meyer says we build our own myths. We

live in the flatlands and the myths are our mountains, so we build them to change the contours of our lives, to make them more interesting."

"I haven't had such a dull life so far. I invested some of my very good years in Ellis, of course."

"Right now is your very best year, maybe."

"I see what Meyer means about myths. I mean you take some bored little suburban wife who plays bridge at the club every Thursday, she can dream that she and her tall brown tennis pro have something going, something unannounced, that they can never dare admit to each other. And that's her myth. If she tries to carry it to the point of its actually happening, it will blow up in her face."

"Like that, I guess."

"And right across the front of her, just above the cleavage, she's got a lot more of those runny little blisters. Hey, Travis?"

"What?"

"I didn't call you up to talk about the blisters on the doctor's bride. I had something profound to say. About us. Now it sounds trivial, I guess. The point is, I don't really want to think about us, about you and me, in the way I thought I would always have to think about somebody I was falling in love with."

"Love, Annie?"

"Let me just barge ahead and leave explanations until later, okay? Being in love has been to me a case of being up to here in plans. Whatever you might think, I wasn't being some kind of opportunist with Ellis. He was a very autocratic man, and he was very very experienced as far as women are concerned. I was dumb about him, and it is still sort of blank in my mind the way he hustled me into bed that first time. Then a person says, Oh, hell, whatever harm is done is done, and you get hung for a sheep as high as for being hung as a lamb. I think it goes like that. And I got to love him. He was a dear man in lots of little ways nobody knew about because he kept himself so much to himself. But let me tell you that anybody who had the wives he had certainly wasn't an unattractive man. I hope you are following all this. Anyhow, with love came plans. I worked it all out. Some day he would divorce Josie and marry me, and do it soon enough so I could have a child with him, and the child would make him a warmer person to be with. Then came the news about the cancer, and so that plan was shot to hell. Right? So there was another plan. I would nurse him and care for him and he would live a long time, and the sickness would purify him. It would burn away the nasty. Then he was killed and I was really really down. But I put my life back together, and I am a very fulfilled woman, businesswise. Now here I am falling in love, and I don't find myself planning anything about us, and that makes me wonder if it is love, really. All I think about is that maybe our lives are like the end of some long period of planning. I am here and you are there, and we are going to see each other now and again until we are too old and rickety to make it across Florida. But I know I am falling in love because I think of you and I turn hollow inside, and the world kind of veers. You know? Like it goes a little bit sideways for an instant. Hey, I wanted to tell you all this as if it was something important. And when I stop talking to you, I don't want you to feel any kind of obligation to say anything about love. Men hate being pinned to the wall like that. If you feel it, someday you'll say it, and that will be okay. And if you don't ever feel it, that will be okay too, as long as you don't ever try to fake it."

"Listen, I—"

"Don't say anything, dear. I can talk enough for two. Any time. Anywhere. So go back to sleep. Good night." *Click.*

I reached and put the phone back. We had been hooked together for a time by General Tel, and the softness of her voice in my ear in the darkness had recreated for me a world long forgotten, when I had stretched out on the leather couch in the hallway, phone on my juvenile chest, and while the family was in the next room listening to the radio, to Fred Allen or Amos and Andy, I was linked to the erotic, heart-stopping magic of leggy Margaret who, at fourteen, kissed with her eyes wide wide open.

I remembered the previous night when, with her head resting on my chest, Anne had stared off into some thoughtful distance. I could look down and see the black lashes move when she blinked. I could see a tiny slice of the gelatinous eyeball. You can repeat a word over and over until it means nothing, until it becomes just a strange sound. You can do the same thing looking at a familiar object until you see it in an entirely different way. Here was a strange wet globe, a shifting moving thing of fluids and membranes and nerves, tucked into muscle that could move it this way and that, that could shutter its lid to remove any dust, to moisten the surface of it. It had looked at me and relayed images of me into the gray suet of the brain behind that eye, where they would remain, instantly available whenever she remembered me. I stroked the dark hair. The wet eye blinked again. The dreaming thoughts behind it were unfathomable. I could never truly reach them, hers or anyone's. And mine would always be as opaque to others.

The phone rang again and she said, "I was so darn busy exposing my beautiful soul, Travis, I forgot to tell you another thing I called about."

"Such as?"

"I talked with Prescott about the drugs for Ellis. He told me that after he got back to Stamford he had a call from Josie. She knew he had flown down to check Ellis over, and she called to find out how he was. He told her what he thought Ellis's life expectancy was, and it depressed her. He knew that Josie still had a certain amount of influence with Ellis, so he told her to tell Ellis that there was really no point in his being so damned brave about his pain and to encourage him to make a connection and buy something. I think she must have tried to do that, because in early July he had several calls from her, and they all made him cross. Crosser than usual. He just didn't like people meddling in his life."

"But it was okay if he meddled in theirs."

"Exactly. That's just how he was. You know, you are really very good at sizing up people. It makes me nervous, in a way."

"Exactly how?"

"Well...anybody who is really good at reading people can be very good at finding the areas where they are vulnerable and then taking advantage of that vulnerability. You know what I mean."

"I will have to get Meyer to explain me to you."

"Can't you do that yourself?"

"Not as well as he can. According to him I take all emotional relationships much too seriously."

"It is very nice for a person to be taken seriously."

"I had this same conversation with a girl named Margaret before you were born. She was fourteen. She wanted to be taken seriously."

"And did you?"

"To the point where I couldn't eat and I walked into the sides of buildings."

"I'm jealous of her. And so, good night again, my love."

Once again she hung up quickly, before I could equivocate.

Meyer says that if I could, for once and all, stop my puritanical ditherings about emotional responsibility, I would be a far happier and less interesting man. In childhood I was taught that every pleasure has its price. As an adult I learned that the reprehensible and dreadful sin is to hurt someone purposely, for no valid reason except the pleasure of hurting. Gretel, in her wisdom about me, said one night, "You are never entirely *here*. Do you know that? You are always a little way down the road. You are always fretting about consequences instead of giving yourself up totally to the present moment."

Add those ingredients together and stir well, and you can come up with a lasting case of psychological impotence. Meyer said to me, "You spend too much time in the wings, watching your performance onstage, aching to rewrite your own lines, your own destiny."

"And just what the hell is my destiny?"

I can never forget his strange smile. "It is a classic destiny. The knight of the windmills. The man rolling the stone up the mountain. The endlessness of effort, Travis, so that the effort becomes the goal."

Right, in a sense. But Meyer is not all that infallible. There are times. Annie had been totally *now*. An immersion. So vital and hungry I had no need to be the man in the wings. I turned on the handy projector in the back of my head and ran through a box of slides, of still shots of her in the underwater green of the towel over the bed lamp, when she was biting into her lip and her eyes were wide and thoughtful, and she was shiny with the mists of effort. Being the neurotic that Meyer believes I am has the advantage of giving me a far narrower focus of pleasure than if I did not truly give a damn. The *now* is that unexpected, unanticipated place where the mind and the body and the emotions all meet in a proper season, destroying identity, leaving only an intensity of pleasure that celebrates all parts of that triad: body, mind, and spirit.

It is the difference maybe between gourmet and gourmand. In a world of fast food chains, the gourmet seldom eats well. But this again is too much of a celebration of sensitivity: "Oh, my God, look at how vulnerable and sensitive I am!" Which becomes a pose. And turns one into that kind of gourmet who looks for sauces instead of meat.

The only suitable attitude toward oneself and the world is the awareness of pathetic, slapstick comedy. You go staggering around the big top and they keep hitting you with bladders, stuffing you into funny little cars with eighteen other clowns, pursuing you with ducks. I ride around the sawdust trail in my own clown suit, from L. L. Bean's end-of-season sale: marked-down armor, wrong size helmet, swaybacked steed, mended lance, and rusty sword. And sometimes with milady's scarf tied to the helmet, whoever milady might be at the time of trial.

Meyer has pointed out that condition, that contradiction, which afflicts everyone who thinks at all: The more you strive to be sensible and serious and meaningful, the less chance you have of becoming so. The primary objective is to laugh.

8

Friday morning I drove the Rolls pickup up past Deer-field Beach, turned inland on 887, and after nine miles of nothing much, I came to Ted Blaylock's Oasis, look-ing not much shabbier than the last time I had seen it.

The long rambling frame structure paralleled the highway, obviously built a piece at a time over a long period. Most of it had a galvanized roof. The sign out at the edge of the right-of-way had been assembled in the same manner, one piece at a time. THE BIKER-BAR. Happy Hours 3 to 7. *Customizing—Trikes, Shovels, and Hogs.* Chili and Dogs. *Service on Carbs, Brakes, Tires, Spokes, Tanks, Frames, and Springers.* Tank art. Body Art. *Paraphernalia.*

I could look right through the open shed structure at one end, and it looked as though Ted had put up some more cabins out back. Men were working in the cement-floor shed, and I heard the high whine of metal being ground down. One portion had a display window with decals of trade names pasted on it and racks of shiny chrome accessories visible between the decals, next to some motorcycles in rank, new and shiny bright. There were some dusty motorcycles parked in front of the center part, in no particular pattern, along with a couple of big brutish pickups, on top of their oversized tires, and a rack with a few bicycles. As I got out of the car, somebody dropped a wrench and it rang like a bell as it bounced off the floor.

I went in through the screen door and it slapped shut behind me. Ceiling fans were whirring overhead. The combination bar and lunch counter stretched across the back of the room, with a dozen stools bolted to the floor in front of it. There were a half dozen wooden tables, each big enough for four chairs. There were new posters behind the bar, big bright gaudy ones, showing semi-clad young ladies who, according to their expressions, were having orgasmic relationships with the motorcycles over which they had draped themselves. Another poster showed a cop beating on a biker's skull and had the big red legend ABATE.

Three of the brotherhood were on barstools, all big, all fat, all bearded. They wore sleeveless tank tops, denim vests with lots of snaps and pockets and zippers, ragged jeans, boots, a jungle of blue tattooing on their big bare arms, and wide leather wristlets, studded on the outside of the wrists with sharp metal points. Their vests were covered with bright patches and faded patches, celebrating various runs, meets, and faraway clubs. Their helmets were on a table behind them. All three heads were going thin on top but had long locks down almost to the shoulders.

They stopped talking and gave me the look. It is supposed to instill instant caution, if not terror. The girl behind the counter gave me a different kind of look, empty as glass. She was apparently part Seminole, thin as sticks, wearing white jogging shorts with red trim and a tight cotton T-shirt with, between the widespread banty-egg lumps of little breasts, the initials F.T.W.

I said to her, "Ted around?"

"Busy."

"You want to tell him McGee wants to see him?"

"When he's through in there, okay?"

"Coffee, then. No cream." I took the end stool, and the mighty threesome lost interest in me and went back to their conversation.

"Well, what that dumb fucker did, he put in that time pulling out what he had and fittin' in them Gary Bang pistons and that Weber carb and all, and when he got it all done, that shovel wasn't worth shit. Man, he couldn't hardly get out of his own way. We come down from Okeechobee first light Sunday, rammin' it all the way, heads all messed up from that shit Scooter was mixing with ether, Whisker and me racing flat out. I come in maybe fifteen seconds behind Whisker and we could have took naps before Stoney come farting in. After all that work on it, he was so fuckin' mad, he jumped off'n it and just let it fall. And then he run around it and kicked it in the saddle, screaming at it, and he was still so mad he run over to a tree and swung on it and cracked his middle knuckle and got a hand that swole up like a ball. We like to had a fit laughing. That old boy just ain't handy, and that's all there is to it."

"Hey," said the one in the middle, "we got to move it, you guys. See you around, Mits."

"Sure thing, Potsie. Have a nice day, guys."

They worked their helmets on as they walked out, swung aboard, and started their engines, and after some deep *garoong-garoong-garoong* revvings they went droning and popping out onto the empty highway, turning toward the west, riding three abreast.

Mits gave me sly glances as she cleaned the counter where they had been. I said, "Wouldn't hurt to just let him know."

"You selling anything?"

"I'm an old friend."

She shrugged and went out. She was back quickly. "Hey, you can go in. He asked her and she said it was okay you could watch."

"Watch what?"

"He's into body art, and this one is kinda pukey, but it's what she wants, I guess. Go on through to the second room there."

When I opened the door and went in and shut it behind me, Ted looked up from his work and said our traditional greeting. "Hi, sarge."

"How you, lieutenant?"

"Come see what you think of this."

He had his wheelchair rolled up close to a cot which was elevated on four concrete blocks. A doughy broad-faced young girl lay on the cot. Her denim shorts were on a nearby chair. She wore a yellow T-shirt, and she was naked from the waist down. Ted had his tray of needles and dyes close at hand. There was a broad strip of masking tape placed to keep her big dark bush of pubic hair pulled down out of the way so that he could start his design right at the hair roots. It was almost done. It was a pattern of three mushrooms, growing up that white-as-lard lower belly, chubby romanticized mushrooms, the kind under which would squat a Disney elf. There was a book open nearby with a color drawing of three mushrooms growing in a cluster. Ted had simplified the drawing somewhat.

He went to work. The girl compressed her lips and closed her eyes. The needle machine buzzed. The window air conditioner rattled and thumped. She snorted and her belly muscles quivered.

"It's wearing off again," she said. "Jesus!"

"Almost through. Hang on."

It took about five minutes more. The buzzing stopped. He caught a corner of the tape and ripped it free.

"Ouch! Goddamn it, that hurt!"

"Stop being such a baby, Lissa. Go look at yourself."

She swung her legs off the couch and slipped down to the floor and walked over to a narrow wall mirror. She had a white hippo rump, a bushel of meat jiggling and flexing as she walked. She stared at herself and giggled and said, "Wow. This's gonna blast ol' Ray right out of his skull."

"I can believe it," Ted said.

She came walking back and picked up her shorts. Before she put them on she gave me a speculative look and said, "Whaddaya think?"

"Well, I'd say it's unusual."

"You bet your ass it's unusual. And I got your word of sacred honor, right, Ted? Nobody else gets the same thing?"

"Not from me, they don't. Even if they get down on their knees and beg."

She put her shorts on and fastened the snaps.

He said, "Here, I forgot. Rub this into the design now and when you go to bed and in the morning. It's an antiseptic cream. For three or four days. Don't forget. No, go in the can and do it, hon. I'm a little tired of looking at you."

— 94

She shrugged and left, slinging her big plastic purse over her plump shoulder.

When the door shut, Ted said, "Play your cards right, Trav, and you could cut a piece of that." He rolled himself over to the sink with his tray of equipment.

"'Mirror, mirror, on the wall. Who's the fairest one of all?' I think I'd be overcome by all that gentle beauty. You know, you're pretty good at that, Blaylock."

"Necessity is the mother of income. Tattooing is very very big lately. You should see my dragons and snakes. The mushrooms took a little over an hour. For eighty bucks. I've got one crazy broad for a customer, I've put over a thousand dollars' worth of dye under her hide. Very strange stuff. No anesthetic cream for her. The thing for her is that the pain of the needle is a turn-on. It's all a marine motif. Dolphins and pirates and old ships, mermaids, things like that. I wish you could see her. Unlike dumpy little Lissa, she's got a hell of a nice bod. Too nice for what she's having done to it."

I sat down beside his desk, and when he came rolling over I got a better look at him. He was even thinner than before. His color was bad and his thinning hair looked dead.

"You feeling all right?" I asked.

"Not too damn wonderful. Like they told me in the beginning, I'm severed so high up, I got what they called a limited life expectancy."

"Where's Big Bess?"

"Well, there was a very very flashy Colombiano pistolero came in, and he really took to her, she being about twice his height and weight, and she was tired of waiting on a paraplegic crip, so now he has her stashed down in the Hotel Mutiny there, eating chocolates and watching the soaps, while he is out around town gunning down the competition. But I've got Mits, my little Indian, and she is a wonder. She's quicker and better and a lot cleaner than Bess. And my God, that little bod is strong. She can pick me right up and walk with me. Loyal as hell. I wonder why I put up with Bess for so long. Or she with me."

"Business going okay?"

"Real well. I really like this body-art work."

"You draw pretty pictures."

"That was what I was going to be, several thousand years ago. I had two years at Parsons." I knew we were both thinking of what had come after that. Basic training, OCS, battlefield promotion, and finally a morning of hard cold rain and incoming mortar fire when I had helped carry the litter down the hill and prop it in the weapons carrier.

"In the VA hospital," he said, "I did a lot of sketches of the guys. I wanted to try to be a commercial artist—not enough mobility to make it. Then this came along. I studied up, mail-ordered the gear, started practicing on my friends. It's a gas. Want one on the arm? Eagle? Anchor? Hi, Mom? Semper Fidelis? F.T.W.?"

"No, thanks a lot. I always figure a tattooed man either got so sloppy drunk he didn't know what was happening, or he needed to have a tattoo to look at to reassure himself he was manly. That F.T.W. is what's on the T-shirt out there, on Mits. What is it?"

"It's been around awhile, Trav. It's the outlaw biker's creed. It stands for Fuck the World."

"Oh."

"Something special on your mind?"

"I shouldn't come out here and ask for favors."

"This is the second time in...what is it?...
Anyway, lots of years. I just hope to hell there's something I *can* do."

I leaned back and rested the heel of one boat shoe on the corner of his desk. "What I need to know is how much the bike clubs are into the drug traffic."

He closed his eyes for a moment. It accentuated the death look of the long bones of his skull. "So far, the question is too loose. The answer is too complicated."

"Ramble a little."

"Well, take the Fantasies. The insignia is the black fist and the yellow lightning, with a red circle around it. With the local affiliated clubs they could maybe put five to six hundred machines on the road, as against the two thousand the Bandidos could mount out west. Now most of these guys are factory workers and warehousemen and mechanics and such. They have meets and shows, smoke pot, wear the sincere raggedy garments and heavy boots, get tattooed, sport a lot of chains and medals, grow big bushy beards, zoom around on weekends with their so-called foxy ladies hanging on behind, drink a lot of beer, smoke a lot of pot, blow coke. What they have, Trav, is a kind of brotherhood hang-up. Anybody is in trouble, they all help. They look a hell of a lot nastier than they are. It's a charade. You get hard with them, they'll stomp you flat into the ground. But if there's no provocation, they have nothing to prove.

"Now as to trafficking in drugs, the story is a little different. There are the club officers, with what the law calls no visible means of support. The officers are the link between the troops and the drug importers and distributors, the money washers, the mafia accountants. Now say we take some group leader captain, call him Mother Machree, and he gets hold of one of the troops, Tom Baloney, and he tells Tom that when he gets off work at the body shop he is to go to the corner of First and Main and sit idling his engine and somebody will hand him a package, and he's to run it up to such and such a corner in Hialeah, weaving around through the back streets, shaking any tail, and get there at seven on the nose and hand it to the woman in the red dress who asks him how many miles he gets to the gallon in that thing he's riding."

"What's the payoff to Baloney?"

"That's one of the points I want to make. He gets the knowledge that he has been full of brotherhood and loyalty, and he knows that Mother Machree will toss five hundred bucks into the pot for the next beer bust. But the troops are getting restless. They know that maybe Mother got six thou for setting up that foolproof run, and there's the feeling around that maybe the officers are getting too far into the business. Some of them have taken to wearing the corporation garments, blow-dry hairstyles, limos with Cuban drivers. Too much separation between the officers and the troops. That is the kind of bitching I hear. They are being used, and they know it."

"Do any of the troops do any retailing on their own?"

"It could happen, but I don't think it would be a big thing. It really wouldn't go with the image they try to project. It would have to be a situation where there was a heavy cash-flow problem, a man out of work. Or maybe a favor for a friend."

"Suppose a man in Lauderdale got a call that somebody would meet him at such and such a time way up the line, over a hundred miles away. And when he went up there to buy, the man who called him wasted him, and though there were no witnesses, maybe the machine the biker was using was identified as to make."

"Recently or way back?"

"Two years in July."

"That's very heavy action, Sergeant McGee. What kind of machine?"

I dug the piece of paper out of my shirt pocket. "The man who saw the track says it was the rear K-One-twelve of a set of ContiTwins, deep enough to indicate a quarter-ton machine, so he guessed a BMW Nine-seventy-two."

"Pretty reasonable guess. But it could have been an HD, or a Gold Wing Honda, or a Kawasaki KZ series, or a big Laverda or Moto Guzzi, or a GS series Suzuki, or an XS series Yamaha. All burly machines. Big fast bastards. But sweet and smooth. You almost can't stress them. And they could all wear ContiTwins. Where did it happen?"

"Up near Citrus City, on the turnpike. A man named Esterland who was dying of cancer."

"I think I remember news on the tube about that. Sure. But there wasn't any mention of drugs or bikes."

"Not enough to go on, so it didn't get in."

"Where do you come in, Trav?"

"A little favor for the guy's son. Ron Esterland. By the way, he's an artist too. Had a big sellout show in London."

"Hey, I know the name. Didn't make the connection. Saw some color plates of his work in *Art International*. Pretty much okay."

"So what should I do next?"

"I don't understand why the buy should have been set up so far out in the boonies. But I can tell you that any one of those kinds of horses I named would be owned by somebody known to the brotherhood. Up by Citrus City and from there on up, it's a different turf. Up there you've got the Corsairs. But there's a lot of interclub contact, when bikers from both clubs go to out-of-state rallies and rendezvous. I think that maybe, if it was nearly two years ago, it's become part of the legend."

"How so?"

"Trav, these people go back to a kind of tribal society. Myths and legends. Whoever was involved would keep his mouth shut and make his woman keep her mouth shut. But after a long time there's not much heat involved. Maybe his woman has switched riders. With lots of beer and grass and encampments in the night, the word gets out. A little here and a little there, and it gets built up into something a lot wilder and more romantic than it was. Do you understand?"

"Sure. I think so."

"If you can find a legend that seems to fit and then unravel it all the way back to the way things really were, you can maybe—just maybe—come up with a name. And even that won't mean much. It'll be a biker name: Skootch or Grunge or BugBoy. And there's turn-over among the troops. Some get into heavy action and get put away. Some of them, when the fox gets pregnant, decide to pack up and get out."

"Can you find out if there's a legend about Esterland?"

"I can listen. I can poke around a little but not much, because it makes these people nervous. I get along fine because I carry good merchandise, and my people do good work, and the prices are right, and the law has never learned a thing out here. And if you learn anything from me about that little party..."

"You don't need to say it. Now, something else. A couple of biker movies a few years ago. *Chopper Heaven. Bike Park Ramble.*"

"Saw them when they came on the cable. What do you want? Some kind of critique?"

"Whatever."

"The outlaw bikers came off meaner and nastier than they are as far as tearing up civilians is concerned. And they came off a little more clean and pure than they are the way they act within the group. Enough stimulation, and they get into gang-bang situations. And if anybody finks to the law, man or woman, they can be a long slow time dying in the piney woods. Technically there were very few mistakes. A lot less than usual. I understand they used outlaw bikers as technical advisers. The sound track was too loud. And those pack leaders were just a little bit too evil to be real. They came out close together, those two movies, at least five years ago. Probably seven years ago. The straight clubs are still bitching about those movies because they think the civilians can't tell the difference between outlaw and straight. I see they still run them on syndication, late at night. Why do you ask?"

"Ted, I'm just rummaging around in this thing, kicking stones, shaking the bushes. The fellow who wrote and produced and directed those two movies stood to maybe get hold of a lot of money due to the killing of Esterland."

"How could that be, for God's sake?"

"Esterland's daughter was dying, in a coma. No chance of recovery. If Esterland survived her, most of the money would go to a foundation. If he died first, the daughter would get it; and then it went to the mother, who was still legally married to Esterland, on the death of her daughter a couple of weeks later. And that movie person, Peter Kesner, is or was close to Mrs. Esterland."

"Way way out there on the end of a long stick, pal."

"For two and a half mil, net, you can think up some very strange things. People will take a lot of pains over that kind of money."

"Did Kesner need money that bad?"

"I'll probably go out there and see what's going on. I haven't really decided. I'm on expenses, but I don't want to waste my friend's money."

"I heard over the grapevine you'd tapped out, Trav."

"In what way?"

"The quiet life. The straight life. Peddling boats or some damn thing. Heard you got scuffed up and turned into a nine-to-five person. When I heard it, I said there was no way. I said you were too used to conning the world, knocking heads, saving maidens. I said that you could lose an arm and a foot and an ear, but when they rang the bell, you'd still slide down the pole and hop onto the truck."

"Meyer said the same thing, but in a slightly different way."

"How is that old egghead?"

"As hairy and belovèd as ever. He's being entertained by a chain of small newspapers."

"That's nice."

"You'll be in touch?"

"I get even a whisper, I'll give you a call. Look, send Mits on in with a Doctor Pepper. Thanks."

I went out and found her rinsing glasses and told her what Ted wanted. She nodded and I said, "He doesn't look too great."

She straightened up and turned to face me. "He isn't too great. That's for sure. These last weeks, he's been going down. It makes me nervous."

"Can you get him looked at?"

"I've tried. You better goddam believe it."

"I believe it. He is a strange and special guy."

"I know."

"He's very fond of you, Mits."

"I know that too."

"Look, here's my number. Any real bad turn, you can phone me and I'll be out here with a doctor."

"You can't get a doctor to make a house call."

"How much would you like to bet?"

The shiny black eyes looked me over, and suddenly the impassive brown face broke into a big smile that wrinkled the nose and squeezed the eyes almost shut. "No bet. Thanks."

When I went out, there were two large bikers staring into the front of my pickup. They had opened it up.

"Something I can do for you?"

They turned to stare at me. Whiskers and hair and hard little eyes, like professional villain wrestlers.

"That's a Merc you got in there, right?"

"Close. It's a big Lincoln."

"Custom heads?"

I edged past them and closed the hood. "Yes, and some other goodies."

"What'll it do?"

"Absolutely no idea."

"Too chicken to take it all the way?"

"Not exactly. The needle sits against the pin at one twenty."

"Why do you keep the outside looking like shit?"

"I wasn't aware that it did."

One looked at the other and said in a higher voice, "He wasn't aware that it did. Look, you use it to run something? Is that why it looks cruddy?"

"Right now, I run myself home. Okay?"

The near one grabbed me by the arm and pulled me back as I started to step up onto the running board. "Maybe you're not through answering questions, Ace."

It made me feel tired. I took his hand off my arm. "Friend, it has been nice having our little chat here. I do not want any childish hassling. Nobody has to prove anything. Okay?"

The screen door opened and Ted came wheeling out onto the concrete walk. He said, "Hey, Mike. Hey, Knucks. What's happening?"

"You know this guy?"

"I know him. So?"

"Do you know he's got a smart mouth and a funny-looking truck?"

"My sincere recommendation, Knucks, would be don't mess with him."

"Don't mess with Ace here? You kidding? This cat is over the hill."

I looked at Ted, wondering why he was setting me up. I said, "What are you trying to do?"

He shrugged. "It's been dull around here, sarge. And good old Knucks here has a nasty habit of trying to grope Mits every time she walks by."

With an inward sigh I moved a few inches farther out of range. I'd been working out faithfully of late, and was right at two-oh-five, which is a very good weight for my six foot four. I look as if I would go about one eighty. The big advantage I had over these too-lardy fellows was a great deal of quick. Quick is what counts. Without the quick, they get to hit you in the face, and that is both demeaning and discouraging. Also, it hurts a lot. The secondary advantage is, of course, quite a few years of scrabbling around, learning that the healthiest attitude is to inflict maximum pain in minimum time.

And the way to create an opening is to create rage. I smiled at them. "Knucks? Ah, *you* are Knucks. You better recheck your tendency to grope the ladies. You look faggoty to me, pal."

He came roaring and swinging, big roundhouse right and left blows, too smart to be a headhunter. At least not yet. He wanted to cave my ribs in first. I trotted about twenty feet backward, just out of range, and when I estimated he had picked up enough speed to compensate for the heft of him, I clapped both hands on his right wrist, rolled backwards, got my feet into his belly just as he was tumbling over me, and gave him a very brisk hoist, while still clinging to the wrist. He whomped the dust like a sack of sand dropped off the top of a building. As I released him, rolled to the side, and came up, I guessed from the sound of impact that good old Knucks was out of the game.

I focused on Mike, coming at me at a half run, right fist cocked. I had time to decide whether to go under it, inside it, or outside it. Outside seemed best, but he waited so long I had to do a Muhammad Ali lean to get my face the final inch out of the way. I felt the breeze of it. He ran on by and was just starting to turn when I heel-stomped him in the back of the knee. He went down and came up, fighting for balance, arms spread wide. I hopped very close, braced my right heel, and pivoted so as to put my hips, back, shoulder, and arm into a very short straight right that went wrist deep into the bulge a few inches above his very fancy brass belt buckle.

He lay down in a fetal position and began throwing up. Knucks was sitting up cradling his right arm. His face was all screwed up like a schoolyard child trying desperately not to cry. His arm came out of the shoulder at a slightly unusual angle.

Ted said, "You're not getting older. You're getting better."

"They might not take kindly to all this, later on."

"You heard me advise them not to mess with you."

"They are fat and they are slow. Not exactly a proud victory."

"And they are not legitimate members of any club, Trav. Anybody moves against me, and the Fantasies take care of it. Right, Knucks?"

"Jesus, Ted! Jesus Christ! I can't stand it. Help me, somebody."

By then the mechanics had moved in. They gave me quick looks in which wonder and disbelief were mingled. Mike was moaning to himself and trying to sit up. They were being given all necessary assistance, so I waved to Ted and Mits and got into Miss Agnes and drove off eastward toward the coast, wondering if this would become one of the ongoing legends and be distorted out of all relation with reality. Showdown at the

Oasis. Fat and slow and dumb. Dumb was the most serious sin. Without the dumb additive, they would not have charged, would not have tried to hit. They would have waited, circled, grabbed, and given me a very bad day. Pale-eyed stranger whips over five hundred pounds of angry meat in a shade over fourteen seconds. It had worked very very well, better than I had any right to expect. So I should not get carried away and come on fearless with the next couple of bikers, who might very well be just as quick and just as able. Or might feel more comfortable with knife or gun or piece of pipe.

What I did not want, most of all, was to become some kind of symbol of challenge, so that their buddies would look me up to take a chop and try their luck. I wanted no part of any OK Corral syndrome. I had long outgrown that kind of testicular lunacy. People who become legends in their own time usually have very little time left.

9

On Saturday morning I saw that the *Byline* was gone and knew Meyer would have a shortened cruise rather than none at all. I had some ideas to throw at him. He always seems to know which ones to field and which ones to let roll on out to the warning track. I took a swim, took a beach walk, and intercepted a Frisbee with the back of my head, an incident that seemed to strike horror into a group of fourteen-year-old ladies. I gave it back, into the wind, with all the wrist flick I could put on it, and by great good fortune it stood still after it reached them. They stared at it, and one of them reached out and picked it out of the air.

So it made a game. Three of them on one side, one of me on the other. It is a great game for running, stretching, and leaping. Usually in any group of teens, one out of three will give promise of growing up into a dog. But not one of these. Comely maidens all, and very competitive. They whirred that championship plastic at me with sincere attempts to whack my head off with it. They were practicing catching the Frisbee behind their back and under a leg, and I served up floaters to give them a sense of achievement. Their brown leaping bodies and half-formed breasts and hips instilled in me such a wistful lechery, I wondered if it might be best if I turned myself in. They could put me away where I'd do no harm.

The game broke up. We had never exchanged a name. They went trotting into the sea, and I went walking back to Bahia Mar. After my shower, I got out the battered old looseleaf address book and sat in the lounge in my robe, turning pages, looking for the right California connection. And in the L's I found Walter Lowery, both his business phone in San Francisco and his home phone in San Mateo. I brought the phone on the long cord over to the curved yellow couch, swung my feet up and tried the San Mateo number, got a recorded announcement, got a different number from information and entered it in my book, and tried it.

"Hello?" said a cautious female voice.

"Marty?"

"No. This is Ginny. Who is this?"

"My God, you sound all grown up, Gin. This is T. McGee, your honorary uncle in Florida. Your father around?"

"Hi! I'll get him. Hold on."

After a long minute he came on and said, "Obviously, sir, you are an impostor pretending to be a friend I used to have."

"Time flies, friends flee, temperance fuggit. Look, maybe I'm coming out there."

"People usually know whether they are coming out or not."

"Then let's say I will be out. *When* is not certain. I am out of touch. You still have the office in Los Angeles?"

"Yes, we do."

"Is Lysa Dean still a client?"

"Let's say she doesn't have as many legal problems as she used to. But yes. We're still on a retainer arrangement."

"And you do remember recommending me to her?"

"Indeed I do. Let's say she was very satisfied with your performance professionally, and furious as hell at you about something else, which she never explained."

"I get the impression she's doing a lot of game shows."

"Indeed she is. At very good rates. She's in demand because she is really very quick and often very funny, which is rare out here with most actresses. And she gets some cameo roles now and again."

"She gave me the impression—back when I knew her—of knowing everything about everybody out there."

"Gossip is a hobby with Lee."

"Did she ever marry that forty million dollars from Hawaii?"

I heard him sigh. "She came close, buddy. Really close. He was on the verge of getting his annulment through the Vatican when his wife came down with leukemia. So what could he do? He settled a nice little bundle on Lee, and they kept up the relationship, and he died of a heart attack last year. His wife is still living."

"Lee live in the same place?"

"Same house. Beverly Hills. She redecorates it every twenty or thirty minutes." I read him the address out of my book and he confirmed it.

"Have you got her unlisted number?"

"Before we go into that, Travis, if she feels toward

you like I think she feels toward you, you won't get past hello. Secondly, it is quarter to ten out here, and she won't even lift the edge of her sleep mask or take out an earplug until noon."

"So I'll call her at four o'clock my time. And I will never tell her where I got the number. And I will try to keep her from hanging up on me."

"I'll give you the number if you tell me what you did to make her so furious."

I thought it over. It certainly wasn't in the kiss-and-tell category. "Well, Walter, our business was finished. She had the photographs and the negatives back. I was at her place to pick up the money I had coming, by agreement. She started worming around on my lap, starting to shuck herself out of her tight knit pants, and I suddenly wanted no part of her. So I gave her a big push and she went flying back and landed on her fanny on a white furry rug and rode it backward all the way across the room. I told her I would take the short count on the money but I would like to skip the thankful bang, as it would mean very little to me and less than nothing to her. So I left, dodging elephants from her little collection. And she knew a lot of ten- and twelve-letter words. Knew them real loud."

"Mother of Moses in the morning," he said in an awed hushed voice. "I doubt there's three idiots in the world have turned that down. Maybe there's only one. And you think she won't hang up?"

"Time has passed, Walter. Woman's curiosity. Maybe she has a little feeling of disbelief. Maybe it didn't really happen that way."

"Can I ask you why you want to talk to her?"

"To get a line on some other people out there."

He waited and when I didn't go into it any further, he said, "If they've had any connection at all to the Industry, Lysa Dean will know when and where they got every traffic ticket."

I wrote down the number he gave me, and then we chatted a little while about old times, old places, old friends. He said it wasn't the same out there, wasn't as much fun. The money had gotten too heavy. You get a budget over twenty million dollars, a lot of the fun goes out of moviemaking. But people were getting in trouble as often as before, and he was kept busy. He said Ginny had grown into a truly beautiful girl, and if she ever tried to get into the Industry, he would shave her head, bind her feet, and have all her teeth extracted. Marty got on to tell me how much they both missed me, and why not come out once in a while, and I said that from now on I would.

That is one of the great troubles, I thought, after I hung up. The people you have great empathy with are never conveniently located nearby. Many are, but the rest are scattered far and wide. You see them too seldom. But you can always pick up right where you left off. You know who they are. They know who you are. No reintroductions required.

I took the robe off and worked with the weights until I needed another shower. Had a drink, fixed a light lunch, went to bed and set the alarm for four.

When it awakened me, I looked in the address book and checked out her new number and dialed it. I had made some notes beside her name. Little things she had told me, accidentally or on purpose. I looked at the notes as the phone rang.

A woman's voice answered by repeating the last four

digits of the number, on a rising intonation of question, "Three three five five?" She had a subtly Japanese way of handling the consonants.

"Lysa Dean, please."

"I will see if she is in at the moment. May I say who is calling?"

"Tell her I have a message from Walter Lowery's office."

"You may give me the message, sir."

"My instruction is to give it to her personally."

"Just a moment, please."

I sat listening to the electronic humming.

"Who are you?" demanded Lysa Dean. "What the hell does Walter want told me on a Saturday? That I'm being audited again? I already for Christsake know that." The throaty, furry, flexible voice had a steely ring behind the fur.

"I scampered out of your life in a hail of elephants, love."

"What?"

"This is Lee Schontz, isn't it? From Dayton, Ohio. Would it have been 1610 Madison Street? Was daddy a fireman? Do you photograph well in the buff, love?"

"Could it be...No! McGee? Is this you, McGee, you rotten dirty son of a bitch?"

"Lee, it's so damn wonderful to hear your voice."

"Let me sit down. Jesus! You got me out of the shower. What the hell do you mean, calling me? What a nerve! Where did you get this number? I had it changed two weeks ago. Did you get it from Walter? I'll tear him to ribbons!"

"I wouldn't put a friend on a spot like that. I got your

number from another source. You remember how resourceful I am, don't you?"

"Look, let me go get a robe on and take this in the bedroom." Several minutes passed. She came back on, a half octave lower. "Now I'm comfy. Are you in Florida, dear?"

"Aren't you going to hang up on me?"

"No, dear. I shouldn't be angry at you. You did me a great favor, actually. You made me take a good close look at Lysa Dean. And I wasn't too enchanted with what I saw. I saw myself through your eyes. And I felt cheap. Yes, cheap. I thought that anything Lysa did was acceptable because it was Lysa doing it. But it wasn't, was it?"

"How much of that is bullshit, Lee?"

"Practically all of it, Travis. Nobody else ever made me that mad. I steamed for months."

"But you got over it."

"Hell, yes. My dearest hope would be that you have thought about me for years and years and you want to come out here and pick up on what you turned down a long time ago. I would lead you on, baby, and then I would cut you right the hell off at the pockets. Or nearby."

"Wouldn't blame you a bit."

The voice softened. "You know what really hurt me? What really really hurt me? The way you said that making love with you would mean less than nothing to me. You were wrong, dear. Wrong, wrong, wrong. I was *infatuated* with you. And it would have meant a great great deal to me. I was going to prove to you how much it meant. Oh, hell. This sounds like bullshit too, doesn't it? I guess it is."

"Heard about your bad luck with Mr. X in Hawaii. Sorry it had to come out that way."

"Thanks, dear. Louie was an okay person all the way. He couldn't leave Muriel once she got sick. It would have poisoned our marriage, building it on that kind of luck. But he was very good to me. I've sort of forgotten what the wolf looks like."

"I ran into you twice on game shows, when I was spinning the dial. You were in a little box up in the air, looking very very good."

"I'm keeping well, they tell me. I can't exactly pass for twenty. Or even twenty-seven. No mere slip of a girl. Can't get away with the cutesy stuff any more. Elfin old me. I work because I like it, dear. Are you still slipping about, doing shifty things for people?"

"It's a living. Salvage consultant."

"Boy, you sure salvaged me that time. I'm forever grateful."

"How's Dana Holtzer?"

"Great. Her husband finally died. She's Dana Maguire, and she's still making babies. She found out she's good at it. Four, and one in the oven. Darling kids."

"Say hi for me when you see her. I want to know something about a couple of people you probably know. I guess I want to know everything you might know about them."

"Who?"

"Josie Laurant Esterland and Peter Kesner."

"That's what they mean when they talk about a bucket of worms. Look, are you in town? Could you come over here?"

"I'm in Florida."

"Oh, heck, I thought you could come over and maybe

we could level with each other, and I'd cancel my tennis date and we'd sort of mess around a little and get reacquainted. With no cutting off at pockets or anywhere else. Afternoons are fun. Look, it will cost you a hell of a phone bill if you listen to all of this."

"Let me ask a couple of questions, and then maybe I'll come listen in person."

"Okay."

"Are they together?"

"God only knows. That is what is called a volatile relationship. They are somewhere in Indiana or one of those states there in the middle, making a disaster movie."

"A disaster movie?"

"A financial disaster. That's what they call those around here lately. Disaster movies. Never never work in something your boyfriend is directing. Romance ends."

"What kind of a movie is it? What about?"

"It is rumored to be about balloons."

"Balloons?"

"You know. Little baskets hang under them, and they have gas burners, and they are all pretty colors, and you go sailing away over the pretty farmland, saying oh and ah. Hot-air balloons."

"It's an independent production?"

"Like practically everything else except for comicbook stuff like the Empire series at Fox. And it is pretty well established here, among those who like to snigger, that Josie is helping bankroll it. I hear they had a long long struggle with script, and finally Peter rewrote it himself, poor lamb. Then they scrounged some bank money and some money from the distributor and went out on location a few weeks ago. And they've had rotten weather. They are together in the balloon picture, but elsewhere, as in the sack, I don't know. Hey, you better come out here, McGee. I'm getting such a nice little rush out of just talking to you. Really. You're filed under Unfinished Business."

"I don't know. Bits and pieces have to come together. I'm like an old blue tick hound, running back and forth at the edge of the swamp, nose in the air, wondering if there's a trail worth following and kind of hating the idea of going into the mud and the snakes and the gators."

"Goodness, how quaint! How picturesque! I hope that when you are trotting back and forth with your tongue hanging out, you'll get downwind of me. I'll be sending out a message."

"What's happening to ladies? What's happened to buttons and bows, and shy sidelong smiles, and demure blushes?"

"You must be some kind of old-time chauvinist. What's the matter? We alarm you?"

"Sort of, I guess."

"When you were solving my little problem were you thinking of it in terms of swamp and snakes?"

"I think so. Walk into the back of anybody's skull, be they born-again, big mullah, or resident of the death house, and you'll come to the edge of a swamp that stretches as far as the eye can see. It's part of the human condition."

"ow cynical!"

"really. Meyer says that knowing it is there is ttle. Beware of those turkeys who really re absolutely pure, decent, honest, God-fearing, hard-working, patriotic Americans. They'll slip a rusty blade into your belly, look upward, and proclaim it God's will. They'll believe they've done it for your own salvation."

"Then you have no need to beware of me, my dear. I am impure, indecent, dishonest, lazy, and permanently randy. You can trust me all the way. I've got a swamp you wouldn't hardly believe."

I thanked her for her help and broke off with cheery goodbyes. I had not known how she would react to me. I had inflicted such a deep wound in her pride, it was probably still draining. There she was at that time, Lysa Dean, a genuine celebrity, a sex symbol, a box-office draw, mobbed wherever she went, star player in the erotic fantasies of a million men she would never meet, and when, out of gratitude, out of affection, she tried to bestow upon a nobody from Fort Lauderdale a warm morsel of all her international magic, giving him a memory that would make him vibrate for the rest of his life, the dreary ungrateful damn fool had turned it down. And, given the insecurity of the aging actress, I could guess that the rejection haunted her in the bleak hours of the night when the sleeping pill had worn off. She wanted to get her hands on me, and there were two ways she could go. She could either build me up to an overpowering urgency and turn it all off, or she could really devote herself to proving what a hell of a deal I, in my ignorance, had turned down. Prudence said to stay the hell away from her. I remembered her slanted green eyes, very handsome, and merciless as a questing cat.

10

At noon on Sunday Annie phoned me and told me she had just had a full hour of good sun right out in front of her cabana, had come in and had her shower, and was stretched out on the bed under the fan, letting the moving air dry her off and thinking of me.

"Cut it out, Annie!"

"Saturday morning I got word that they're going to let me have the extra wing I've been asking for. Twenty more rooms over on the other side, two-story. The architect is coming down."

"That's nice."

"We've been out of balance here. When we're full, we have more bar and dining room and kitchen capacity than we're using. I hate to encourage a lot of outside business coming in, just to eat and drink. Sooner or later that creates problems. If we make it with our guests, it's more like a club. If it could possibly be done by December, I can really show them one hell of a season next year. Already we are reserved almost full for the first quarter. Are you interested at all in this kind of stuff? I have nobody else to brag to."

"Of course I'm interested, Annie."

"I bet. It's exciting to me. It is kind of like farming. I mean you have a nice harvest of tourists coming up, and all of a sudden you get a tornado, or a red tide, or a big oil spill, or the country goes on gas rationing. So it's always a little bit nervous. Or a hurricane will come and wash us away. We're pretty exposed here."

"Sooner or later one will. Just hope it's later."

"Very cheery."

"Any chance of you ever getting away, Annie? Like for a week or two. A little boat ride to no place in particular?"

"Not anytime real soon. I fired my assistant manager. He kept telling me how wonderful I am and slicing me up whenever I turned my back. Caught him at it. I've got a new guy now. And I think he is going to work out. He hasn't had a lot of experience, but he knows food and liquor service and he gets along with the guests and the employees. It looks as if by maybe sometime in July I could give him a trial run, by going where he can't ask me questions. Is July okay?"

"Great. Maybe I'll bring the *Flush* around and pick you up over there and we'll flip a coin for which direction we go. North or south."

"Beautiful. I wouldn't want to stay on a boat too long. I spent too much time on the *Caper* with Ellis. There's no place to put anything, and no real privacy. It was like the walls were closing in."

"The bulkheads."

"The walls, honey. Walls and floors. Kitchen and bathroom. Upstairs, downstairs. Inside and outside. Ellis was so damn picky about being seamanlike, I decided after he died that the whole thing is a crock. I lived aboard until it got sold, and I called everything by the civilian name for it, and it made me sort of happy."

"I want to ask you something else. You told me Josie called Ellis a couple of times. Several times, I believe you said. Early in July. At that time she must have been terribly concerned and depressed about the condition of her daughter, Romola."

"Oh, she was. Of course."

"You said that the phone calls from her made him cross."

"I see what you mean. I knew that they weren't about Romola or any change in her condition, because he always told me things like that. And news of his daughter would make him either very depressed or very jubilant. Not cross. That's why I think she must have been urging him to buy something for pain, the way Prescott had asked her to do."

"Josie was willing to do that in spite of her major worry?"

"Look, she couldn't do anything about her major worry. There was Romola all hooked up to a life-support system that was even breathing for her, all tubes and wires and things, and nothing to do but wait. She didn't die, legally, until August tenth. I would guess that Josie was very restless. She'd welcome anything that diverted her from her worry. I would guess that she wanted Ellis to come back to her and stay with her. Maybe she brought that up too. And that was what made him cross. He always told me she was a very nice woman, and absolutely impossible to live with."

"I might be going out there."

"What for?"

"Josie Laurant has been financing a motion picture project for Peter Kesner. She's acting in it, I think."

"Oh, God, that's terrible!"

It was a lot more reaction than I had expected. "Terrible?"

"I should have told you. Ellis, through his banking connections, arranged a personal report on Peter Kesner. An absolutely, totally unreliable person. A disaster area. He had the discipline to make those two little films that got rave reviews and made a lot of money, but it went to his head and he blew the whole thing. They gave him a big-budget film to produce and direct, and he went way over budget and it turned out to be a dog. They gave him a chance to do a little picture, like his early two, and it was so completely bad they never released it at all. By then his money was gone, of course. Tax judgments, the whole thing. It was clear that Josie was supporting him. I remember when Ellis dictated a three-page single-spaced letter to her, telling her to have as little to do with Peter as possible and saying why. Knowing Josie, I knew she'd turn it over to Kesner. I told Ellis I thought that would happen, and he said he wouldn't mind if she did. There was nothing actionable in the letter. It was all fact. He said maybe it would give Kesner a better look at himself. When I typed it I softened it a little bit, but he caught it and marked up the original and had me type it all over again. What this really means, I guess, is that the money Josie got from Romola's estate is down the drain, or soon will be."

"Ellis didn't put any strings on it?"

"He talked about it, but he never got around to doing it. He talked about setting it up as an annuity for Romola, but then when we were both certain Romola was going to die before he did, he put all his attention into refining that foundation concept of his. Which never got used."

"Important question: Would Kesner know the terms of the will?"

She thought for a moment. "I would certainly think so. Josie knew, long before we moved down here from Stamford, that Romola would get the bulk of it, and if Romola died first it would go to a foundation. Yes, she asked me and I told her about it. I think she was wondering what would happen to her support, to that fifty thousand a year, and I didn't blame her for wondering. I told her I thought she would get a hundred thousand and that would be the end of it. Yes, I told her that's what she would get. And anything Josie knows, Josie tells anybody she happens to find sitting next to her at the table."

"And so Kesner was vitally interested." There was a long long silence. "You still there?"

"Yes, I'm here. I had a kind of an ugly thought."

"Such as?"

"You remember how Romola got hurt?"

"Nobody ever told me. I assumed it was a highway accident."

"It was a bicycle accident, yes. She was way over by Thousand Oaks, twenty tough miles from home. There were witnesses. She was going along pretty fast on a ten-speed. A dog rushed her and she tried to dodge, but she hit the dog and went over the handlebars and fractured her skull on some curbing. What she was doing out there was a big mystery. Josie thought she was in class in UCLA. It turned out—I don't really know how they discovered it—she was using a little house out there owned by a woman who was temporarily in London, doing a screenplay over there for a British company. The neighbors had seen Romola coming and going for a couple of months. They said she rode the bike a lot. Oh, I remember how they found the house. Romola's little car was there, some kind of an MG. And with her car keys in her pocket she had a key to the little house. There was evidence she had been staying there for some time. She had moved some of her things from the Beverly Hills house to the little house, without Josie noticing. She had not been in classes since early February. She was an exceptionally beautiful girl. I saw her just once, when she was fourteen, and she was breathtaking. The extraordinary secrecy was very strange. It was a place of assignation, apparently. But there wasn't any real urge to find out who because she was in such critical condition."

"And the ugly idea?"

"Maybe it's too ugly. Peter Kesner knew that Ellis had terminal cancer. And he knew that Josie would get a lump-sum settlement that wouldn't be enough to support him for very long. And he knew Romola would inherit. He was perfectly capable of seducing Romola. And that would have made her very very careful to keep it a secret from her mother. I'll bet you a dime that lady screenwriter is an old pal of Peter's. It was the screenwriter's bike, by the way."

"Yes, that is an ugly idea. And if the fall had killed her outright, then when Ellis died of his problem, the foundation would have gotten the money."

"But she hung on. And suddenly Peter realizes that if Ellis should die before Romola, he will still be in clover. Or even better off than before. He can finance another chance at moviemaking, possibly. But, Travis, it is one long long shot, isn't it, to try to connect Peter Kesner with something that happened so long ago near Citrus City?"

"Very long."

"I didn't call you up to talk about that!"

"What did you have in mind?"

"Do you want five hundred guesses?"

"I give up."

"That's sort of what I had in mind."

"Once I get onto the Alley it is only eighty-four miles. But aren't you a working woman on weekends?"

"All I have to do from now on is take one of my famous walks through the bar area and the dining room between seven and nine, check a couple of empty rooms at random, and take the totals off the register tapes. A grand total of—call it forty minutes. And as soon as I hang up I am going to have a nice nap, and then I am going to put little dabs of scent here and there. Park at the far right end of the lot and take the path down past that fountain with the stone benches, and you'll come out right behind my place, and the rear door will be unlocked. Welcome, darling."

And she hung up before I could change the plan in any way.

I stayed in her place with her Sunday night, in the queen-size bed under the fan, with a yellow towel over the lampshade and with pretty good surf thudding onto the beach in a steady rhythm all night long.

We knew a lot more about each other, the things that quickened and the things that delayed. She was joyfully diligently sensuous. She just purely enjoyed the living hell out of it. She was a kid, and bed was the big candy store, and she had the keys to every cabinet.

At one point, resting, she said, "Look, do you mind about me and Ellis?"

"In what way?"

"Him being so much older. I'm younger than his son. Did I tell you that already?"

"I think so. So what?"

"You take a younger woman who moves in with a well-to-do old man, it looks as if she's going where the money is. I don't give a damn what most people think, but I want you to know that it wasn't like that. It really wasn't. Two years before he got sick we went down to a meeting in New York when there was an industry-wide convention. He always picked me when there was work he wanted done just right. By then I was almost over a rotten affair with the man I had wanted to marry until I learned he had a boyfriend on the side. Ellis landed a huge consultant contract at the convention, and we had wine in his suite—I lived across the hall—and he managed to hustle me into bed somehow. I told him I had to quit. I wasn't going to be a sleep-in secretary to anybody. He said if I had to quit, I had to quit. Okay. The next day I quit, and he said the fair thing to do was to stay on until he could find somebody just as competent. Later he said that inasmuch as I was quitting anyway, and as long as we had been to bed together once, it would be stupid not to continue while he looked for a new girl. I felt a little bit crawly about him being so old. But it turned out to be all right. Then on account of the chemotherapy and the radiation, he all of a sudden couldn't. He was sorry and I was sorry, but, as I told you before, I had a moral and emotional commitment to him. He was mean, but he never cheated me. He never lied to me. And he was always pleased when I looked nice, so it was fun to dress up for him. And because I never did really quit the job when I said I would, I felt I owed him. And I had to believe it was a kind of love that kept me with him. Hey! Are you asleep?"

"No. Heard every word. Understand the whole thing."

"And now what do you think you are doing?"

"In the immortal words of Burt Reynolds, something has come up."

"Which, all things considered, love, is very very flattering."

"I know."

By twenty minutes after dawn I was on my way back across the peninsula, yawning and singing, beating time with the heel of my hand on the steering wheel. Roll me over, in the clover.... With 'is 'ead tooked underneath 'is arm, 'e 'aunts the bluiddy tower.... Never let a sailor put his hand above your kneeeee.... And other tender love songs and ballads of the years gone by.

When I awakened in my own bed at noon, I put a call through to Ted Blaylock. Mits answered in a small uncertain voice. He had lost consciousness Saturday evening and had been rushed to Broward Memorial. His condition was not good. She had just come from there. She was going back in the late afternoon.

"What is it?"

"Kidneys. That's what he's been afraid of. You saw how kind of yellowish he looked."

"I noticed, yes. Can I get to see him?"

"He wants to see you. He told me how to get you by phone, but I didn't even try on account of I don't want to do anything to tire him out. Anyway, I don't think they'll let you in. I told them I'm his wife."

"Does he have something to tell me?"

"I think so."

"Get him to tell you, then. I don't want to tire him. You can tell me. You got a ride in?"

"One of the guys is taking me and waiting."

"What room is he in?"

"Why?"

"So I'll know where to wait for you when you come out."

"I can only be with him like five minutes. I guess if you want to come meet me, five o'clock would be okay. Across from the main entrance."

I got there at four thirty. I looked around the area and I found a big silver and black Harley Davidson parked in the shade, a thin brown Indian-looking fellow standing by it, smoking, leaning against a tree.

"You bring Mits in?" I asked him.

"You McGee?"

"Right."

"She told me you'd be around. I'm Cal. I'm her cousin. She's really nuts about that Blaylock. You the one messed up Knucks and Mike?"

"They kept pushing me."

"They're like that. Be a long time before they do any more pushing. You tore up Knucks's shoulder pretty good. And Mike is in the hospital, this one right here,

— 128

for observation on account of something might be busted inside. He can't keep food down. A lot of people are glad they got wiped out. They get too much kicks out of beating on people."

"I have the idea those two are dumb enough and ugly enough to take another try at me when they feel up to it, but not with the bare hands."

He nodded. "Sure. That would be the way they go. But they been given the word you're under the protection of the Fantasies."

I looked at his rear mudguard and saw the emblem. "That's nice. I really appreciate it. That pair doesn't fill me with terror, but I don't like having to look around behind me all the time. Why the favor?"

"You did the Fantasies a favor, okay? Knucks had been told about groping Mits. He was told not to do it. It was like some kind of a joke to him. Mits is my first cousin, so she's in like an affiliate. Fantasy Foxes, under our protection. Like the Oasis is under our protection because Blaylock has been a true friend to the club. So some people were going to get around to Knucks and maybe break his hand or something. But you worked him over. So if you want, you can wear the pin. There's one for associates, without the red circle around it."

The keen dark eyes stared at me, and I knew I was on very delicate and dangerous ground. Ridicule is unforgivable. But I had the feeling I'd been transported back to one of the schoolyards of my youth, where if you belonged to the right group, the big kids wouldn't beat you up and take your lunch money.

"I'd be very honored to have the pin and wear it, Cal."

The tension went out of his shoulders. "I'll see you get one. What my squad captain did, he checked you out with Blaylock, and he got a good reading. Hey, here she comes. I guess things aren't so great."

Mits came slowly toward us. Though she was expressionless, tears were running down her brown cheeks. She was in jeans and a blue work shirt, both too big for her. Her helmet was slung on the machine, next to Cal's.

She acknowledged my presence with a nod, went to Cal, held his forearm in her two hands, and rested her forehead against his shoulder for a moment. "In't gonna make it," she said in a muffled voice. "Din't hardly know me at first. Then he came back, like from far off, like from being dead."

She took a deep breath and let it out, and then turned to me and said, "Other things are going bad. Inside. Like he knew they would sooner or later. But, damn it, this is sooner. It isn't fair."

"Can we get going now?" Cal asked.

"I can see him another five minutes at six o'clock. I think I better stay here."

"Maybe I can get back. I don't know, Mits. I'll have to get off work."

"I'll stick around and run her home, Cal."

She looked at me dubiously. "Sure you wouldn't be too much put out?"

"Sure."

Cal handed her her helmet, swung aboard, cranked up, and went droning out of the shade and into the road and away.

She looked around and saw a bus bench in the shade and headed toward it. I followed her. She took cigarettes out of her shoulder bag, offered me one which I refused, and then lit up, sucked the smoke deep, huffed it out to be pulled away by the late-afternoon breeze.

"They said I should expect him to die tonight or tomorrow."

"Soon."

"Everything has gone bad. They say he had to be in pain for a long time, saying nothing about it. I knew he hurt. He'd make a sniffy sound if I lifted him wrong. How old do you think I am?"

The question startled me. "Nineteen? Twenty?"

"Hah! I'm twenty-eight, man. Half Seminole. A skinny Seminole, you can't tell the age. With the fat ones you can tell. Okay, except for my little brothers when I was growing up, nobody in my whole life has ever really needed me except Ted. I mean *really*. He turned that place into home for me. So now what? I have to make some kind of plans, get some kind of work. But I can't even think about it."

"Don't try. There'll be time to think about it."

"McGee? What was he like when he was young?"

"I knew him in the service."

"That's what I mean."

"He was a good officer. He didn't showboat and draw fire. When stupid orders came down, he'd drag his feet until they were out of date. He tried to make sure everybody got shelter and rations and transport. He didn't mind the kind of goofing off that didn't matter, but if anybody didn't do their job when it did matter, he'd chew them out good. He was an okay officer, and he was down in a little ravine helping a medic slide a wounded man onto a litter when he got a mortar fragment in the back, right through the spinal cord."

"Did he ever laugh, joke, smile?"

"As much as anybody."

"Did he have a girl?"

"I don't recall hearing anything about her if he did."

"It's been a lot of work taking care of him. It makes a long day and into the night seven days a week."

"Must have been very hard."

"I would have done it if it was twice as hard. Oh, I asked him if there was something I should tell you. It doesn't make sense to me. I hope it does to you. His mind seemed to be kind of wandering. Here is exactly what he said: 'Tell Sarge there is a legend about how Dirty Bob and the Senator made it all the way in fifty hours flat out, popping Dexamyls, and then faded away.' Mean anything?"

"Not right off."

"I think his head has gone all weird. I held his hand. It was like ice."

"Say it again?"

"'There is a legend about how Dirty Bob and the Senator made it all the way in fifty hours flat out, popping Dexamyls, and then faded away.' He made me say it twice too."

I found that interesting. It meant the message was significant in the shape and form it was told.

"Could those be biker names, Mits?"

"Oh, sure. I've heard about Dirty Bob, but I don't know where or when. And when they take a long hard ride, they do it on uppers and coffee. Night and day, they really go. And it's safer there's two at night, riding side by side, with the two headlights showing, the two tail-lights in back."

"Fifty hours would be how many miles?"

"All the way acrosst. I knew a cat went from Toronto to Mexico City without sleep. A while back, there was kind of a thing about setting records. But it's dumb. People got killed. You can lose your best troops that way." She picked up my wrist and looked at my watch. "I think I'll head back in there. I'll stay as long as they let me. You sure you don't mind?"

"You go ahead. I'll wait. Good luck."

"There isn't any more of that left. But thanks."

She came back at ten after six, dry-eyed. "Look, you want to take off, it's okay. They're going to let me set with him. They got curtains around the bed. He doesn't know me any more, or know anything, I guess. But everybody has to be somewhere, and I might as well be here."

"You going to get anything to eat?"

"I couldn't eat."

I gave her my number again. "You call me when you want to leave. It will take me fifteen or twenty minutes to get here. Is that all right?"

"I hate to have you doing this for me."

"If I didn't want to, I wouldn't."

There was a nod and a fleeting smile and she turned and went back to the hospital.

The phone woke me a little after three in the morning. She was waiting by the bench where we had sat. She climbed up into the Rolls, chunked the door shut, and said, "He died at a quarter to three. He stopped breathing and then tried to kind of rise up and fell back with his eyes half shut and his mouth open. I got his stuff here in my bag they took from him. The watch and ring and wallet and keys."

"I'm sorry, Mits."

"F.T.W."

"What? Oh. Right."

"I signed a couple of things there. I signed them Marilyn O. Blaylock. They didn't ask for any ID. I always liked the name Marilyn. I think what they do, maybe, they get to collect from the VA somehow."

"Probably. Did he have any living relatives?"

"I never heard of any at all."

"What will happen to the place out there?" I asked as I started up, heading north.

"He said he had it all worked out, but he never said how. His lawyer has the papers on it, he said. Man name of Grudd up in West Palm."

We rode in silence. She sighed heavily. "Oh, God, somebody's got to go through all his stuff and decide what should happen to it."

"Maybe Mr. Grudd has instructions. Better contact him first."

"First thing."

"Hungry?"

"Like some kind of wolf."

So I pulled into 24 HOUR CHICKEN and she ate one of the big breast baskets all by herself, with fries and a chocolate shake. I told her I was going to be given a kind of associate-type pin that put me under the protection of the Fantasies, that Cal was going to get it for me.

She studied me for long moments as she sucked up the shake, cheeks hollowed by the effort. "What could save your life and save your ass, you shouldn't try to be funny about, okay?"

"I wasn't trying to be funny."

"There isn't anything funny about that Knucks. He is genuine through and through crazy. Someday they are going to put him away."

"Cal is going to get the badge to me. I've been voted in."

"I know. Because it got the message to Knucks about not messing with me any more. At least I hope it did. I hate being grabbed like that. And he's so rough, he hurts a lot."

"Have you got people close by?"

"Not close by. They're all down near Monroe Station on the Trail. Lots of brothers. When this thing is settled, I might go down there awhile, sew up some tourist skirts, get a good rest, go frogging."

"It would probably be good for you."

"What the hell would you know about what's good for me?"

"Excuse me all to hell, lady."

She came sliding over and put her hand on my arm. "Oh, Jesus, I'm sorry. I didn't mean it. Look, I'm hurting and I want to hurt back, but I shouldn't be hurting you."

"Forget it. No harm done."

She had nothing to say the rest of the way. She got out with helmet and shoulder bag and thanked me. I waited until she got the door unlocked and turned and waved.

By the time I tucked Miss Agnes away and biked from the garage back to the *Flush*, there was a faint pallor across the eastern sky, close to the horizon line. I chained the bike up and went walking on the empty beach, not too healthy a night activity of late. Some of the jackals cruise our area from time to time, and have shot an innocent man in the head, raped a woman on the beach, cut a man up while removing his wallet and watch. Sub-human freaks, looking for laughs.

I stashed my sandals where I could find them, rolled up the pants legs, walked the water line. The sea thumped in and slid up the sand, pale suds in starlight.

I walked and thought about the lieutenant. I could never feel easy about his gratitude toward me. If I hadn't helped carry him down the hill in the rain, somebody else would have. And maybe he would have been better off not being carried at all, being left there. But he didn't think so. I had run into him again by accident, fifteen years after he was wounded. It had been up to him to recognize me. He was fifty pounds lighter and a hundred years older than I remembered.

Okay. Okay. Okay. But, by God, it seemed that an awful lot of people were into dying. The "in" thing this year, apparently. No chance for practice. You had to do it right the first and only time you got to do it. And you were never quite certain when your chance was coming. Stay braced at all times.

11

The *Byline* did not come hulking into the marina until midmorning on Thursday the twenty-third. Meyer and Aggie were standing up in the bow. I went along with the yacht, keeping up easily at a walking pace. They both looked several shades darker and very content.

"Lovely cruise," Aggie called. "Just lovely."

I helped with the lines and went aboard when the crew had rigged the gangway. They greeted me. I kissed Aggie on the cheek and asked them how far they had been.

"Just up to Jupiter Inlet," Meyer said. "We anchored in a very secluded cove. And we had a nice time. And then we came back."

"I admire the way you seafarers put up with the rigors of the deep dark ocean blue."

"Don't be snide, darling," Aggie said. "No one needs to be bounced about on a lot of angry ugly waves in order to enjoy a cruise. Don't you agree, Meyer dear?"

"Aggie, I always agree with everything you say."

"Mary time?" she asked. "Below or up here? It *does*

seem nice up here, don't you think, Travis? Raul, *tres marías picantes, por favor.*"

She sorted herself out on a sun chaise on the upper deck, crossing her long tanned elegant ageless gleaming legs arching her magnificent back just a little, tossing that rich ruff of hair back, favoring me with a slow and sardonic wink. It was not invitation. It was confirming our mutual approval of the effort that had made the tight pink bikini feasible, with only the smallest roll around the middle. She was a big glorious engine, and a very smart tough lady who, a bit belatedly, had come into her own in every way and was enjoying every moment of it.

"Aggie is flying out from here at one o'clock," Meyer said, "instead of cruising back to Miami."

"I was going to be a day late," she said, "but after two phone calls, I learned better. One of the media monsters is nibbling at my poor little string of papers, salivating. Wants to stick us in with all their magazines and television stations and bulk carriers and tampon factories and give me a fat consultant contract."

Meyer spread his hands apart and said, "Aggie, it depends on what you want. If you take the cash, put it in tax-frees after paying capital-gains taxes, you could have over half a mil a year with very small tax to pay on it. You could spend a lot more time aboard this vessel."

"What I want, dear man, is to run my world better than anybody ever ran it before, or will again. A business person, making business moves all day."

"So you shouldn't sell."

"I seem to have a business I can't sell," I said.

— 138

They both stared at me and Aggie Sloane said, "*You* have a business? How quaint, dear boy! Of what sort?"

The drinks arrived, and I took a swallow before I turned to Meyer. "You heard me talk about Ted Blaylock."

"Yes, of course. The crippled lieutenant."

"He died Monday night."

"Sorry to hear it."

"An attorney named Daviss Grudd, two s's, two d's, phoned me and told me about it Tuesday afternoon. That whole enterprise of his, Ted Blaylock's Oasis, Inc., was in a closely held corporation. Very closely held. One hundred shares of stock outstanding. So he left fifty to me and he left fifty to a skinny little half-Seminole woman named Millicent Waterhawk, called Mits, one of the famous Fantasy Foxes. And I can't sell that damn stock or give it away until there has been an appraisal of the value of the whole damn thing, and God only knows how long that is going to take. Grudd says the thing has got to keep operating or the value of the shares left to Miss Waterhawk will go down, and Grudd said that there is a note in his office to me from Blaylock, saying that it was the only way he could think of to protect Mits's interest and he was sure I would make sure she didn't get a tossing."

I jumped up so quickly I splashed some of my drink on the back of my hand. In a higher than normal voice, I said, "I don't *like* all this! My God, when it got so you couldn't rent a car or check into a good hotel without a credit card, I had to sign up. I had to have a bank account to get the credit cards. I keep getting into more and more computers all the time. Boat papers, city taxes, bank records, credit records, IRS, army records, census records, phone company records.... God damn it, I feel like I'm getting more and more entangled. Like walking down a dark corridor into cobweb after cobweb. I didn't sign up for this kind of lousy regimentation! I don't want to be a damn shareholder, owner, manager, or what the hell ever. I'm getting smothered."

They were both staring at me. "There, there," said Aggie. "Poor baby." She turned to Meyer. "Poor baby doesn't comprehend the modern way of guaranteeing anonymity and privacy, does he?"

"Tell him, dear," Meyer said, looking fatuous.

"Sit down, Travis. The computer age, my rebellious friend, is strangling on its own data. As the government and industry and the financial institutions buy and lease more and more lovely computers, generation after generation of them, they have to fill them, they have to use lots and lots of programs, lots of softwear to utilize capacity. How am I doing, Meyer?"

"Very nicely."

"Meyer taught me this. What you should do from now on, Travis, is to make sure you get into as many computers as possible. Lots of tiny bank accounts, lots of credit cards, lots of memberships. Have your attorney set up some partnerships and little corporations and get you some additional tax numbers. Move bits of money around often. Buy and sell odd lots of this and that. Feed all the information you can into all their computers."

"And spend my life keeping track of what the hell I'm doing?"

"Who said anything about keeping track? If you can get so complicated you confuse yourself, imagine how confused the poor computers are going to be."

"Is she putting me on, Meyer?"

"She's giving you good advice. If you try to hide, you are easy to find. You are leaving only one trail in the jungle, and the hounds can follow that one. Leave forty trails, crossing and recrossing. The computers are strangling on data. The courts are strangling on caseload. Billions of pieces of paper are floating around each month, clogging the inputs, confusing the outputs. A nice little old lady in Duluth had twelve post office boxes under twelve different names, and had twelve social security cards and numbers, and drew checks on all twelve for eight years before they caught up with her. And they wouldn't have, if she hadn't signed the wrong name on the wrong check five years ago. The government seeks restitution. She says she lost it all at bingo. Think of it this way, Travis. With each new computer that goes into service, your identity becomes more and more diffuse and unreal. Right now today, if every man, woman, and child were put to work ten hours a day reading computer printouts, just scanning the alphabetical and numerical output of the printers, they could cover about one third of what is being produced. Recycling of computer printout paper is a giant industry. We're all sinking into the oblivion of profusion, and one day soon we will all be gone, with no way to trace us."

Aggie began to giggle and gasp. "Millicent Waterhawk," she said in a strangled voice. "Your business partner."

"What's so damn funny?" I asked.

Meyer started laughing, and pretty soon I had to join in. It was such a dreadful blow to my self-image that it took me a while to see any humor in it. But there was a lot, I guess.

The funeral service was on Friday noon in the little Everglades settlement of Bonahatchee. There was a better turnout of the Fantasies than Mits had expected. She was obviously pleased that almost a hundred and fifty machines had assembled at the Oasis and had rumbled at slow funeral pace to Snead's Funeral Home in Bonahatchee and, subsequent to the eulogy and service, had followed the hearse out to where the flowers covered the raw dirt mound of the pre-dug grave.

All the brothers and sisters wore black arm bands. After the graveside service things began to break up, and they milled around for a time, talking to people they hadn't seen since the last biker funeral, then peeled off in twos and threes, roaring past the two state trooper cars which had apparently been summoned just in case, no doubt by nervous residents of the town, unstrung by the bearded, burly, helmeted visions which made such a powerful and flatulent sound as they moved through the town slowly in columns of four.

Daviss Grudd came over and introduced himself after the service. Mits had pointed him out to me and said he rode a 900cc Suzuki with a new Windjammer fairing for touring. She had to explain what she meant. He was a smallish man with big shoulders and a big drooping mustache and a voice like something in the bottom of a barrel. I introduced him to Meyer. He followed us back to the Oasis, which was closed for the day. He brought in the portfolio he took out of a saddlebag, and the four of us sat at one of the tables in front of the bar.

"Meyer," I explained, "is my adviser in business matters."

Mits said, "I can't believe I'm gonna *own* half this place. I never owned anything in my life."

"The cash situation is pretty good," Grudd said. "What you've got to have here is management. Ted, for all his kidding around, was a good manager. It has always looked messy around here, but it does turn a dollar."

"I wouldn't want to manage it even if I could," I said quickly.

"Who kept the books?" Meyer asked.

"Ted did," Mits answered. "They're in his desk drawer. You want them?" Grudd nodded, and she went and brought them back. Checkbook, journal, ledger, inventory sheets, payroll, withholding, state sales tax, ad valorem tax records.

"I've got the corporate books, minute book, and so on."

Meyer flipped pages, ran his thumbnail down columns of figures, went backwards through the checkbook. Then he said, "I can make a couple of preliminary judgments."

"Hey, I like how he talks," Mits said.

"Pay a good manager what he would be worth, a manager who can get along with and attract the kind of trade the place caters to, and there'll be damn little left over for dividends. If there is anything left over, it should go into replacing equipment and maintaining the buildings. At first glance I see a very clean debt situation. There are nine acres of land with a seven-hundred-foot frontage on a not-very-busy tertiary road. Land value, twenty-five to thirty thousand. Liquor inventory, fifteen hundred. Motorcycle and parts inventory, about ten thousand to twelve thousand at cost. Liquor license, how much?"

"Maybe twenty thousand if we can move it somewhere else," Grudd said.

"Shop equipment and tools, say five thousand. Let me see, that would come to about sixty-five to sixty-eight thousand. My advice would be to liquidate."

Mits glared at him. "Now I don't like the way you talk. No damn way do we liquidate. No way!"

I don't know whether or not he was going to try to talk her into it. Two big machines came in, popping and grumbling. Mits jumped up and looked out and said, "Hey, it's Preach and Magoo."

"Top officers of the Fantasies," Grudd explained. "Let 'em in, Mits."

Preach was tall and thin and wore a gray jump suit with a lot of silver coin buttons. He had long blond hair and a long thin blond beard. Except for the little gold wire glasses he was wearing, he looked like folk art depicting Jesus. Magoo was five and a half feet high, and about four broad, none of it fat. If he could have straightened his bandy legs, he would have been a lot closer to six feet. His arms were long, large, sinewy, and bare, with a pale blue tracery of dragons, fu dogs, and Chinese gardens under the tan. His head was half again normal size, with a brute shelf of acromegalic jaw. The expression was at once merry and sardonic, happy and skeptical.

Preach put his hands on Mits's shoulders and looked down into her small brown face with warmth and compassion. "Mits, Mits, Mits," he said. "A bad thing, eh?

Couldn't make it in time, kid. We're sorry. We were in Baja when we heard. Flew back."

"I wondered," she said. "It's okay. You know Daviss Grudd. This is Mr. Meyer and this here is Travis McGee."

"Preach," he said, and stuck his hand out to me, ignoring Meyer. His hand was thin and cool, the handshake slack. I saw his eyes flick down to take in the metal badge Cal had slipped to me, and I saw a trace of amusement. "McGee, meet Magoo." His was a hot beefy grasp. "Heard about you," Preach said. He turned to Grudd. "What did Teddy do with it?"

"Half and half. Mits and McGee. An even split."

"Interesting," Preach said.

Mits broke in. "Mr. Meyer thinks we ought to sell it off."

Preach studied Meyer. "What would give you thoughts like that, book man?"

Meyer smiled at him. "Common sense. Blaylock didn't draw salary. And he slacked off on maintenance and repair. Some of the cycle inventory has been around a long time. Once you start paying a manager and picking the place up, there won't be enough left over."

"Whose friend is he?" Preach asked Grudd.

"He's with me," I said.

Preach wheeled around and studied me again. "You tell your friend Meyer that management will be provided."

"He says management will be provided, Meyer," I said.

"Are you being a little bit smartass, McGee?" Preach asked.

"Just enough so you'd notice."

"I notice you," he said. "Grudd, you folks deal the cards or something. I'm going walking with the Mc-Giggle twins here."

We went out in back where the cabins were, the brush tangled around them. Magoo's big arms hung down to his knees. He hopped up and sat on the trunk of an ancient red Mustang convertible, top long gone, rusting in the grass, dreaming of hot moonlight nights in the sixties. Preach leaned against a cabin, arms crossed, smiling at me, the Jesus eyes blue and mild. I perched my rump on the edge of a concrete birdbath with seashells stuck into the top of it in a design.

"What's your action?" Preach asked.

"Favors for friends, when I have to. This and that."

"Big old bastard, aren't you?" It didn't need an answer. He continued, "It doesn't take too much to handle a pair of fat dummies. Maybe there's a couple more fat dummies you could bust for me. I mean not just as a favor. Cash in hand."

"No, thanks."

"What if you've got no choice?"

"What does that mean?"

"That means that if you don't want to do me a favor, Magoo here and some of his friends will do me a favor by breaking your elbows. It's known to sting a little."

I smiled at him and shook my head. "If you give the orders, friend, tell them to kill me. You'll sleep better."

"You think so?"

"Whatever gets broken will mend, one way or another. And I would not come back at you from the front, Preach. Something would fall on your head, maybe. Or something you picked up might blow up. Or you could be in a room that catches fire and the door is locked.

If I came at you from the front, I might not get you. And I would want to be absolutely sure. So, as far as taking orders are concerned, do you want me to tell you what you can go do in your helmet?"

He pushed himself away from the cabin, stretched and winced, and said to Magoo, "We better do more riding, you know that?"

"I know it," he said. "The last fifty miles my ass was getting sore. I mean, how much chance do we get lately?" Preach studied me. "Testing, testing. Blaylock told me about you one time. Said you don't push. Neither do I, so I understand you. I've got an idea or two about this place. But I want to know something. Are you fixing to make any moves on Mits?"

"No."

"What ideas have you got about this place?"

"Once the legal estate thing is settled, I want to see how quick I can unload my half in any way I can unload it."

"How are your civil rights, McGee?"

"I don't know what you mean."

"I mean if you are a convicted felon, I can get you a pardon so you can vote again."

"That's nice, but I'm clean."

"That's nice because you should keep owning half. It could be a nice thing for you."

"In what way?"

"You won't have to come anywhere near it. You won't know anything about it. You won't know that we'll have some nice little pads built back here, and a lake dug, and an airstrip, and a meeting room put in, like a little convention center. And the whole place will be wired so a rat can't sneak in without turning on the red lights. Somebody will bring you what you have to sign, on corporation things. You and Mits will sign a management contract with somebody. I don't know who yet. The books will show a loss, you'll get dividends in cash you won't have to report. They could be nice dividends."

"Mits gets the same deal?"

"Maybe. Maybe not. Why should you care?"

"I care."

He moved toward me and put his hand out. "We can get along." We shook hands again. "You handle a bike?"

"Not for a few years. But I can if I have to."

"Why were you out here the other day, McGee?"

In the next ten silent seconds I shuffled through all my choices, all the ways I could go. "I was hoping Blaylock could give me some kind of a lead on a biker who beat a sick old man to death near Citrus City nearly two years ago."

"There's been a lot of that going around. I would be very disappointed in you if this has anything to do with law enforcement."

"It has to do with the old man's son taking a screwing in the will."

"No law?"

"I'm helping out. A favor for a friend. My line of work."

"Blaylock help any?"

"He came up with two names: Biker names. Dirty Bob and the Senator."

Preach turned to Magoo and said, "Anybody like that in the Corsairs you ever heard of?"

"God's sake, Preach, ever since that goddam movie there been Dirty Bobs sprang up all over the place."

"That's where I heard it!" Preach said. "That movie,

that *Chopper Heaven*. The name they called the boss biker was Dirty Bob."

"And," said Magoo, "they called his buddy the Senator. Can't remember what their names were, their real names."

"That pair was supposed to have ridden all the way from California in fifty hours, without sleep, using uppers," I said.

"Then hell," said Preach, "maybe what you're looking for is the same two that was in those movies. The originals. I heard they were both Hell's Angels out there. Or Bandidos. I forget which. Dumb damn moving pictures. Any club goes around ripping up the civilians like in that movie, the smokeys would stake out the highway and shotgun those fuckers right out of their saddles." He gave me the broadest smile I had yet seen and said, "There's quieter ways of ripping off the civilians."

As we entered the room where the others were, Preach hung a long thin hand on my shoulder. "We're getting along just fine," he said to Mits and Grudd. They both looked relieved. "McGeek here decided he might just keep on owning this garden spot. Mits, you keep hanging in."

"Sure thing, Preach."

"Gruddy baby, I will be in touch anon."

"Fine."

"Come on, Magoo. Put your sore ass back to work."

They went booming back out onto the highway, kicking up pebbles, riding hard and fast.

Grudd said in an uncertain voice, "He's...a very unusual man."

"What does he do, actually?" Meyer asked.

"Don't ask. I don't really know. He's got an office in Miami. Karma Imports. He's got some kind of leasing business."

I said to Mits, "He wants to make a lot of improvements here, bring in a manager."

"Anything he wants to do suits me fine," she said. "Shall we just...open up here and keep going?"

Grudd nodded. "Probably best. He'll move quick, I think. Mits, you go through all Ted's personal stuff, will you? Sort out the giveaway, and the stuff that has value, and the stuff you have questions about. Keep a list. I'll be back Monday. No, make that Tuesday. I have to be in court on Monday."

We all had to be leaving. Mits walked out with us. She said, "This is going to be one rotten weekend, guys. There was a squeak in the left wheel on his chair. I oiled it three times but it didn't go away. I'm going to be hearing that squeak coming up behind me....Thanks for everything, guys, okay?"

In the old blue Rolls on the way back to Bahia Mar, I told Meyer about my talk with Preach. "I don't think I want any under-the-table dividends from an operation I have to stay away from."

"What will he be doing out there?"

"God knows. Home industry, maybe. A little pharmaceutical plant. Smugglers' haven. Wholesale distribution point. National headquarters for the outlaw bikers."

"Grudd is frightened of the man. Through and through."

"I got what I wanted from him. The back trail is very tricky, very old and cold, but if it leads where I think it is going to lead, it goes right back to Peter Kesner.

Back to Josephine Esterland. Now I want to see those biker movies."

After I was alone aboard the *Flush* I could not account for my feeling of unrest, uneasiness. It had begun the instant Preach had put his hand on my shoulder. It had not been friendship or affection. It had been a symbol of possession. He and Magoo had walked me out into the weeds, raped me in some kind of deft and indescribable way, and walked me back in, announcing that I had enjoyed it. I wondered if I had been blowing smoke when I told him I would go after him if they busted me up. Testing, testing. Was pride enough? Maybe I'd spent too much of myself in too many hospitals over the years. Did Preach think I meant it when I said it? If I wasn't really certain I meant it, then I would try to be careful to keep my elbows intact. It is the new warning system. They hold it on a concrete block, one man on the wrist, his feet braced against the block, and they give the elbow a smack with an eight-pound sledge, crushing the joint. If they do them both, you end up being unable to feed yourself. The Italians do kneecaps; the dopers do elbows.

I looked in my little book and tried the Miami number for Matty Lamarr. It was five after five. They said he was retired and living in Guadalajara. They gave me an extension number for Lieutenant Goodbread. He was on another phone. Yes, I would hold.

"Goodbread," he said. The voice gave me a vivid recall of that big face, with its useful look of vapid stupidity.

"McGee in Lauderdale."

"McGee? McGee. Oh, sure, the smartass that kept

me out of trouble that time with that great big rich important general. You kill somebody?"

"Not recently. But I met a biker today who seems to be trying to put some kind of arm on me. He's boss man of a biker club, the Fantasies. And he operates down in your area, maybe even legitimately. People call him Preach."

"Under that arm could not be such a great place to be, McGee. There are some people around who want harm to come to him, enough to gun down anybody in the area. His name is Amos Wilson. He owns Karma Imports. Many arrests, no convictions at all. He has access to lots of bail. I thought he was pulling out of the biker scene."

"What is he?"

"Believe me, I can't nail it down. It's easy to say what he *might* be into. He might be big in imported medicinals. Or he might be importing people from unpopular countries. Witnesses disappear. The feds tend to forget things. He isn't in any known pattern."

"What would he want with a big tract of land out in the boonies, with lots of security, an airstrip, and so on?"

"This is just a guess, friend. What I *really* think is that he and his animal pal, name of Magoo, they run a service business for people who are into untidy lines of work. Those people need transport, security, communications, and muscle. I think he is once removed from the action, and it is a smarter and safer place to be than out front where we are aiming at them."

"Will you nail him for anything?"

"I used to say that sooner or later we get everybody. But nowadays, that is hopeful bullshit. We don't. We're short on money and troops. There are too many groups on the hustle. Nobody is in charge any more. People like Preach, they jump in there, right into the confusion, develop a reputation, and take their fees to the bank in wheelbarrows, and sometimes they own the bank. I really envy Matty down there in Mexico. I told him to save room for me."

"Thanks for the time and the information."

"What have I told you? You ask me about a very smart one with a lot of moves. Times keep changing. Every month a better way to bring in the hash, the grass, and the coke. Every month people getting mashed flat by the competition, or sent out swimming with weights on, or crashing tired airplanes in empty areas zoned for tract houses, where only the roads are in. Preach runs an advisory and investment service, maybe. With a place to go when you're too hot. Maybe he settles disputes between A and B and can arrange with C to get D killed. What I would say is unlikely is that he is out front on any of it. He can lay back and take a percentage of what nine groups are bringing in, and do better than any one of them in the long haul. I hear rumors he is buying old office buildings, little tacky ones, and fixing them up and renting them pretty good. But, like I said, I would stay way clear if I were you. There are people who'd like him dead, him and Magoo both. It's always good to stay out of a target area."

"Thank you very much, lieutenant."

"Some day I'll need a favor from you, McGee. I'm just building up my equity."

12

Saturday I visited my neighborhood travel agency, put the houseboat in shape to leave it for a time, had a long phone talk with Annie Renzetti and another with Lysa Dean. Sunday morning in Miami I boarded the L-1011 nonstop to Los Angeles, sitting up there in first with the politicians, the airline deadheads, and the rich rucksacky dopers. There is more legroom, the drinks are free, and the food is better. Also, somebody else was paying. I had the double seat to myself.

I was aware of the flight attendant giving me sidelong speculative glances as she roved the aisles. She was a pouter-pigeon blonde with a long hollow-cheeked face which looked as if it had been designed for a more elegant body.

Finally when she brought me a drink she said, "Excuse, me, Mr. McGee, but I feel almost certain I know you from somewhere."

"Maybe from another trip?"

She looked dubious. She frowned and held a finger against her chin. They like to identify and classify all their first-class passengers. Tinker, tailor, soldier, sailor....She couldn't figure the stretch denim slacks, knit shirt, white sailcloth jacket with the big pockets and snaps, boat shoes.

When I did not volunteer more information, she went on to the next drinker, probably convinced that I was just another doper, running Jamaican hash to the Coast. I sipped and looked down through scattered cloud cover and saw the west coast of Florida slip back under us, six miles down. We'd had our life-jacket demonstration. I've never been able to imagine a planeload of average passengers getting those things out from under the seats and trying to get into them while the airplane is settling down toward the sea with, as Tom Wolfe commented, about the same glide angle as a set of car keys.

Had drinks, ate a mighty tough little steak for lunch, got into LA before lunch their time, found my reserved Hertz waiting, studied the simplified Hertz map and found my way through traffic to Coldwater Canyon Drive, found the proper turnoff on the second try, and stopped outside the pink wall, with the front of the little Fiesta two feet from the big iron gate.

An Oriental looked inquiringly at me through the bars of the gate. "McGee," I called out.

"You Messer McGee, hah?"

"Messer McGee, pal. Miss Dean expects me."

"I know, I know," he said and swung the gates wide, showing a lot of gold in his Korean smile. "Drive by," he said. "Park anyplace. Miss Dean in the pool, hah?"

The plantings were more luxuriant than I remembered. They'd had a few years to grow. Her big pink wall was due for repainting. I remembered Dana telling me that a Mexican architect had done the house for

Lysa and her third husband, in a style that could be called Cuernavaca Aztec. I walked around to the pool-side. It was quiet and green in here behind the wall, and the city out there was brassy, smelly gold, vibrating in sun, heat, and traffic, already into midsummer on only the twenty-sixth of April. When I went around the corner of the house, the world opened up, and I could see the cheese-pizza structures of the city under the yellow haze, far beyond the pink wall that crossed the lower perimeter of her garden. She was swimming a slow length of her big rectangular pool, using a very tidy crawl, with no rolling or wallowing, sliding through the water with the greased ease of a seal in an amusement park. She saw me and angled over to the ladder and climbed out. She was wearing a pink bathing cap and an eggshell tank suit of a fabric so thin that, sopping wet, it fit her like skin, showing the dark areolas around the nipples and the dark pubic smudge. She yanked her cap off and shook her blond bleached hair out as she came smiling toward me. She stood on tiptoe and gave me a quick light kiss on the corner of the mouth, flavored with peppermint and chlorine. She tossed the pink cap into a chair, picked up a giant yellow towel, and began using it.

"Well!" she said. "How about you? You look fantastic."

"We're both fantastic."

"Look, I have to work on me. I have to think about me all day every day, Diet, exercise, massage, skin care, hair care, yoga."

"Whatever you're doing, it works."

I followed her over to a marble table, out of the sun. And after a slender Korean maid brought a Perrier for her and a rum and juice for me, Lee went into the house and came out ten minutes later with her hair brushed to gleaming. She was wearing lipstick and a little tennis dress.

"I really hated you, McGee."

"It wasn't a really great time for either of us."

"These are better years, amigo. I was very hot back then, getting lots of scripts to choose from, spoiled rotten. Also I was trying for the world boffing championship. The all-American boffer. Anything that came within reach. And I seldom missed. As I did with you. Anyway, my psychiatrist pulled me out of that swamp. What I decided about you, McGee, was that if you were some sort of funny-looking little guy with pop eyes and no chin and a dumpy little body, you wouldn't have turned me down. You wouldn't be turning anybody down. You would take what you could get and be grateful. So, my friend, your reluctance wasn't based on character. It was based on appearance. And that puts us both in the same line of work."

"Actors?"

"Get used to it. We're out front. I don't need to work, dear, but I keep right on scuffling. I don't want anybody to ever say to me, 'Hey, didn't you used to be Lysa Dean?' You do your share of posing, both for yourself and other people."

"You're smarter than I remember."

"Maybe I started thinking with my head instead of my butt."

"Looks good on you."

"And you are here to talk about Josie Laurant and Peter Kesner."

"I think I'm going to go at this a different way than I planned at first, Lee."

"Meaning?"

"I was going to keep the bad part of this to myself and con you along a little, here and there. But I find you just enough different to let me drop the whole bundle in front of you."

"Go ahead."

"Before I do, let me tell you one thing. Aside from the people whose help I had to have, I have never mentioned one word about your problem with the photographs and the blackmail."

She nodded. "I know. I expected the worst after you walked out. I thought maybe you were justifying your own actions to come. Like hanging onto a set of prints and doing an interview for *Penthouse*. I held my breath for a year. You get used to backstabbing in this business. Finally I decided you were straight, and I thank you for it."

"It would be nice if you would keep all this just as quiet."

I liked the fact there was no instant promise. She thought it over, frowning. "Well, okay. It'll be hard for me, but okay."

"You know anything about Ellis Esterland?"

"Just that he was a rich plastics tycoon, and he and Josie had the daughter with the strange name who died as a result of a bad accident. Rondola? Romola! Josie must have lived with her husband for ten years. They never did get divorced. A legal separation, though. They lived in the New York area and she did some theater work, not much, and then came back out here after the separation. Didn't he die a couple of years ago, in some strange way?"

"He was beaten to death. He had terminal cancer at the time. No arrests, no clues. He and his ex-secretary were living on a boat in Fort Lauderdale at the time. He drove inland alone and was killed. The reason for his trip is not known."

"I heard that Josie inherited a pretty good slug of money when Romola died. And that the money was from her father's estate." She tilted her head, took off her dark glasses, and looked at me with those vivid slanted green eyes. "Josie was involved with his death?"

"I don't know. Here is how it looks right now. It looks as though Josie, through her friendship with Anne Renzetti, the secretary, knew everything there was to know about Esterland's financial setup, his will and so on. And whatever Josie knew, Peter Kesner knew. Josie was supporting Kesner. When it became evident that Romola was a hopeless case, and if she died first Esterland's money would go to a foundation, it was in Kesner's interest to make sure Esterland died first. A problem in elementary mathematics. A couple of million is better than a hundred thousand, and worth taking some risks for."

"Josie, no. Forget Josie. Peter, yes. But how would he work it?"

"Very very carefully. He has contacts among outlaw bikers based on those two movies he made several years ago."

"For low budget, they were very good."

"Though I can't prove it and probably nobody ever will be able to, I think those two bikers who were in one or both of those movies rode all the way across the country, set up a meet with Esterland, and beat him to death. In the movie or movies they were called Dirty Bob and the Senator."

"I remember. Very tough people. Authentic tough, you know. You can always tell authentic tough from acting tough. Bogart was acting tough, but he was also a very tough-minded man on the inside. Nothing scared him, ever. Those bikers sort of scared me a little."

"Would they kill people?"

"If the price was right, yes."

"How do I find out what their real names are?"

"You find out from me, right now. Be right back." She went in and came out five minutes later with a thick, well-thumbed, paperback book. "My bible," she said. "The basic poop on five thousand motion pictures. All the statistics." She checked the index, found the right page. "Here we are: *Chopper Heaven*. The part of Dirty Bob was played by one Desmin Grizzel. My God, can that be a real name? It probably is. And the Senator by one Curley Hanner. Let me check that other one. What was the name of it?"

"*Bike Park Ramble,* I think."

"Sounds right. Yes, here it is. Same fellows. It was a sort of Son of *Chopper Heaven* and not quite as successful."

"Any way I could get to see the movies? Just one would do. Either one."

"I can call around the neighborhood. People are getting big collections of movies on videotape, the home-television kind and the three-quarter-inch commercial. I can show either one. I get tapes from the shows I'm on."

"If it wouldn't be too much trouble."

"Why am I doing you favors anyway? Okay. After lunch?"

"Had it on the airplane."

"It'll just be a salad. Choke it down. Or the Snow Princess will snap a gusset."

She led me on into the terrazzo silence I remembered, where there was dark paneling transplanted from ancient churches and portraits in oil of the owner. There were white throw rugs, and sparse white furniture, and a large wall cabinet of glass and mirrors containing a collection of owls in pottery and crystal, in jade, wood, ivory, bone, and silver.

I stopped to admire them. "Used to be elephants," I said.

"They're in the bedroom."

She led me to an alcove off the dining area where there was a window table for two overlooking the pool, the long slope of the garden, and the city beyond. The Korean maid brought the salad in a big wooden bowl, fresh spinach, with cheese and mushrooms, some bits of bacon, a dressing of vinegar and oil with an aftertaste of garlic. Tall nubbly glasses full of iced tea with mint.

In Lee's casual conversation, in her expression, in her tone of voice, in the way she held herself, she seemed to be making an offer of herself, to be advertising her accessibility. And because any actress is such a mannered thing, such an arbitrary construction, I could not tell whether she was merely being her habitual self or inviting mischief.

"Who occupies the secretarial suite these days?"

"There's not as much to do, of course. Not like it used to be. A darling young man comes in and works in there three days a week. The letters and cards keep coming, thank God. A lot of it from those late late late late shows, the pictures I made at the time they were filming *Birth of a Nation*. I had my eighteenth birthday on location. I was aching to look at least twenty. Can you imagine?"

She smiled at me over the rim of the iced-tea glass, green eyes as frosty as the glass.

It took her three phone calls to locate a home videotape of *Chopper Heaven*. A boy on a bicycle delivered it. Her little projection area was an alcove off the bedroom. Two double chaises faced the oversized screen on which the television image was projected. The set and projector were between the two double chaises. The sound came out of two speakers, one on either side of the screen. There was no window in the alcove. Daylight filtered in through the drawn draperies in the bedroom.

I watched the eighty-minute show with total attention. Peter Kesner was given the writing credit, directing credit, producing credit. The sound track was old-fashioned hard rock. And loud. Hand-held cameras, grainy film, unadjusted color values from scene to scene. But it moved. It was saying that this biker world was quick, brutal, and curiously indifferent to its own brutality, almost unaware of it. The characters seemed to want things very badly and, when they got them, discarded them. The dialogue was primitive but had an authentic ring. The bikers' girls were sullen and slutty. After death and bombings, Dirty Bob and the Senator rode off down the highway toward the dawn, bawling a dirty song in their hoarse untrained voices, over the rumble of the two big machines.

She got up and turned it off and pushed the rewind key. "Interesting," she said. "It doesn't hold up. At the time it was more daring than it is now. It cost a million and a half and grossed maybe fifteen to twenty."

"Would Kesner have made a lot of money?"

"Darling! This is the Industry! The really creative people are the accountants. A big studio got over half the profit, after setting breakeven at about three times the cost, taking twenty-five percent of income as an overhead charge, and taking thirty percent of income as a distribution charge, plus rental fees, and prime interest on what they advanced. If he had made a million, including fees for his services, I'd be surprised. Peter lives *very* well. I'm surprised Josie could afford him. Anyway I remembered the picture as being better. Some of *my* old ones seem to be much *better* than I remembered. Odd, isn't it?"

"Did you ever meet those two? Grizzel and Hanner?"

"On a talk show several years ago. They were a disaster. They came stoned to the eyeballs. Big noisy smelly fellows, thrashing around and saying things that had to be beeped off the air, thinking they were hilarious, apparently. One of them grabbed me by the behind and actually left big dingy fingermarks on my yellow skirt. I told him if he touched me again, I'd cut his heart out and fry it. I meant it and he knew I meant it. I didn't know their names. They were just Dirty Bob and the Senator."

I knew I would recognize them if I saw them again anywhere. Dirty Bob, a.k.a. Desmin Grizzel, had a full black beard and a moon face with high cheekbones and such narrow eyes it gave him an Asiatic look, like a Mongol warlord. The full beard was a fringe beard, growing thick around the perimeter but not very lush around the mouth. It looked to me as if he had done his own tricks in the motion picture. If so, he was very quick and spry for a man of his considerable bulk.

The Senator, a.k.a. Curley Hanner, had a long narrow face, a long narrow nose, a tight little slot of a mouth. His eyes were so close together it gave him a half-mad, half-comedic look. His little slot mouth turned into a crazy little V when he smiled. On the right side of his forehead there was a deep, sickening crevasse, as though he had stove it in on the corner of something. Black thinning hair, and a black thin mustache that hung below his chin, like an oldtime gunfighter. Throughout the movie they had both worn thin red sweat bands just above the eyebrows. They were ham actors and could have spoiled the picture if the director had let them.

"Where did Kesner find that pair?"

"No idea, Travis. The story was that he'd auditioned some very hard-case types from the Bandidos and Hell's Angels, picked a half dozen, and then let them fight it out for the two parts. But that was probably some studio flack's idea of exciting copy. I heard that Kesner got a motorcycle and went riding with one of the outlaw clubs, and that's where he got the idea for the picture and found the people to play in it. You saw how many there were altogether. Fifteen or twenty."

"And Kesner is on location now?"

"Out in farm country somewhere. With Josie. Making a balloon picture. Hot-air balloons."

"How do I find out where they are?"

"You have me, dear. Girl guide to the wonders of the Industry. Let me phone. You stay put." She gave me a pretty good rap on the skull with her knuckles when she went behind the chaise. She went to the bedroom phone, sat small on the side of her big bed, her back to me, as she hunched over her phone list. I got up and roamed over to a wall rack which seemed to hold scores of videotapes. It was too dark to read the titles. There was a little gallery light over the rack and I pulled the chain. The titles were visible. They ranged from X to XXX. With a very few R-rated here and there. I could hear her on the phone. There was a shallow drawer under the middle shelf of the rack, and on nosey impulse I pulled it open. And there was the little white Prelude 3 System massager, fitted with what I believe is called the Come Again tip. Beside it a small vial of lubricant. I slid the drawer shut and went back to the chaise, then remembered the light, went and turned it off, and stretched out again.

Scenario for a lonely lady. With frequent insomnia. Slip in here from the bedroom, put on a dirty tape with the sound turned low or off, and surrender to the throbbing hum of electrical ecstasy.

No obligation for dull conversation before or after. No awkward emotional entanglements. No jealousies. No involvements. Just an interwoven pattern of as many climaxes as she cared to endure, and then turn off all the machinery and go back to bed, to a sleep like death itself. The modern female, making out with no help from any male. I had never felt more superfluous—which in itself is a comment.

She came back in and sat on my chaise near my knees, facing me. "Well, I know where they are, almost. In Iowa, at a place called Rosedale Station. It's northwest of Des Moines and southwest of Fort Dodge, somewhere off U.S. Route Thirty. What you have to do is fly to Des Moines and get a car there, and it would be maybe sixty miles."

"Now I have to come up with an approach."

"What do you mean?"

"Nobody there in Rosedale Station, neither Josie nor Kesner nor those two bikers—if they're there—would have any idea who I am or what I want. And I can't exactly go up to Josephine Laurant and say, 'Honey, your stepson Ron hired me to find out who beat old Ellis to death.' What I am talking about is some kind of a cover story. People making motion pictures keep a good guard up to keep the local hams and autograph hounds away. I can't exactly start cold and ingratiate myself."

"What is it you want to do when you get there?"

"I don't know. Mill around. Make friends. Trade secrets back and forth. Beat heads. Lie a lot. I don't know. I improvise. If you have made some good guesses about something that happened in the past, you can usually stick the pry bar into the right crack. If nothing much happens, you know you guessed wrong."

She tilted her pretty head and studied me. "Who should you be? I'll have to think about that. Let me see. You should have some authority of some kind, so they'll have to be nice to you."

"I know nothing about their line of work. Or about hot-air balloons."

"Hush. I'm thinking." With doubled fist she struck me gently on the knee, again and again. Lips pursed, eyes almost closed. "Got it!" she cried.

"I give up. Who am I?"

"It so happens I own a nice little piece of Take Five Productions, sweetie. And some of their nice letterhead.

We do daytime game shows. So let's go to the darling secretary's office and compose a letter."

Mr. Peter Kesner
President, Major Productions
On location
Rosedale Station, Iowa

Dear Peter,

This will introduce Travis McGee, one of the consultants on our new and exciting project for prime-time television, tentatively titled THE REAL STUFF.

As you may or may not know, I have an ownership interest in Take Five Productions, and I have had the privilege of being in on the planning phase of this new program scheduled for next fall on ABC.

It is our intent—and I know you will keep this confidential—to go behind the scenes of the entertainment industry, not only in America but around the world.

From backstage ballet to the back lot of the carnival, to big band rehearsals, to animal training, to moviemaking. We will go for action and pictorial values, and we have no intention of skimping on the budget. Some very excited sponsors are waiting in the wings to see what we come up with as a pilot for the show.

In discussions here, it occurred to us that the picture you are making, about hot-air balloons and the people who fly in them, out there in the lovely springtime in the heartland of America, might make a very vivid episode in our projected series THE REAL STUFF.

I hope I am not imposing in asking you to give Mr. McGee the run of the sets and to answer his questions. I am certain

he will be considerate. Should we want to use clips from your
rushes, I can assure you the compensation will not disappoint
you.

I wish you all manner of luck with your picture. And please
say hi to darling Josie for me.

Affectionately,

Lysa Dean

She read through it again and signed *Lee* with a
flourish, a swooping curlicue thing that went back under her name and crossed itself in a figure eight
stretched out on its side.

"Such utter crap!" she said. "But you know, it is just
ridiculous enough to appeal to that freak. Especially
the hint about money. Can you carry it off, do you
think?"

"Provided you tell me the kind of questions I should
be asking."

She did not hear me. She was staring into the middle
distance. Finally she said, "You know, it really might
make a program. I'm going to take it up with Sam."

13

I got into Des Moines late on Monday night, stayed over in a motel near the airport, and drove to Rosedale Station on Tuesday morning, the twenty-eighth of April. I drove through soft gray rain, the wipers thudding back and forth in slow steady rhythm. The flat fields and the hedgerows and the ditches beyond the shoulder of the highway were green, the bright new green of springtime.

My road atlas said that Rosedale Station had 2,812 people. It had a railroad track, grain elevators, a central school, a dozen churches, a dozen gas stations, a new downtown shopping mall, a couple of fast food outlets, a lot of white houses and big trees, and a very few traffic lights.

I drove around in the rain until I came upon a brick and frame structure called THE ROSEDALE LODGE. FINE FOOD. It had its own gravel parking area to the right of the entrance. I pulled the rental Buick into a slot and trotted under the dripping trees, up onto the veranda, and into the front entrance hall.

There was a tall thin old lady behind the oak registration desk. I asked her if there was a vacancy.

"You with that movie bunch?"

"I'm not *with* them. But I have some business to transact with them."

"Then you're with them, the way I see it. I've got a single. It's fifty dollars a night. In advance. Food is extra."

"Is Mr. Kesner staying here?"

"Yes."

"Is he in now?"

"I wouldn't know and I won't ask."

"Is something wrong?"

"Nothing is wrong with the people around here. Do you want the room or don't you?"

"I'll take it for one night. Why are you being so rude?"

"Let's say it's catching."

She slapped my key down: Room 39. I paid and signed in, using the Burbank address of Take Five Productions.

"Third floor, all the way to the back on the left," she said.

"Would it be against your house rules to tell me Kesner's room number?"

"Twenty-five and -six," she said, and turned away.

"Pretty good room rate," I said.

"When you people go back where you belong, it will come on back down to normal."

"Welcome to Rosedale Station. Nice little town."

"Used to be," she said, and went into the switchboard alcove, pulled an old-fashioned plug, and let it snap down into its recess.

I took my duffelbag on up to 39. There was a big tree outside my single small window. Through the leaves I could see a neighboring lumberyard. My wallpaper was a design of crossed ropes and little old sailing ships, in brown, gray, and blue. My single bed was hammocked in the middle. The toilet and shower shared a three-by-six closet. The sink was in the bedroom, beside the shower-room door. There was an oval mirror over it. I had to stoop to look at myself. The backing was coming off, so that my image was fragmented. The spit-colored eyes looked back at me with more calm than I felt. I did not look like your ordinary consultant-type person. I looked more as if I worked with a sledge out in the sunshine, turning big rocks into little rocks. I took my shirt off and scratched my chest and thought about the tragicomic inconsistencies of the emotional life of McGee. A repressed libertine. A puritanical wastrel. A lot of names rolled around in my skull. Old ones: Puss and Glory and Pidge and Heidi and Skeeter and Cindy and Cathy. New ones: Gretel and Annie and Lysa.

Ah, the eternal compulsion to leap into a marvelous stew of boobs and butt, hungry lips and melting eyes, rolling hips and tangled hair. But I had to pause before the leap, like some kind of shy farm girl interrogating the traveling salesman after they have dug their nest in the side of a haystack: Wait, Walter! Is this for real?

Lysa was the peach which had hung long on the tree, gone from green to ripe to overripe, bursting with the juices that had that winelike tang of early fermentation. She had made all the moves she knew, and she knew a lot of moves. But I had bicycled around the ring, keeping her off with a long cautious left jab, avoiding the corners, slipping, rolling, tying her up. I had wanted her so badly I had felt as if I was carrying paving blocks around in the bottom of my belly. But of course it wasn't for real, and it wasn't forever. I had the sap's record of spurning her once before, and apparently I was out to win the world title for sapistry.

And here I was on a rainy day in a sorry little room in a country hotel, a long long way from that lady of Sunday evening, that queen of the game shows who had wanted merely a jolly cluster of bangs in the night, topped off with steaks and a swim and a farewell bang for luck. But I had left her to the tireless throb of her Prelude 3 System and the technicolor stimulation of her blue movies.

Maybe what I was saying to myself by sidestepping a quantum bang was that I wanted but one lady at a time. Regardless of what Annie's reaction would have been, it would not have been anything I would have wanted to tell her. That did not improve my image. I wanted the free ride and I wanted to be paid in my own coin—meaningfulness or sacrament, or some kind of spiritual dedication—something that would give Hefner the hiccups. What gave me pause was the thought that for a fellow of my hesitations, I had sure cut myself a wide swath through a wall of female flesh, dragging my canoe behind me. Cheap apologist is the phrase that comes to mind.

I put on a fresh shirt and went down the stairs and found rooms 25 and 26. I could hear murmurous voices in there, which stopped when I knocked. A tall, strong, dark-haired young girl with a glassy look in her wide eyes opened the door and said, "Yeh?" She was wearing a very faded purple T-shirt with a drawing of Miss

Piggy on the front of it and, as near as I could judge, nothing else.

"Peter Kesner in, please?"

"Whaddaya want with him?"

"I've got a letter here for him."

She whipped it out of my hand, said, "Stick aroun'," and closed the door smartly. I waited at least five minutes until she opened the door and beckoned me in with a motion of her head, a lift of her shoulder.

Peter Kesner was sitting on an unmade bed, folding the letter into a paper airplane. "How is that old bag, Lee Dean, holding up?" he asked.

I didn't answer because my attention was riveted on Purple Piggy. She was putting one foot carefully in front of the other as though walking an invisible tightrope. She made a right-angle corner and went six feet, made a right angle in the other direction, and walked until she came to a low solid oak table against the wall that apparently was intended for use as a luggage rack. She swiveled onto it and assumed the lotus position. She rested her head back against the wall and closed her eyes, her hands, palm upward, resting on her thighs, which looked uncommonly meaty and heavy for the rest of her.

"Don't mind Freaky Jean," Kesner said. "She's having one of her ninety-degree square-corner days." He glided the airplane toward her, and it hit the wall beside her and fell to the bench.

"What's she on?"

"She is into Qs. Like they were popcorn. How's Lee? I haven't seen her in a year. She's a money head. Pieces of this and pieces of that, and she puts them together nice. She's going to own as much of California as Bob Hope."

"She looks fine. She looks great."

He yawned and picked up a bound mimeographed script and riffled the pages. "I shouldn't tell you this because maybe you can come up with some pesos which we sure God need, but I think this thing is becoming a turkey. I should never have farmed out the script. Should have done it all myself. When you start with a piece of shit, no matter which way you turn it, form it, shape it, revise it, you end up with the same piece of shit. But the pictorials are great, when they happen. Jesus Christ, we are either getting rain or we are getting winds over nine miles an hour. And over nine, those balloon-club freaks won't fire them up. Can you imagine? And if the weatherman says a front is fifty miles away and moving in on us at fifteen miles an hour, they won't even take the gondolas out of the trucks. And if we get an absolutely beautiful day, say five-mile-an-hour wind, bright sun, warm and pretty, they will fly in the early morning or the late afternoon. And that is all, period, fini. Everything by FAA regulations, and they have saddled us with a resident FAA spook to make sure about getting every i dotted and t crossed. What we are doing here, McGee, is running too fast through the money and too slow through the film. And pretty soon I am going to have to take *Free Fall* back to LA, do the studio shots, and try to fake the rest from what we've gotten so far."

I swiveled a straight chair and sat there astride, arms crossed on the back of it, staring at him with an attentive questioning look, waiting for more. He wore jogging shorts and ragged blue canvas shoes. I guessed his age at fifty. Once upon a time he had been in shape. He had long ropy muscles, blurred by fat. He had dead-white skin and a lot of curly black hair on his body, even on the tops of his shoulders and down the backs of the shoulder blades. His face and forearms and the top of his bald head were deep tan. His trimmed beard was speckled with white hairs. He wore two heavy gold chains around his neck, one with some kind of a tooth hanging from it, and a thick gold chain around his wrist. His eyes were deep-set, and he wore Ben Franklin half glasses with little gold rims.

"I admire your early work, Mr. Kesner."

"Make it Peter, please. What have you seen, Travis?"

"*Chopper Heaven*, of course. And *Bike Park Ramble*. Very significant contributions to popular culture, Peter. I was very impressed with the quality of the performance you got out of those amateur actors, Grizzel and Hanner particularly."

He beamed at me. "It was long years ago, Travis. When I was young and hungry. They were existentialist films, both of them, tied into the significance of the immediate moment. Desmin Grizzel is still with me, by the way. He's working on this picture. Not in front of the camera. He's sort of a personal gofer. The Senator, Curley Hanner, is dead, of course."

"Dead? I didn't know that."

"It was covered in the trades and on the wire services. Accidental death. A year ago. He was coming down the coast road, working out a new machine, a Moto Guzzi Le Mans One Thousand. They were just north of Point Sur, really winding it up, very early in the morning. Desmin estimates a hundred and twenty-five to thirty miles an hour. The Senator was out front by fifty or sixty yards when without warning he ran into a cloud of sea gulls, just as he was starting to lean into a curve to the left. Dirty Bob thinks one of them took him right in the face shield. He straightened and went out over the edge. Low tide and it was three hundred feet down to a shale beach. That was his fourth crackup and his last. Over two thousand bikers came to the funeral, some of them all the way from across the country. There was TV news coverage. Where were you?"

"I have to travel outside the country often."

"Consultant. That's the way to go. What do you want to see? What do you want to know?"

"Is everybody staying here in this hotel?"

"God, no! We'd be out of money already. We leased some pasture five miles north of town when we first got here. Nearly everybody else is out there, with the mobile units, vans, house trailers, campers, pickup trucks, and so on, sitting out the rain, bitching, gambling, freaking out. Oh, we were real big when we came to town. We were going to put Rosedale Station on the map. They were all smiles. But, you know, the crew likes a little fun, and there are some townie girls who've learned how fun-loving they are, and there are some townie dudes who got broken up in little arguments about this and that. Now things are very cool, and they talk about us from the pulpits. And overcharge us."

"I've got an eighteen-dollar room upstairs for fifty dollars."

"And the old bat behind the desk was happy to see you?"

"Not exactly."

"Okay, for Lee's bad idea for a program, what are you looking for?"

"Behind the scenes, how problems are solved. What goes wrong with the balloon scenes until you get it right."

"We are up to here in what goes wrong. We can show you lots of that, McGee. One trouble, we're down to eight balloon teams now. The rest of them got sick of waiting around and took off. We had thirty teams here at one time. Freaky Jean here, she dropped out of one of the teams that took off. Right, Jeanie? Hey, you! Jeanie!"

She opened her eyes slowly and took long seconds to focus. "Wha?"

"Where'd the buddies on your team go?"

"Wha?"

"Forget it. Look, I got some more script work here. Afterwards, I can take you out and introduce you to the kids. About noon or a little after. So kill some time and I'll get back to you. If you want, pal, you can take Jeanie here along with you. She's a real workout."

"Not right now, thanks."

"Feel free, any time. Courtesy of the house."

"Thanks. What's the theme of the picture?"

His face changed, and he looked demented. "The free flight in the hot-air balloon is the symbol of the yearning for freedom, like any dream of flying. We see the life-worn female, trying to reenter the freedom of her youth, seeking it in blue skies, searching and yearning, but the dream of flying contains implicit within it the dream of falling. Age is a falling away, a manner of dying."

"Oh."

"Gallantry in the face of disaster will underline the symbols of her life, the young lover deserting her, her child dying, the man who wants to take her on this last splendid voyage."

"Lysa Dean said that Josephine Laurant is starring in the picture."

The demented look vanished and the odd face scowled. "She will by God win awards with this role if she will for Christ's sake keep saying the lines the way they are written, not the way she thinks they should have been written."

"She's an investor?"

He stared at me. "Why do you ask?"

"Lysa said there was a rumor around."

"There are always rumors around. Yes, we are both investors, friend. We are both betting our asses and all we own in this world on a fine artistic venture which will, because of its message, be a commercial success. I know how to combine those two elements. I bombed out on two films because they wouldn't let me go my own way. They controlled me. They turned those two films sour. Now it's like the old days. Complete artistic control, casting control, direction, production, writing, everything. Because we staked everything, the two of us, the distributor and the banks came into the picture for nine mil, and wished upon me a godawful little ferret-faced money man to watch every cent spent, checking every scene against the story boards, setting limits on the number of takes, cutting down the camera angles on both units. So all my wonderful control doesn't mean shit. And it keeps raining. Look, let me get to work here."

So I left, taking with me the memory of Freaky

Jean's placid young freckled face, of the dazed mind riding atop the ripe maturity of the animal body.

At a little before one o'clock I rode out to the rented pasture in Kesner's rented car. He was a ragged driver, accelerating too soon, braking too late, wandering over the center line, talking with his hands. The rain was dwindling. Sunshine was predicted for afternoon. Kesner was full of optimism.

The thirty or so vehicles were parked in random order under a long roadside row of big maples. The pastureland had been trampled into mud paths that followed the traffic pattern. They had wangled a hookup to the power line, and the wires led down to a temporary meter on a pole. There were camera booms and camera trucks standing in the drizzle, their vital parts shrouded in plastic. There were lights shining through the windows of some of the trailers. People wandered around in rain gear. Kesner led me to the cook tent, to a large helping of excellent beef stew on a paper plate, served with a big tin spoon and a cup of india-ink coffee. He settled for just the coffee and a banana.

He introduced me as "A television person who can maybe set us up for some exposure on a network show, so be nice to him."

I couldn't retain the names. They came too fast. Chief cameraman, second unit director, script girl, lighting technician, some actors, some balloon people. Everybody seemed very cordial. And then Dirty Bob came in, in a shiny orange jump suit with water droplets on the shoulders and chest. Unmistakable bland moon face, the fringe of beard now flecked with gray, the small Mongolian eyes, slitted and slanted.

"Hey, Desmin. Meet one of your fans. This is Travis McGee."

I stood up and shook hands with him. His hand was thick, dry, warm, and so slack it felt lifeless. As Kesner explained why I was there, Desmin Grizzel stared out at me through those little blueberry eyes set back behind the squinty lids. And I looked back at him. There was something going on behind those eyes. He was perhaps adding something up, something he had heard, measuring me in all the ways I didn't fit the present role. Or maybe it was some primitive awareness of a special danger.

I sat down, and he sat down with us.

Kesner said, "I gave Kitty the changes for the pink sheets. Did they get that goddam duplicator fixed?"

"Early this morning. She's caught up on back stuff."

"What's with Josie?"

"She come in here for lunch today. Now she's doing backgammon with Tiger in her trailer."

"What about the fellow from Joya's balloon?"

"It turned out it was pneumonia, and they run him on down to Des Moines in Jake's wagon."

"Jesus Christ! It's clearing and I want to do number eighty-one. Jesus Christ, is he in that one?"

"No. I checked it out with Kitty. No scene, no lines, nothing. That's why I didn't call in."

"How did the special project go after I left last night?"

"Mercer thinks it's pretty much okay. He just doesn't like the Mickey Mouse equipment and no chance to make cuts."

"Where's the girl?"

"Linda's looking after her."

"Good thinking. McGee, if you're through, I'll go introduce you to Josie. Dez, what you do is get people going on makeup and have Kitty get the pages distributed for number eighty-one, and get those balloon crews ready to go out there to the takeoff area soon as the sun comes out."

I followed Kesner through the mud to Josie's big dressing-room trailer, stepping with care. She let us in, and he kissed her on the cheek and said, "We'll be able to roll this afternoon. Here's what we'll be doing, if we stay lucky."

When he introduced me, she gave a vacant nod and began skimming through the script pages. I found it hard to believe she was as old as she had to be. A small woman, dainty, dark, fragile, with a lot of energy and vitality in her expression, in the way she moved.

She moved her lips as she turned the pages. Suddenly she threw her head back, dashing the dark hair away from her forehead. She threw the pages at Kesner's face.

"I told you! I will *not* do that. I will not!"

"Not do what?"

"I will not go up in that goddam wicker basket!"

"And I told you fifty times, damn it, that you *will* go up to eight feet off the ground. The damn balloon will be anchored! I want you up there with Tyler for your scene, the big one. The lines that are going to break hearts." He picked up the pages. "Look. Right here. Where it's marked. That's where we take you out of the basket and put Linda in. We back off for a low angle and get Linda when she jumps out of the basket into the net. Then it goes on up and we pick up the fall after they throw out the dummy, and all the rest is process. Eight feet in the air, for God's sake."

"I don't like the height. It could get away somehow. It would kill me. It would stop my heart. No."

"I'm telling you, there will be three ropes this big around tied to that basket and tied to three trucks on the ground."

"The propane will blow up."

"It is safe! Absolutely safe! I know what I am doing."

She switched emotions instantaneously, from indignation and fury to cool sardonic query. Posture, expression, voice quality—all changed.

"Do you now, darling? Do you really know what you are doing? Do you really understand the extra risks you're running?"

"What would you rather have me do, mouse? Wind it all down or try to keep it going?" It seemed to me that he gave her some look of warning, some sign to be careful.

After a moment of hesitation, she said, "It makes me nervous."

"You don't have to know anything about it. Or even think about it. Okay? Maybe you don't even have to think about being in the basket way up there in the air, eight feet. Maybe Linda would be better all the way through. Go back and do your scenes over with her. Her skin tones are better by daylight."

"You son of a bitch! She's a stuntwoman. She's no actress."

"Listen! You were run out of the industry because nobody could trust you not to fuck up and spoil scenes and cost big money. For God's sake, it's *your* money you're wasting!"

"So I'll waste it if I want to!"

"I'll use Linda for the whole thing. I need a picture in the can more than I need your famous face, lady."

She hesitated. "Three real strong ropes?"

"Big ropes. This big around."

"I better start to get ready."

I followed him back out into the mud and along the row of vehicles to a yellow four-wheel-drive Subaru parked next to a big cargo trailer and a small house trailer. A woman sat in the doorway of the house trailer, mending the toe of a red wool sock. She wore bib overalls over a beige turtleneck. She looked lean and husky, with big shoulders and a plain, intelligent face, red-brown hair combed back and tied.

"Hey, Joya," Kesner said. "This here is Travis McGee, who is a consultant, and he'll get us some prime-time exposure for free, if we're lucky. Joya is the boss lady of the balloons we got left."

She had a muscular handshake, a direct, crinkled smile, a pleasantly rusty voice.

Kesner said, "I'd like to get them off the ground in maybe two hours. The weather looks okay."

"The forecast looks good," she said.

He drew in the dirt with a stick. "The wind is going to keep coming out of the southwest. Did I say wind? The breeze. Five knots and fairly steady, they tell me. So right here we do a tethered scene with Josie in the number-one balloon. Then we get her out, then Linda jumps into the net, then you balloon people take it up, and I want about five hundred feet on it when the dummy gets tossed out. We'll cut from Linda jumping to the free fall at five hundred feet. Now when we take the low angle on the dummy coming out, I want to see balloons up there, not placed so they'll get in the way of the cameras. I want enough of them in the scene so in the editing, we can go back to where we had them all going nice that day, remember?"

"Sure."

"So the closer together and the closer to the number-one balloon, the better. So what you do is establish the placement and the order of takeoff, and when you get the gear spread out, I'll set up the camera stations. Okay?"

"Fine."

"I want to put Simmy with a camera in the number-three balloon, so that better be the one to come off last, so he can get wide-angle stuff of the other balloons and the fall. I want him back in the basket and low, so the other cameras don't pick him up."

"Upwind, then, about two hundred feet from number one, with a simultaneous takeoff, and Red has such a nice touch on that burner, he can hold it anywhere you say in relation to number one."

"I'd say a little higher, but not so high the envelope gets in the way of his camera angle. With the set of the wind, he should get the kind of landscape we want to show below number one. Joya, please, honey, it has to go right the first time."

"Do everything I can."

"Sorry to hear about Walter."

"He'll be okay. We thought it was some sort of flu, and then he began to have trouble breathing. They've got him on oxygen and full of antibiotics."

"Leaves you shorthanded."

"We were already shorthanded. There's just me, Ed, and Dave."

"So here is your new man. Travis McGee. Consultants are supposed to be able to do anything. Give him the speedy balloonist course. Okay with you, McGee?"

"Fine with me."

There was something in her quick glance which I could not identify. It seemed like some kind of recognition. It gave me the strange feeling that she knew I was an impostor, here for some private purpose. It made me wonder if I had seen the woman before, known her in some other context. But I am good about faces, and I knew she was a stranger. I knew I had not misinterpreted some kind of flirtatious awareness. It gave me a feeling of strangeness, wariness, distrust. Proceed with caution. She either knew something about me she had no right to know, or she was making some kind of very poor guess about me. In the glance, in her body language, in her voice, there was the sense of a secret shared, a private conspiracy.

14

The mist was gone, the sky brightening, and the encampment came alive, with people trotting back and forth from chore to chore, engines grinding as they moved vehicles into position.

Joya told me where to wait for her, and after she had organized the positions and told people the timing she came back to me.

"McGee, I hope you are a quick listener, because I don't have much time. Stop me any time you have a question, any time anything is unclear, okay? We like to fly in the early morning before the thermals begin to kick up, but this should be a similar situation. The air is cool enough to give a nice lift. We've got a nice launch site here. The direction of the breeze will hold, and the first thing in the way is that line of trees at least a half mile off."

A truck pulled up to us, and two men hopped out and started to wrestle the wicker basket out of the back. Joya introduced them. I helped them with the basket. They lifted a big canvas sack out of the basket, set it on the ground, and began pulling the seventy feet of canopy out of it. It was very brightly patterned in wide vertical yellow and green stripes.

"It's ripstop nylon," Joya said. "We stow it into the bag in accordion folds, inspect it when we fold it in, inspect again when we spread it out. We check the deflation port and the maneuvering vent."

"Whoa."

"The maneuvering vent is a slit on the side, up beyond the equator, ten or twelve feet long. You pull a cord and let hot air out to descend. When you are just about on the ground, you pull the red line for the deflation port, and that opens the top of the balloon and collapses it. It has a Velcro seal. They are checking the numbered gores and the vertical and horizontal load tapes. As owners, we're authorized to fix little melt holes with patches. And the places where damn fools walk on the canopy. Bigger damage has to have FAA-authorized repair."

When they had the big bright envelope spread out, downwind, Joya and the two men brought the propane tanks from the truck and slipped them into the stowage cylinders in the corners of the basket. They bolted together the support frame for the burners, hooked up the fuel lines from the ten-gallon tanks to the burners, then tilted the basket onto its side with the frame and burners toward the spread-out envelope.

At the other locations Joya had selected, the teams were doing the same things, getting set for a coordinated launch. They seemed to be trim and attractive people in their late twenties and early thirties. There was an earnestness about them, a cooperative efficiency, that reminded me of the sailing crowd, of preparations for a regatta. About half of them were women.

As the men were hooking the load cables to the tie blocks, Joya showed me the small instrument panel and explained it to me: variometer for rate of ascent and descent, pyrometer for temperature up in the crown of the balloon, compass—which she said was not very meaningful because there was no way to steer once you were aloft. There were gauges on the top of each propane tank. She showed me the sparker used to ignite the propane and to reignite it quickly should the flame go out. There was a small hand-held CB radio strapped to the side of the basket, which she said they used for contact with the chase vehicle.

She showed me the red line for deflation and the line to the maneuvering vent. She ran through a checklist with her ground crew and then turned to me, shrugged, and said, "Now we wait until it's time to inflate. Nothing else we can do at the moment, Mr. McGee."

When I asked her how that was arranged, she said we could walk over and watch them at the number-one balloon. They brought out a power-operated fan, and two crew members held the mouth of the balloon wide open as the fan blew air into it. One crew member held a line fastened to the crown of the balloon and kept watch to see that it didn't roll in any kind of side wind that would twist the steel cables at the mouth. When the balloon seemed about three quarters inflated, they started the burner, and it made a monstrous ripping, roaring sound as it gouted flame into the open mouth of the balloon.

She leaned close to me to holler over the burner sound, "Flying, you use over twelve gallons of propane an hour, enough to heat ten houses. George is working the blast valve. See. Now there's a lift."

The roaring stopped. The balloon lifted free of the ground and slowly swung up, righting the basket as it did so, and another man climbed into the basket. The basket was tethered to a truck and to a smaller vehicle. George pulled on the blast valve, giving it a three-second shot of flame up into the balloon, waited, and then did it again.

"Short blasts are the way to do it," Joya explained. "You don't get any reaction for maybe fifteen or twenty seconds, and then you get the lifting effect of the new heat."

She took me closer to where we could look up into the balloon. It was blue and white and crimson, segmented like an orange, and there was enough daylight coming through the fabric to dim the long blue flame of the burners. The sun broke through. Kesner was walking around, arguing, waving his arms. Josie Laurant arrived, leading her small entourage, and Kesner picked her up and put her in the basket. I couldn't hear what she was saying, but she was visibly angry. They brought the camera boom close and wanted the area cleared. I went back to the number-two balloon with Joya.

There was no diminution in my awareness of her special attitude toward me. She carried on a second conversation at a nonverbal level. She was telling me that she and I had some sort of arrangement. And, in addition, she was curious about me. It seemed an unemotional curiosity, speculative and slightly anxious, expressed by the quick sidelong glances, the set of the mouth.

The number-one balloon lifted to the limit of its tether. The breeze kept it canted toward the northeast.

Kesner yelled through his bullhorn. They seemed to be having trouble over there, doing the scene in between the blasts of the burner needed to keep the balloon aloft at the end of the tethers.

"You want to take this flight with me, Mr. McGee?"

"I don't know anything about it. I wouldn't be in the way?"

"I like the extra weight. Dave was going to come along. Let me ask him."

She went over to the truck and in a little while she came back with leather gloves and a helmet. "He says sure. See if these are okay. If you lose balance or something, you might touch the burner or the coils that preheat the propane. Helmet is standard for landings. They can get rough. The thing is to face the direction of flight, hang on, and don't leave the basket. That's important. Without your weight it could take right off again and get in trouble. Look, do you want to try it or not?"

"I'd like to try it, but not very much."

She studied me and smiled. "That's an honest reaction. This should be a routine flight. What do people call you?"

"Travis. Or McGee. Or whatever, Joya."

"Joya Murphy-Wheeler. With a hyphen, Travis. Mostly what you have to do is keep out of my way, which isn't easy, and admire the view."

We killed time for an hour, and finally they took Josie down to ground level and let her out, and put another propane tank aboard and another smallish dark-haired woman dressed like Josie.

"That's the stunt woman," Joya said. "Linda." She said the name the way she might say "snake."

They took the number-one balloon back up again to twenty feet above the ground. Linda held the burner support, straddled the side of the basket. The man with her, who had been in the long scene with Josie, grabbed for her and missed as she toppled over the side. She fell neatly into the safety net, bounced up, clasped her hands over her head, duck-walked to the edge of the net, grasped it, and swung down. George stood up out of his concealment in the basket and hit the blast valve for a few seconds. The balloon sagged down anyway, and the crew grabbed the edge of the basket. The actor climbed out and then was told to climb back in. The dummy was brought aboard and stowed. After a small conference, Linda climbed aboard too, and Kesner yelled through his bullhorn, "Joya, get your people ready to go."

It took about thirty minutes to get all seven balloons inflated. They seemed to come growing up out of the field like a crop of huge poisonous puffballs. The gas blasts were almost constant. Joya had arranged the signals. When number one took off, number three followed almost immediately, staying near it, gaining a little height on it. Joya's crew people, Dave and Ed, held the basket down and made bad jokes about what I might expect of the flight.

"Weight off!" Joya ordered. They removed their hands. We had positive buoyancy, and she blasted for eight or ten seconds. A little while after the blast ended, we began to lift more rapidly, following the first two in their mated ascent.

"I'll have to try to stay close, for the sake of the cameras, but then we'll peel off."

"I thought you said you couldn't steer these things."

"You'll see." She worked the blaster valve, ripping the silence with that startling bray, a snorting sound that shot the blue flame high into the envelope. Without that noise, there was a strange silence. We were moving with the wind, so there was no wind sound. I heard the other balloons blasting in short staccato sequences, then heard the wicker of the basket creak as she rested her hip against the edge. The ground had dropped away. Behind us I could see the pattern of vehicles, of the muddy paths, the trailers and trucks.

"There!" Joya said.

I looked where she pointed and saw the lifelike dummy ejected from the number-one balloon, about seventy feet above us and ahead of us. I heard the rattle of the clothing as the dummy fell, turning slowly. It seemed to pause and then pick up a terrible speed as it dwindled below us to smack into the tough pastureland.

We held position for a little while until Joya said, "I think they have enough." She pulled the line to the maneuvering vent and bent to watch the variometer scale, explaining that we were too high to use visual reference points to indicate altitude. She let us sag downward until it seemed to me that our descent accelerated. At just that point she began feeding it short intermittent blasts. The harsh sound startled me each time until I learned to watch her gloved hand on the lever.

The others were far ahead of us, much higher and leaving us well behind. "Higher wind speeds aloft," she explained. "They'll be coming down soon, to fly close to the ground. That's when it's best. You'll see."

She gave all her attention to stabilizing the balloon

at the height she wanted, explaining that as we came down we were pushing cooler air up into the envelope, thus decreasing lift. She leveled it out at about twenty feet above the ground. The breeze carried us along at I would guess ten miles an hour. Now and again she would pull the blast lever for a short sequence of that ungodly racket, and in a little while I began to comprehend the rhythm of it. If there was a tree line ahead she would give a two-second blast which, thirty seconds later, would lift us up over the trees.

We moved in silence, looking at the flat rich country. We heard the birdsongs, heard a chain saw in a woodlot, heard horses whinny. Children ran and waved at us. We crossed small country roads and once saw our reflection in a farm pond.

"What do you think?" she asked.

"There aren't any words," I said. There weren't. In incredible silence between her infrequent short blasts for control, we moved across the afternoon land, steady as a cathedral, moving through the land scents, barn scents, the summery sounds. It was a sensation unlike anything else in the world. It was a placid excitement, with the quality of an extended dream.

We beamed at each other, sharing pleasure. It made her strong plain face quite lovely. It was the instant of becoming friends.

At last she bumped it up to two hundred feet, where her exquisite coordination was not as imperative. We used the wrench to cut an almost empty tank out of the line and tie in another full one. She explained that we had wasted gas by using the maneuvering vent to drop us down, but she had wanted to get down quickly and get away from the others. From our altitude I scanned the horizon and could see but two of the others, little round pieces of hard candy way off to the west of us. "Divergent winds at different altitudes," she explained.

She perched a hip on the edge of the basket again, one hand overhead on the blast lever. She glanced at the control panel, then looked at me with the questing look she had concealed before.

"Travis, I can't add anything to what I told them on the phone."

Moment of decision. The proper thing to do would be to express all the confusion I felt, to take her off the hook, to correct her misapprehension. But there was a flavor of conspiracy, and I did not want to sidestep anything that might become of use to me. Apparently she and I were having a clandestine meeting, hanging up there in a wicker basket under a seventy-foot bulge of rainbow nylon, moving northeasterly across middle America.

I took my time with the response, knowing it was make or break. "They said they felt it would be better if I got it from you, rather than secondhand from them."

"I thought they were taping it. There was that little beep every few seconds."

"Listening to a tape and listening directly to a person are two quite different experiences, Joya. So if you don't mind..."

She shrugged, sighed. She pointed out a small deer, bounding toward a woodlot. And then she told me the story.

They had been going to leave when a lot of the others left. But she had been concerned about what had happened to her friend, Jean Norman, who was staying at the hotel with Kesner. There was a large trailer at the far end of the leased pastureland, fixed up like a bedroom set. There the withered little technician named Mercer used a video camera setup with a videorecorder, and with Dirty Bob and Jean and Linda, who was gay, they made cassettes, masters, which were flown to Las Vegas, where a distributor paid three thousand apiece for them and could then duplicate a thousand copies a day, title them, package them, and send them out. They kept Jeanie on pills and paid so little attention to her that she heard more than they realized. She signed releases every time, and they gave her a little money every time. Lately they had been bringing local girls into the action, making them think it was going to be some sort of screen test. The girls got some false reassurance from the presence of Linda and Jeanie, but the fake rape turned out to be real rape, and the screams were real as well. With enough Valium in them to quiet them down, they would take the money later on and sign the release and never dare reveal what had actually happened, hoping only that no collector in Rosedale Station ever bought one of those X tapes and recognized his neighbor's daughter or granddaughter in the jolly tattooed clutch of Desmin Grizzel.

"I haven't got any proof at all," she said. "I shouldn't have gotten involved. But I think it is rotten. And they should pay somehow for what they did to Jeanie, if for nothing else. She told me bits and pieces when she was sort of lucid. And I put it together. I don't think Josie Laurant knows about it. I like her. Kesner and Dirty Bob are monsters. Like I told your people on the phone, we're cutting out. Dave is driving the chase car and Ed is driving the truck with all our gear. I don't even want to take you back to where we left from. It's going to get very dangerous around there. The people around there hate the movie people and us too. If any one of those girls talks about what happened to her, it could start a shooting war. It's almost a shooting war now. One balloon came in with three rifle-bullet holes right through it, but little holes won't bring a balloon down. From now on it's up to you people."

"How did you know I was the one?"

"They said somebody would be here today, somebody with a cover story, to look around and decide whether it is worth further investigation." She looked up into the envelope and down at the variometer dial, gave a five- or six-second blast, frowned at me, and said, "Anyway, you *look* like the sort of person I expected them to send. What will you do?"

"Try to nail down the violations. Interstate transportation of obscene materials. There's a corrupt organizations statute that might fit."

"Will they go to prison for a long time?"

"Probably not."

"One of those girls was fifteen."

"If she would testify against them, it would be a big help. Lots of nice charges there, with the locals in the driver's seat."

"She probably wouldn't ever testify."

"Well, we're very grateful for the help of any citizen."

"You're welcome. I've got to get back anyway. I've taken too much time off work. I'm from Ottumwa. All four of us are. We're shares on the balloon. It's a Cameron. We've got about four thousand total in it. We really wanted to see it flying in a movie. But I don't think there'll be any movie. I tried to read that script.

It doesn't make any sense at all. I think Peter Kesner is crazy."

"What do you work at?"

"Oh, I'm a systems analyst, and I do some computer programming. It's kind of a slack time right now, so they let me off work. I think we better come down, and I think I see a good place. And there's the search car." She pointed it out to me, the Subaru with a yellow and green target painted on the roof, running along a road that paralleled our course.

She took the CB out of the straps, extended the aerial, and spoke into it. "Breaker Thirty-eight, this is Joytime, calling Little Sue. Come in, Little Sue."

"Little Sue sees you, Joytime."

"Take your second left and go in about two hundred yards, and that should be about right, Little Sue."

"Got you. See you there."

She made a face at me as she packed the CB away. "Not what you'd call good radio discipline. But it gets the job done."

She turned her attention to the descent, checking the stowage of loose equipment, checking on helmets, reading the surface wind, telling me where to stand and what to hold on to. She worked the maneuvering port line, bringing us down at a steady angle, clear of any obstructions. We passed the parked Subaru, twenty feet in front of it and a few feet higher than its roof. Ground speed seemed to increase. At the instant the bottom of the basket bumped the earth, she yanked the red line to empty the envelope and turned the fuel tank valve off. We bumped along for perhaps a dozen feet and stopped.

She scrambled to keep any part of the nylon skirt

from touching the hot burner. Dave, round, redheaded, and heavily freckled, came trotting up, saying, "Great work, Joya. Real nice. You like it, Mr. McGee?"

"It's fantastic."

A pack of farm children arrived on bicycles and hung back at a shy distance until Dave and Joya gave them chores. She bled off the fuel pressure, and then we emptied the envelope by holding the mouth closed and squeezing the air out toward the apex. Dave disconnected the pyrometer, and we packed the envelope in the bag, inspecting it as it was accordion-folded in. Everything fitted on or in the Subaru. As I helped fold, lift, and carry, I wrestled with my conscience and with my liking for guile. Guile won. So I was not going to walk her a little way down the road and confess. I walked her a little way down the road and asked for the name of the fifteen-year-old, knowing what a useful lever I might make of it.

"Karen," she said. "Thatcher? Or Fletcher? Hatcher! That's it. Karen Hatcher. Blond. With some baby fat."

"Thank you for the balloon ride, Joya."

"It was a good private place to talk. I . . . I'll be watching the newspapers. I hope you smash them flat. I really do."

So we said goodbye to the farm kids, and Dave made a rendezvous with the truck, let Joya off there, and we moved the basket and the rest of the gear into the truck. Then Dave drove me back to Rosedale Station. The last of the breeze was gone. The late afternoon was utterly still.

There was no one behind the desk at the Rosedale Lodge. I was tall enough to bend over the counter and lift my key out of the box. I went up the stairs, walked silently down the corridor to rooms 25 and 26, listened at both doors, and heard no sound. I went up the next flight to my fifty-dollar room and sat on the edge of my narrow sagging bed.

There could not, I realized, be any clean resolution of this whole thing. Ellis Esterland had been killed twenty-one months ago. And what he had been killed for was long since down the drain, flushed down by an erratic and talented middle-aged woman, misled by her parasitic friend, Peter Kesner. Circumstances changed for the folks in the black hats, just as they did for the white hats. And the gray. Their universe continued to unfold. The Senator flew over the cliff with a sea gull in his face. Up until now I had not been able to feel any particular personal imperative at work. Annie Renzetti had dropped delightfully and unexpectedly into my arms, but possessing her did not act as a spur to action, to learning what really did happen to Esterland.

In my blundering about, with my dull uncomprehending smile, my earnest clumsiness, I had inherited half a motorcycle haven and tattoo parlor. And now I had joined the FBI, or the equivalent. I had begun to feel a little bit like Sellers in his immortal *Being There*. I felt no urge to enrich either Ron Esterland or myself. And no urge to punish Josie Laurant any more than she was going to be punished by the gods of stupidity at some time in that future which was getting ready to crash down on her. I was a fake consultant in the employ of Lysa Dean, queen of the game shows. I represented, to Kesner, a chance for free promotion of a motion picture that would probably never be shown in the unlikely event it was ever completed.

I had zigged and zagged until, finally, I had completely confused myself. I had spent some of Ron's money and had myself a nice balloon ride, and I wished heartily that Meyer would happen along, listen, and tell me what to do next.

At least, now, there was a sense of personal involvement. The misdeeds of the vague past seemed unlikely. What is the penalty for killing a dying man? But I had seen Freaky Jean, Joya's ex-friend, and I could visualize blond Karen in her baby fat as, under the lights of the improvised little studio, she came to the horrid and ultimate realization that the creature of her nightmares, Dirty Bob himself, was going to jam that incredible ugliness right up into her while the women watched and the wizened little man came closer with the camera and the hi-fi rock masked her yelps and hollers, her pleas for mercy.

The fracture line was, of course, somewhere between Peter Kesner and Desmin Grizzel. And I could improvise a pry bar of sorts. Perhaps there was another vulnerable area between Josie and Kesner, labeled Romola. Daughter lost and gone. Twenty months gone.

Time to try to close the store.

15

I drove my rental Buick back to the pasture five miles out of town. Kesner's car was there. Clouds were bulging up to interfere with the last of the sunlight. There was the usual amount of milling about, but there appeared to be fewer vehicles.

After asking three people where I could find Kesner, I finally located him in Josie's trailer. She was not there. He let me in, went back to the couch where his drink was, and continued his conversation with a thick-bodied man of about fifty who sat bolt upright in a chair and had no drink at hand.

"What's your name again?" Kesner asked him.

"Forgan."

"Forgan, this is Travis McGee. He is here as a consultant for Take Five Productions. He is representing one of the owners, the famous actress Lysa Dean. I ask you, Forgan, would they be interested in doing a network feature on this operation here if we were some kind of scumbag ripoff?"

Forgan gave me a single brief glance, his brown eyes

as still and dull and dead as the glass orbs in a stuffed bear.

"I want to talk to a woman named Jean Norman," he said.

"I told you, they're *looking* for her. They're *looking* for her. Jesus!"

"Where's Mrs. Murphy-Wheeler?"

"Forgan, why do you keep asking me the same shit over and over? I told you before, she was on flight today. We did one of the big scenes. They're coming back in now, one at a time. Eight balloons." I saw Kesner stiffen with sudden realization. "Hey, you flew with her, McGee! She back?"

"That's what I'm supposed to tell you, Peter. They were all packed up to take off after the flight, so they wouldn't have to come back here. She has to get back to work, she said. Back in Ottumwa."

He smacked his fist into his palm. "Goddamn! That makes three who broke away today. Those bastards have got me down to five balloons. They're trying to kill me. They've been getting free chow, free propane, and a hundred bucks a day per balloon. What do they want?"

"So Mrs. Murphy-Wheeler isn't returning here?" Forgan asked.

I could see interesting complications if he got to Joya and she told him about me. But I couldn't see anything I could do about it. This man Forgan was official. He had all the rich warm charm of a tax collector. Or of J. Edgar Hoover.

"I told you before, Forgan. Feel free. You and your skinny buddy. Poke around. Ask anybody anything.

But get it over with, because this is a working set and we got work to do, and delay costs money."

I tried to look at Peter Kesner out of Forgan's eyes. The bald tan head, long white ropy body, big flat dirty white feet, lots of dangling gold jewelry, graying chest hair poking out of the pink Gucci shirt, crotch-tight blue jeans, faded, frayed, threadbare, half glasses perched halfway down his generous nose, thick fingers saffroned by the ever-present cigarette. Forgan would second a motion of no confidence.

Forgan stood up slowly and turned toward the door. He stopped and gave me a long official look, memorizing me. Apparently I failed to meet his standards too.

At the door he turned back toward Kesner and said, "Besides this Grizzel clown, how many more people you got working here with records?"

"I wouldn't have any idea. Most of them are hired by my office in Burbank. They have the personnel records there. Major Productions. They're in the book. The production people here on location are all trade union people, guild people. The payroll is killing me."

Forgan stared into space. "I never go to movies," he said softly, and went out and pulled the door shut. The trailer moved a little on its spring as his weight left the step.

Peter Kesner sprawled on the couch, leaned his head back, sighed, took off his little glasses, and pinched the bridge of his nose.

"Sit down, McGee. Sit down and relax. How was it?"

"The flight? A great experience. I appreciate your making it possible."

"I went up with Joya once, and with Mercer, and we took a hell of a lot of footage of going across country in a good breeze at about zero altitude. That lady was scraping the gondola on the tops of the cows and chickens. Like a fun ride at the park as a kid. What I can't understand, why would Joya turn me in on some kind of weird rap about making dirty tapes? She say anything to you?"

I handled that one with care. "Just that she was worried about what was happening to Jeanie Norman."

He hit his forehead with the heel of his hand. "Shit, yes! Sure. They used to be friends. Old Freaky Jean. God only knows what Jeanie thinks is happening around here. She's around the bend, way around. If anybody hooked her, Linda did. Linda has good sources, and she likes big brunettes. It's easy to see how Joya might get the wrong idea from things Jean might tell her. There's videotape equipment around, portable recorders, and Jap cameras. The kids fool with it. It's a professional tool, the way a photographer will use a test shot on Polaroid film before going ahead with the real stuff. A bit player can improvise a death scene or whatever, erase the tape, and try again. You can look at the scene in living color the minute you've finished it. They probably got Jeanie involved with some of their horsing around, and she got the wrong impression, or Joya got the wrong impression of what Jeanie was trying to tell her. I can't afford all this hassling!"

He got up and paced the small area, walking back and forth behind my chair, appearing and reappearing in the mirror over the couch.

"I've got special things to say, McGee. I have special visions to reveal to the world. I can compose scenes within scenes, dialogue behind dialogue. When realities are composed in a certain way, a scene becomes referrent to a Jungian symbolism, and millions of people will be moved and disturbed in a way they cannot understand."

He came around in front of me to stand looking down at me.

"There is such a thing as an artistic imperative. Genius demands the communicative medium. It's my mission to change the world in a way you can't even comprehend, McGee. And I will sacrifice anything at all to that mission. Right in the midst of the bad dialogue in this turkey script I am working with, I can project an instant of magic so precious I will lie, cheat, steal, kill, torture, in order to have the chance to do it. I am beyond any law, any concept of morality, McGee, because I have this gift which has to come out. I have to use everything and everyone around me, for my own ends. A little bureaucratic turd like Forgan can't comprehend the necessity of the mission. The mission is bigger than all of us. So I do what I have to do. When the money gets thin, I have to make more somehow, to keep this project alive. Do you understand that?"

"Not exactly. Maybe I do."

"I can always tell when the chance is there," he said, his voice animated, his expression full of excitement. "I get a big rush, a really stupendous flowing feeling, and I can see all the symbols and relationships as if a fog lifted. I can then move the camera just so much, change the lighting a little bit more, get the people in a different postural relationship to each other. And it doesn't matter what they say. The symbols are speaking and the words mean nothing. This is my chance to do it perfectly and change the world!"

"Now I understand," I said.

He reached and clapped me on the shoulder. "Good! Good! Right from the start I had the feeling you could catch on, Travis. You have sensitivity. Your inputs are open. Desmin thinks you're some kind of fake. It got me worried, and I called Lee Dean and she vouched for you. Are you sore at me for checking you out?"

"Not at all, Peter. Not at all."

The windows had darkened. He turned on two lamps and stretched out on the couch again. There was the sound of a key in the door and Josephine Laurant came in, wearing a white safari suit, with a leopard band holding her hair back and a white silk scarf knotted at her throat.

She nodded at me and said to Kesner, "It's raining again, hon."

"Jesus jumping H. Christ!" he yelled. "What are they trying to *do* to me?"

She knelt on the couch beside him and patted his cheek. "It's all going to be all right."

He pushed her arm away roughly, got up, and walked out without a word. She looked at me and managed a weak smile. "Peter gets very tense when he's working. There's been a lot of rain."

"So I've heard."

"It will really help us if Take Five will give us some advance publicity."

"When is it going to be released?"

"That isn't firm yet. There's an awful lot of editing and dubbing to do yet. Peter always does the film editing personally. It's an art, you know."

"I guess you both have a lot of reasons for wanting it to succeed."

She tilted her head. Her eyes looked old. "Exactly what do you mean by that, Mr. McGee?"

"I guess I meant that you've both invested money in it. And you've been sidelined for quite a long time. And Peter bombed out on his last two tries. I mean it must be very important to both—"

"I don't need that. I don't need any part of it. I didn't ask you in here. Get the hell out! Move!"

She had snatched up a heavy glass ashtray. I moved. I walked through light rain to the cook tent. Desmin Grizzel sat at a corner table for four with Jean Norman. He and I stared at each other until he beckoned me over. I sat across from Jean, with Dirty Bob on my right. He had been in the rain. The corona of gray-black beard was matted. He smelled like an old wet dog. Jean was in dirty white pants and a yellow top. She was hunched low over her plate, eating her stew with her hands. Her mouth was smeared, and gravy ran up her wrists.

"Hearty eater, ain't she?"

"Did Forgan get to talk to her?"

He took his unlit cigar out of the corner of his mouth and stared at me. "What would you know about that?"

"Only what Peter told me. Joya phoned the FBI about you people here making porno tapes before she took off for good."

"Peter told you that?"

"I was there in Josie's dressing room with him when he was talking to Forgan."

"Oh. Nobody here knows anything about any tapes. Jeanie here didn't know a thing, did you?" She ignored him. He pinched the flesh of her upper arm. She winced and looked at him. "You didn't know a thing, did you?"

Her expression was one of intense alarm. "No, Dez. Nothing at all. Nothing."

"Keep eating, princess."

She dipped down again, her chin inches from the pile of stew.

Grizzel smiled at me. He popped a kitchen match with a thumbnail and lit his sodden third of a cigar. There was a curious flavor of latent energy about him. I felt as if I were sitting next to one of the big jungle cats, and neither it nor I had any good idea of what it might do next.

I said, "Peter was giving me some of his ideas about his work."

"So?"

"I couldn't make a lot of sense out of what he was telling me."

"Why should you?"

"Frankly, it sounded spacey. It sounded unwrapped."

He studied the end of his cigar. "I think you should keep your mouth shut."

"I just meant that if there isn't going to be any motion picture, I'm wasting my time here."

"Peter Kesner turned me into somebody, pal. From dirt nothing to somebody. I've got a beach house, pal. I've got great machines, and a Mercedes convertible, a batch of bonds, and a lawyer working on getting me a pardon on a felony I did once. I owe him."

"You can see the reason for my concern."

"It isn't scheduled to rain tomorrow. We'll get going early, with the flying, and we'll wrap up the last location shots, and we'll go back home, and he'll put it all together. It'll be great. So don't sweat it, Ace."

He stood up, slowly, heavily, inspected the red end

of his cigar again, took another drag on it, then leaned and hissed it into the little pile of stew remaining on Jeanie's plate and walked out.

She sat there staring at the upright butt in glum confusion and then stared at me. "Am I gonna be with you?" she asked. "I thought I was gonna be with Dez."

The little dark-haired stunt woman came striding in, directly to the table, directly to Jeanie, ignoring me. She was wearing boots, jeans, a red shirt, a suede vest. She clucked in dismay, scooped up the dirty plate, and went off to scrape it into the garbage can over near the coffee machine. She came back with a damp towel and sat beside Jeanie. Jeanie tilted her face up, eyes closed, as Linda mopped her clean. Jeanie's face was immature, with a spray of freckles across the unemphatic nose, dark soot of lashes lying against the cheek. Linda swabbed the girl's hands and wrists clean, gave her a little pat on the shoulder, a little kiss on the forehead, and took the towel back to the counter. She came back and sat where Desmin had been, braced her chin on broad brown little fists, and looked at me with flinty eyes.

"You want pieces of this turkey for some kind of television?"

"Just to show how things like this are done."

Her laugh was abrupt and humorless. "Things like this are not done like this, fellow. I have busted fifteen bones in this line of work, which comes out to one a year since my first stunt where I fell off a cliff onto the roof of a stagecoach. I know good from bad. These people here are nuts. Peter, Josie, Mercer, Tyler, all of them. The money is almost gone and they keep making up new story lines. Peter calls it free association. How did you get mixed up in this?"

"Lysa Dean sent me here, for Take Five Productions."

"Now there is one hard-case lady. I doubled for her three times. No. Four. Drove a convertible into a culvert. Red wig. Broke my collarbone when the safety belt snapped. Can't remember the name of the film. It was very big at the time. When she was very big. She has—like they say—carved out a new career."

"Linnnnda?"

"Shut up, sweetie. We're talking. I saw you go up with Joya. How'd you like it?"

"Very very much. Not like I thought it would be."

"Me too. I hear Joya cut out, after turning us in for something she made up. She and I never got along at all. She'll be lucky Peter don't send Dirty Bob down to Ottumwa to slap her loose from her shoes."

"Something about tapes, wasn't it? Videotapes?"

"This is no kindergarten, and the people Kesner brought here are not churchgoers. When you have toys around, people will play with them. When you have candy around, people will eat it. If Joya didn't like it, she could have left any time. She didn't have to try to make trouble. She didn't as it turned out. The two they sent here looked around and took off. If they were after like controlled substances, it might have been something else."

"Linnnnda?"

"Hush, baby. You could get to fly again tomorrow, or at least help out with the ground crews, because we're shorthanded again. Make it out here early, like practically dawn." She leaned toward Jeanie and snuffed at her and frowned and said, "You smell musty, sweetie. Linda's going to take you in to the Lodge and give you a nice hot bath." She got up and pulled Jeanie to her feet and led her out, looking back to wave and smile at me.

The babble of conversation and the clatter of spoons in the coffee cups died for a few moments as they left and then picked up again. There was a smell of burning grease, and a drifting odor of garbage. I went back through the night to my car and drove back to town. I stopped at the BurgerBoy microphone, put in my order, and drove around to the window. A plump girl gave me the paper bag and took my money. I drove over to a parking slot, turned off the lights, and let the radio seek out a strong signal.

It was an FM station in Ames, Iowa. When it began on the local news, I was reaching to turn it off when the announcer said, "The two teenagers who died in a one-car accident this evening on State Road One Seventy-five just west of Stafford have been identified as Karen Hatcher, fifteen, and James Revere, seventeen, both of Rosedale Station. The vehicle, a late-model pickup truck, was headed east at a high rate of speed when it failed to make a curve five miles west of Stafford, traveled two hundred feet in the ditch, and then became airborne for another hundred and ninety feet, ending upright in a field. Both passengers received multiple injuries. The Revere boy was pronounced dead at the scene, and Karen Hatcher died while en route to the hospital...Legislators today issued a statement that the anticipated bond issue will not be validated—"

I punched it off. I felt a little curl of visceral dread which slowly, slowly faded away.

It was, I told myself, no part of my ball game. If a plump little girl had gotten herself into more emotional trauma than she and her boyfriend could handle without spilling themselves all over an evening landscape, that was too bad. And this year three hundred and eighty-six thousand people would die as a result of lung damage and heart damage from cigarettes. And that was too bad too. Death and despair and misery were all unfortunate. There were a lot of Peter Kesners and Desmin Grizzels and Lindas and Jeanies and Josephines at large in the world, and my only function was to use some of Ron Esterland's money from his paintings to ease his curiosity about the death of his father. And get back as soon as possible to the pliant pleasures of my executive hotel-manager woman. And figure out what to do with my motorcycle business.

Lecturing oneself does not cure the megrims. It does not create the indifference one seeks.

When I parked and went into the lodge, the old dragon was behind the desk. She said, "You'll have to be out of Thirty-nine by tomorrow morning."

"How about the others?"

"They've been told. All the rooms are reserved. All you people have to be out."

"If that's the way you want it."

"That's the way I want it. That's the way the town wants it. The best thing you can all do is get out of town and stay out, all of you. It might be the healthiest thing you can do."

"Like the Old West, huh? Don't let the sun set on yuh, stranger?"

"Nobody is in any mood for jokes tonight."

"Anything to do with the Hatcher girl?"

She froze for a moment. "I bet you'd even joke about that too. Jamie was my sister's only grandson. You people are vile. You are wicked. You are an abomination in the eyes of the Lord God. Drugs and rapine and fornication and a bunch of *prev*erts!"

"Now wait a minute!"

"I don't have to wait on you, mister."

And there was nothing else to say, because there was no one to say it to. She had ducked out of sight back somewhere behind the counter. It is possible to feel the guilt that is assessed only by association. Maybe each one of us has enough leftover unspecified guilt so that it is always available in case of need.

I plodded up the creaking staircase, through a smell of dust and carpet cleaner, belching an echo of BurgerBoy onions. Before I reached the second floor I heard the yelling and the thumping. The noise was coming from 25. There was a thud, a grunt, a curse, a heartbreaking moan of anguish. I tried the knob. It was locked. I backed off, raised my leg, and stamped my heel against the door just above the knob. It ripped the bolt out of the old wood and swung open just in time to reveal Peter Kesner, in his underwear shorts, holding Josie Laurant against the wall, his left hand at her throat, while he landed a big swinging blow against her left thigh with his balled fist. They both stared at me, Josie through streaming tears.

After only slight hesitation, he went back to the task at hand. His splayed left hand held her flat against the wall. She tried to writhe her hips and legs out of the way, but he kept on thumping her with those big swings.

I took three steps and caught his wrist as he wound up to swing again. "Hey! Enough already, Peter!"

16

"This is a private domestic argument, McGee!" Kesner yelled. When he took his hand away from her throat, she sagged to the floor. She was wearing a pale yellow terry robe, floor length, with a big white plastic zipper from throat to hem. Her face was bloated and streaked.

"It's too noisy to keep private," I said.

He came at me, grunting and swinging. He looked insane. He swung at my head, and I had time to get my fists up by my ears, elbows sharply bent and angled toward him. He was very slow, but those fists were hard and he swung them with all his might. I can move very quickly, and so, as soon as I had read his timing, I was able to let him waste his punches by getting my elbows and forearms in the way of his wrists. His little gold glasses fell off. It was my earnest ambition to pick the right moment, step quickly inside, and chop-chop— left in the gullet and a right hand deep into the soft white gut. But I realized how badly he was wheezing and gasping. The blows were softening. His mouth was sagging open. He was in that peak of physical conditioning which would cause him to get winded by changing his socks. So I let him flail away, and when he took an exceptionally hard, high swing at my head, I ducked below it. He went all the way around, got his legs tangled, and went thumping down like the dummy tossed from aloft.

As he lay there on his face, Josephine Laurant Esterland came crawling over to him on her hands and knees. She raised her fist and popped him in the back of the skull. She shrieked and sat, hugging her fist in her lap, rocking back and forth.

"Had enough?" Kesner asked me in a breathless, hollow voice.

"I give up," I said. The room door was ajar. I went over and closed it. I rolled Peter over, sat him up, helped him to his feet, and walked him over to the bed. He sat there, and I flexed my arms to relieve some of the pain and the numbness where he had hit muscle and bone.

Josie stood up slowly and carefully. She said, in loyal explanation, "He never marks me. I never show my thighs onscreen. They're too short and fat. He never marks me." She turned and glared at him. "Every cent? Every damn cent gone? What happened to the budget? What happened to that mealy little accountant person?"

"Shut up, Josie."

"That means the house is gone too, you son of a bitch. You can't finish without money. You're not half through the story boards. Jesus Christ! It *finishes* me! Don't you care?"

"Shut up and get out of here."

"You are unbelievably mean and cruel. I'll be lame for days. You impoverish me and then you beat me when I object."

"Leave!" he yelled, pointing to the connecting door.

She hobbled to it, head high, slammed it behind her.

"You shouldn't break in on a domestic discussion, McGee."

I straddled a chair, facing him. "How much did you have to pay Dirty Bob?"

"What do you mean? He's on salary."

"Oh, I don't mean for what he's doing now. I mean for the long ride when he and the Senator went over to Citrus City and beat Esterland to death, so he wouldn't outlive his daughter and leave all that good money to his foundation. I'd think he could bleed you forever for something like that."

He peered at me. "Friend, you've got to be covered with needle marks."

"Anne Renzetti knew the terms of the will, and she told Josie. Ellis had terminal cancer, and Romola was going to get all the money, and the support would stop, and Josie wouldn't be able to support you any more. That's when you went after Romola and set up the hideaway where you two could be together."

He looked toward the closed door and back at me. "Lower your damn voice, you idiot! Who are you? I think Dez was right about you. What do you want?"

"Then she had the bike accident, and when you knew she was really going to die, you explained to good old buddy Dez how nice it would be for everybody if the old man went first. Then the money would come to the daughter, and on her death to Josie, and you would be able to stay in the trough."

"Not so damn loud!"

"If you were doing the talking, you could keep your voice down."

"I see what you mean. All right. About Esterland, it just happened to work out lucky for me. I don't know who killed him. You have Dez all wrong too. I wouldn't say there wasn't a time when he might kill somebody, but that's all behind him. He's a good citizen. Who are you anyway?"

"A consultant, like Lysa's letter says. Two birds with one stone. Ron Esterland told me if I ever ran into you, I should ask about his dad, about you arranging to get him killed."

"Friend of his?"

"And of Anne Renzetti. They both think you arranged it, Peter."

"You're getting loud again!"

"Because you're not saying anything interesting."

"All right, all right. That's a very high-strung lady beyond that door there." He lowered his voice even further. "Don't say anything else about Romola, please. It's a terrible guilt load for me. I had a wonderful father-daughter relationship with that lovely child. She was the one who decided it had to turn into something else. Neither of us could stand the thought of hurting Josie. I found us a pad. It wasn't against the law, McGee. I know just how I'm going to handle it in my autobiography. Tender, gentle, sensitive. Two people caught up in forbidden sexual obsession, secret meetings spiced with guilt and shame. Honest to God, when she ran over that dog and fractured her skull, I thought it was God's judgment on both of us. I'll never forget her. Never. She had the most beautiful damn body I've ever seen on any woman."

"That's very touching, Peter."

"So get off me about that other."

"What if Grizzel and Hanner decided on their own to do you a little favor? What if it could be practically proven?"

"Proven?" He studied me, his expression wary and dubious. "Look, I may have done some bitching about the situation, and I suppose somebody could have grabbed that ball and run with it. Would that be my fault? What kind of proven?"

"Not airtight. Ron says his dad went to Citrus City to make a buy of an illegal substance, to relieve his pain, intending to pay with Krugerrands. I don't know the details, but it has something to do with tracing those gold pieces to Hanner or Grizzel or you."

"Not to me! Jesus! No way can that be true."

"There's a rumor around that Grizzel killed Hanner."

"You show up here pretending to be a big fan of my work, and then you hit me with all this shit. Anybody can hear rumors. I heard a rumor too. I heard he had a woman a while back who caught Dez's eye, and Dez was always able to take Curley's women away from him. Then she is supposed to have said something to Dez that she should not have known unless Curley had talked a lot more than he should have, about something involving the two of them. And then Dez waited until the right time. Maybe while he was waiting for the right moment, Curley ran into the sea gulls."

"Have you thought of writing for pictures?"

"McGee, I hate a smartass, especially when he takes shots at my work. Nothing about this conversation is important. I'll tell you what *is* important. I am going to finish this picture. There's enough left to do the final flight scene early tomorrow. With the footage I've got, there are a lot of directions I can go in. I can use voiceover to pull it together plotwise. There are scenes in the can that really sing. On Movieola, no score, they sing. They've got my imprint. A hundred years from now, kiddo, people will be going to see *Free Fall* in the basements of museums, to see the unmistakable mark of Peter Kesner. The dynamics of each scene, unfolding, the people working in a kind of magic rhythmic counterpoint in their relationships to one another, and with the cuts underlining the tempo of the score. We fold up shop here tomorrow and head home, and in eight or ten weeks, eighty-hour weeks, I'll put it together. *That's* what's important, not you coming here bugging me with this Esterland bullshit. What's with this Ron? He didn't make the will?"

"I heard on the radio that Karen Hatcher is dead in a one-car accident. She was fifteen."

"She—who did you say?"

"Come off it, Peter. Joya was right, wasn't she?"

He looked thoughtful. He got up and went over and picked his glasses up off the floor, put them on, nodded, and said, "She was right and she was also wrong. I wanted to know as little as possible about it. Josie knows nothing about it. I happened to know about that one, is all. She was well over fifteen. You could tell from the tits and the rug. This is depressing me. And my arms are sore. Look at the bruises coming up. I'm going to take a line to shape up. I can spare one if you want."

"No, thanks. You go ahead."

He went over to the bureau and put a careful pinch of white powder from a jeweled case onto the smooth bottom of an overturned dinner plate. He chopped it fine with a single-edged blade and scraped it into a thin line, bent down to it, and snuffed it up a soda straw, moving the straw along the line as he took the long slow inhalation, pressing his other nostril shut. It was quick and deft. Not a single motion lost.

He straightened, flexed his arms, worked his shoulders, slapped himself on the belly, and turned and smiled warmly at me. "You did con me, you son of a bitch. You know that, don't you?"

"Two birds with one stone. The Take Five situation is legitimate."

"I know. I checked with Lysa. Tell you what, you bring her to the lab in Burbank in about two weeks, and I'll show you a sequence that will knock your ass right off. That lady in there, let me tell you, that lady in there is giving one hell of a performance. She's hard to handle, but she's a classic talent. Bergman, with a whiff of Taylor. When they are very very good in bed, it shows on the screen. It shimmers under all the lines they say. You see it in the backs of their eyes."

"The Hatcher girl and her boyfriend were both killed."

"Do you realize how much you're boring me?"

"There could be some very real trouble about that, if anybody knows she starred in one of your dirty tapes, Peter."

"Screw her and screw this town. We'll be out of here by lunch. We've only got one of the big location rigs left. And what we do, we have to do it right the first time."

He sat back on the bed.

"What you can do, you can do me a favor by being out there real bright and early. We're down to five balloons and we're short on ground crew to handle them. I've got that Tyler sequence to shoot, where the balloon comes wobbling down with him stretched out dead in the basket, and all frosty from being so high he froze to death. Mercer invented some kind of crystal stuff he can spray him with. I wanted to have the other balloons settling down too, like the way animals gather around a wounded member of the herd, but you can't control the damned things that way, so the way we work it tomorrow, we have them take off from a close formation and then later I'll splice it in to run backward, so it will look like they are coming in, gathering from far off. I wanted it to be a big scene, but with only five balloons left, what can you do? I think I can work in some of the stuff when we had thirty of them taking off, and some bits of that could be run backward too. Will you be out there to help out? Listen, I would really really appreciate it, McGee."

What was there to say? There was no way to tell him what he was, even had I been entirely certain. I had the feeling that neither my vision of him nor his image of himself was particularly close to reality.

I said yes and went up the stairs to my overpriced room. Choice was still open. I could get up in a couple of hours and take off for Des Moines. Or I could go out there in the morning and help out and see what was happening.

I had as much as I was ever going to get out of Peter Kesner. I was personally convinced that Dez had taken Curley along and taken care of that little matter for Kesner, as a favor. Bravado. Help out your friends. It would probably be enough to satisfy Ron Esterland. He had performed the filial duty. Time to head home.

Yet on the very edge of sleep I realized that I was going out there in the morning on the slender chance that I could get some sort of confirmation out of Desmin Grizzel. It was a narrow chance and a big risk to try to trick him into some sort of partial confirmation. He might well want to throw me to the sea gulls, off some inconceivable cliff in the flatness of Iowa.

And also, of course, there was the slender chance I might get to ride in the gondola again, and that would give me a chance to find out if the second ride could possibly be as elegant and hypnotic as the first, moving in that sweet silence across the scents, the folds, the textures of the soft green April country.

17

With the oncoming sunrise a broad gold band along the eastern horizon, the area was coming awake. There was a smell of coffee, truck engines starting, balloonists breaking out the bags, baskets, tanks, spreading the big colorful envelopes downwind, ready for inflation. I was pressed into service on number five as a member of the ground crew, taking the place of a member of that team who had broken his hand landing the previous day. He had a cast and a sling, and he trotted along a half step behind me, telling me over and over everything I was supposed to do. He was very fussy, and he had a high nervous voice.

"The envelope bag has to be stowed on board, stowed in the basket. Fold it up. No, not like *that*. Open it up again. Bring in the sides and fold them flat onto the bottom. Start on that side, and fold the whole thing over. Now fold it again. See. Now put it in the basket. Not *underfoot*. Shove it behind that brace. Right there. Now we have to check the connecting pins and rings. And then the sparker. And then the safety line. If you always check everything twice or three times, Mr. McGee, you will not have those accidents which arise out of carelessness."

The sun appeared and the balloon colors turned vivid as the warmth struck us. Kesner, in feverish energy, was moving camera positions back and forth with orders over his portable horn. Linda and Tyler, fresh from makeup, were sitting on folding chairs, waiting.

"Blow them up! Blow them up, you people!" Kesner brayed.

"He means inflate," said my interpreter. "Put those gloves back on. And fasten the buckle on your helmet, please."

They positioned me out beyond the crown of the balloon, holding a line that was fastened to it, with instructions to counter any movement during inflation if it should show a tendency to roll in any side wind. Rolling would entangle the cables at the mouth and damage the burners.

By the time the sun was up above the horizon, all five balloons were upright, fully inflated, swaying in the morning breeze, estimated at five knots, coming out of the northwest. Number five was vertically striped in broad alternating segments of crimson and light blue.

I was put to work picking up the tools and equipment used during inflation, along with the inflator, and stowing them in the box in the big rugged pickup used by this team. It became clear to me that I was not going to get another ride. They were all waiting for the take-off signal. The tether rope had been untied from the pickup truck bumper. Linda came over and vaulted briskly into the basket. The pilot was a lean man with a deeply grooved face, an outdoor squint. He looked like a cowboy in a cigarette ad. One of the team was on one side of the basket, holding the rim, and I was on the other. Every time the pilot gave the blast handle a twitch, I could feel the sense of life and lift in the basket long seconds later.

The balloons were in a pentagon formation, about a hundred and fifty feet apart. Kesner decided he did not like that. He had one walked to the middle of the area and ordered enough deflation so it would look tired and flabby. He had the other four walked in closer, so that the flabby one was in the middle of the hollow square.

The breeze was freshening slightly, and at that point a caravan of perhaps twenty pickups and vans came roaring down the road. The lead pickup turned directly into the big field, smashing aside the barricade of two-by-fours. They came closer, spread out, came to spinning, skidding stops, and fifty or so young men came piling out. They wore jeans and T-shirts, and they carried tire irons, ball bats, and short lengths of two-by-four. They came toward us in a dead, silent run, and there was no mistaking the dedication and the intent. There was going to be no measured appraisal of guilt or innocence. We were all—balloonists and grips, cameramen and drivers, script girls and lighting experts— going to take a physical beating that would maim and might even kill. This was a mob. They had whipped themselves up. The fact that they looked young, clean-cut, and middle-American did not alter their deadliness.

In the silence of their rush toward us, I heard the prolonged ripping, roaring sound of the burners on one of the balloons. Everyone seemed to realize at the same moment that this was the best chance of escape. "Peter!" Linda screamed. "Peter! Here!" He came on a wild scrambling run, and as she began the long continuous blast of heat into the bag, he dived over the wicker rim, hitting the pilot with his shoulder. The pilot bent forward over the rim, and Peter snatched his ankles and tumbled him out. I swarmed over the rim as it began to lift. The other ground crew member let go. It moved with a painful slowness. Two beefy blond young men came running after us, too late. We lifted just out of reach. Something pinged off the round side of one of the propane tanks and went screeing off in ricochet.

We lifted more rapidly. I looked at the pyrometer and saw it moving close to the red line, and I knocked Linda's hand off the blast valve.

"What are you doing!"

"Melt the top of this thing open, and we'll drop."

She understood and watched the gauge with me. It went on up right to the edge of the red and then began to fade back. The inclinometer needle held steady. I guessed we were at about eight hundred feet. I looked back and down and could see the knots of people, flailing away and struggling and falling. The other balloons were airborne, both at a lower altitude, one ahead of us and one behind us. The flabby one was half deflated on the ground. People were fighting close to the basket of the other one, and it seemed to be deflating. Bodies lay silent in the grass. The cook tent was aflame, as was Josie's trailer-dressing room. As I watched, three of them caught up with a running man and beat him to the ground and kept on beating him.

"They've gone crazy!" Linda said. "Look! There's two cop cars. They're parked down the road there. They're not going to even try to stop it!"

"You people didn't make many friends."

"We brought a lot of money into this hick town," she said. "What the hell has happened to everybody?"

"I can guess. I think the little Hatcher girl told her best girl friend what you wonderful moviemakers did to her, and after the two kids were killed in that accident, the girl friend decided she didn't have to keep quiet any more. She didn't have to keep her word."

"Oh." She turned on Kesner. He was sitting with his back against the wicker, his arms wrapped around his upraised knees, his face quite blank. "I told you that girl was too damned young."

"I didn't ask for a driver's license. She said nineteen." He pulled himself up. He looked back and saw the fires, pallid in morning sunlight. "They don't know what they're doing," he said. "They don't know what they're destroying."

"Hey, we're coming down!" she said.

"We better try to fly low," I said. "Take a look."

The pickups and vans were streaming away from the pastureland, taking the roads that led southeast, that followed our drifting pattern.

"Why don't we go high?" Kesner asked.

"Because these things won't go all that high. The higher you go, the less efficient they are and the more gas they use up. And we'd stay in clear sight even at ten thousand feet, and they could follow us until we come down. If we go low enough, maybe we can lose them."

When we were at fifty feet and descending ever more rapidly, she opened the valve. It continued to sink. The basket brushed the top of low bushes. A red barn was rushing toward us. Kesner pointed at it and screamed. The lift finally took effect, and we rose above the crest of the barn roof, missed the silo, and then, because of the long blast, went right on up to five hundred feet.

"Short blasts, dammit," I said. "You have to use short blasts."

"Run it yourself!" she said.

And so I did, badly at first. The response always came so late, it was difficult to time. When I had the hang of it, I gained some altitude, found the wrench, and changed to fresh tanks. I could see chase cars a mile away on a parallel road, kicking up dust. I took it back down, and soon we came to a big agribusiness installation, a line of tractors, in offset pattern, working a giant expanse. They waved to us.

It was Kesner who pointed out the balloon that was spoiling our strategy. It was above us, in a fresher breeze than ours, well behind us and gaining on us. It was pumpkin and green, with bands of white. The chase cars could follow him easily. I took us up to where we could yell at him to fly low, as we were.

Linda recognized him first. "Hey, it's Dirty Bob. All alone! Wouldn't he be alone, though?" She yelled at him. "If you fly lower, they might lose you. Hey! Fly low, Dez. Low!"

He ignored us. I worked our balloon back down again. He was even with us for a time and then moved a little ahead and a little farther off, to the left of our line of drift.

I kept glancing at him too often. I didn't see the power lines in time. The big ones, the high structural towers, the spiderweb look of the thick cables swooping from tower to tower. Even with a constant blast I did not think we could lift over them.

"Get ready to land!" I said.

"No!" Kesner yelled. "I saw them following us, right over there, past those trees."

"We've got to come down right now!"

I yanked on the line that opened the maneuvering port just as Linda sprang and opened the blast valve. We were too high to risk opening the deflation port at the top by pulling the red line. I jumped at Linda to pry her hand free, but she was too wiry and strong. We started to lift, and I made the almost mortal decision that we were as low as we were going to get. So I went over the side, hung, kicked free, and dropped, facing the direction of flight.

If I had to swear on all the books, I would say it was a forty-five-foot drop, at ten to twelve miles an hour. I went down toward the cultivated brown-dark earth. I dropped, pinwheeling my arms for balance, trying to remember everything I knew about falling, relaxing, rolling. The laws of motion state that a body falls at thirty-two feet per second, but it did seem to take a lot longer. One doesn't get much practice at stepping off the roof of four-story buildings.

I landed on the balls of my feet, inclining slightly forward, and as I hit I hugged my chest, tucked my chin down, and turned my right shoulder forward and down. I felt the right knee go, and the forward momentum took me into a shoulder roll. I went over and right back up onto my feet, where I didn't especially want to be, and then tried to take some big running steps to stay there. But the knee bugged out, and my body got ahead of my legs, and I took a long diving fall onto my belly that huffed the wind out of me and chopped my teeth into the dirt of a corn row.

I pushed myself up, gagging for air, spitting dirt, and saw the balloon angling up toward the wires. Relieved of my weight all of a sudden, it had taken a good upward surge. But it was still going toward the power lines. In retrospect I decided that the upward bounce had not been lost on Peter Kesner. The racket of the gas blast stopped abruptly, and an instant later a figure came tumbling down, falling away from the basket. She had, I would say, seventy feet to fall. She was a tough little woman, athletic and nervy. I learned later that she had done some sky diving, and I think that she spread-eagled her arms and legs in an attempt to stop the tumbling caused by her being thrown out of the basket by Kesner. Maybe the tumbling would have stopped if she'd had more falling room. A lot more room. She made a single lazy turn and landed at a head-down angle that snapped her neck a microsecond before the heavy thud of her body into the soil.

Kesner was higher. The blast was ripping away, jacking that long blue flame up into the envelope. He was going to make it over the power lines. From my angle of sight he was already clear when the basket and cables struck the power lines. There was a stunning crack, loud as an antitank gun, a condensed flash of

blue lightning, and then a big orange ball as the propane tanks blew up. The orange and crimson ball
melted the striped crimson and blue envelope almost
instantly, and a stream of debris came tumbling down
in free fall, one morsel of it the flame-shrouded man-
nikin which had been Peter Kesner, landing under the
power lines, thumping down beside the shredded and
blackened basket with an impact that blew the flames
out and left him smoking for a moment before the
flames began again.

Beyond the lines, high and off to the left, the pumpkin and green balloon floated in the breeze, moving
away from me. Outlined against the blue sky beyond,
I could see the silhouette of Desmin Grizzel from the
waist up, standing there in the hard weave of the
wicker basket, looking back down at us, motionless and
intent. I stood up, favoring the right leg. I was dazed,
and I was sickened by the pale and dying dance of flame
on Kesner's body and the small silence of Linda. Out
of some vague impulse I raised an arm to Desmin Grizzel as he dwindled against the morning sky and saw
him wave in response.

I heard the hard whine of the engines of the chase
cars and looked for a place to hide. I could not run to
the distant row of trees. I hobbled over closer to Linda's
body, stretched out face down, dug with two paws like
a dog, wormed myself against the soil, lay with my face
wedged into the breathing hole. As a final act of guile,
I pulled the wallet out of my pocket and pushed it down
into the dirt at the bottom of the hole under my face.
The earth smelled rich and moist.

They came running, feet thudding, breathing hard.

"Oh, Jesus! Oh, Jesus! Look at that one, Ted!"

There was a coughing sound, a gagging sound, and then a gush, coughing, and another voice saying weakly, "I'm sorry, guys. It was the smell."

I took a deep slow breath and held it. Somebody put a foot against my hip and shoved. "Maybe this one's alive." I felt hands poking at my pockets.

The hands went away. A deeper voice said, in exasperation, "What are you doing, Benny?"

"Nothing."

"Get your hands off her."

"She's got something here on a chain around her neck."

"I said get away from her!"

"Okay, okay, okay. What's the matter with you?"

"Ted, come over here. Look, guys. I think we ought to go back to town and split and keep our mouths shut."

"What about that balloon still in the air?"

"There'll be guys after it. This thing got out of hand. Right? Everybody got too excited. I saw Wicker kill a little old guy. I saw him do it on purpose. Nobody agreed to anything like that. Nobody said anything about setting fires. I saw Davis go down, and it looked as if he was hurt bad. There was a lot of blood on his face. Here we got two more dead people and one maybe dying. It got too big. There'll be television guys and newspaper guys from Des Moines all over the place."

"You remember what we all agreed, Len. It was for Karen and Jamie. It was in their memory. These are evil people."

"'Justice is mine, saith the Lord.' I think we ought to cut out right now, guys."

They seemed to reach an agreement. When I heard

voices again, they were too far away for me to hear what they said. I knew the explosion wouldn't have gone unnoticed. Others would be arriving. I retrieved the wallet. Somebody had scooped dirt onto Kesner and put out his fire. I brushed dirt off me as I walked out of the big field. The knee had popped back in, leaving the tendons stretched and sore, okay for limited and careful use. When I reached the tree line, I found that they were planted alongside a narrow asphalt road. I looked back and saw a glinting of vehicles back near the power lines and some tiny figures moving about in the field.

There was no traffic. I walked and rested, walked and rested, and finally reached a crossroad. Bagley and Perry were off to the east, Coon Rapids and Manning off to the west. A rumpled old man with a harelip and a lot of opinions about that mess in Washington gave me a ride to another crossroads, where a very fat woman in a van upholstered in sheepskin gave me a ride through Rosedale Station and on out to the location. When she stopped, the cops tried to wave her on, but I got out. She drove on. A young officer said, "This area is closed."

I pointed out my rental Buick and showed him the keys. He took the keys and made certain they worked. He wanted to see the rental agreement, and I took it out of the glove compartment. Then he asked for identification.

"What's going on here anyway, officer?"

"All hell has been going on here. How come your car is here and you weren't?"

"I left it here last night when I rode into town with

someone else. I meant to come back and get it, but I didn't get around to it."

"Where did you stay last night?"

"The Rosedale Lodge."

"Are you with this movie company?"

"No way," I said, and from the back compartment of the wallet I slid the folded machine copy of Lysa Dean's letter to Kesner. He read it carefully, his lips moving. He was broad and young and plump, and he had high color in his cheeks, a thick chestnut mustache.

"That Lysa Dean, she is a really quick-witty person," he said. "She's been around. When I was maybe fourteen, I had a terrible case of the hots for her. And, you know, she still looks damned good. What's she really like, McGee?"

"She's a very shy and retiring person, officer. All that sex-pot front is just an act."

He sighed and said, "You'd never know it," and gave me back the letter. "I'm sorry you told me that."

"What *did* go on here?"

"Were you going to use some of the balloon stuff on the TV?"

"I'm going to recommend against it. Was there a fire here?"

We stood and looked out across the field. A lot of the trucks and private cars were gone. There were two television news teams at work, interviewing people out on the field, taking shots of the bright empty envelope on the ground, the overturned basket.

"What they were doing here, on the sly, Mr. McGee, they were making dirty videotapes, conning some of the young people around here to appear on those tapes, paying them for it, making them sign releases. It didn't all come out until one of the young girls they made perform for them got killed yesterday, and her girl friend broke down and told what had been going on. This is a Christian, God-fearing community, Mr. McGee, and a big bunch of the friends of Karen Hatcher came out here early this morning to bust everybody up. And they pretty much did. We've got twelve high-school seniors locked up, and three in the hospital, and warrants for the rest of them. There were two dead right here on the field, two of the movie crew, and another that will probably die. A lot of expensive equipment was destroyed and burned, and from what we can find out, a lot of the movie film was burned up too. A report came in a while back that two or three more got killed running into high-tension lines way southeast of here. Some of them got away in time in balloons, apparently. It's just one of those things that happen. It's a godawful mess. It's hard to say who's to blame in a thing like this. It really is. One of the ones in jail is my kid brother."

"Sorry to hear that."

"Billy would never in this world set out to kill anybody. His dog fell out of the loft one time and broke his back. Dad said it was Billy's responsibility to shoot old Boomer. He plain couldn't do it. It wasn't in him. Of course, he was only twelve. I had to do it for him."

"It all got out of hand, probably," I said.

"That's exactly it, mister. That's exactly it. They don't want people who don't belong here hanging around here, okay?"

"Okay."

"Oh, wait a second. If you know anything about that sideline of making those tapes, maybe they'd want to talk to you some."

"Officer, I got here yesterday morning. All I've seen are balloons."

He nodded. "Okay. You can take off."

18

The world turned further toward summer. Vennerman scheduled my knee in May, and by early June I was walking at a reasonable pace, but only for a mile at a time, and I worked with the weight Velcroed around my ankle every evening—swing the leg up straight and hold it, and let it down very slowly.

In mid-June there were a few unusual days when Florida became almost too hot to touch. Annie Renzetti came over from Naples, and while she was there, making lists of what she'd bring on the promised cruise aboard the *Busted Flush*, Ron Esterland came to town for our long-delayed accounting. He had been out in Seattle making additions and changes in a big show of his paintings which were about to go on the museum circuit, all of them on loan from museums and collectors.

Meyer came over in the morning and got his big pot of Italian meat sauce started, checked it out at noon, and came back at drinking time, toting a sufficient amount of Bardolino.

It made a very good group. Ron and Annie were

obviously fond of each other. He said to her at one point, "You were maybe the luckiest thing that ever happened to that crusty old bastard."

She said, "I'll always owe him. He taught me to do my work as perfectly as I was capable of doing it, and to think about better and easier ways of doing the chores as I was doing them—not to take my mind off them and drift. He used to say—"

"I know," Ron said. "He used to say ditchdiggers are the ones who can design the best shovels."

After we were all bloated with more pasta than anyone had intended to eat, I went and got my expense sheet and presented it to Ron Esterland.

His eyebrows went up. "This is all?"

"I tried. First-class air fare. Car rentals. Steaks. It just didn't last long enough."

"When I saw Josie last week I didn't see any point in telling her you were looking into the old man's death as a favor to me."

"How did she seem?" Annie asked.

"Okay. She misses Peter terribly. She told me there had been some vicious gossip about Peter and Romola, but neither of them had been capable of betraying her that way. She was very busy. She and somebody from one of the agencies were working out a lecture schedule for her and going over her materials."

"Lectures!" Annie exclaimed. "Josephine Laurant?"

"It seems that Peter is becoming a cult figure," Ron said.

Meyer went to his old cruiser, the *John Maynard Keynes,* came back with a clipping he had taken from a small literary journal, and read it to us, with feeling.

"'Perhaps it is too early to attempt an appraisal of

the lasting value of the contributions of Peter Gerard Kesner to the art of the cinema. At the heart of the pathetically small body of work he leaves us are the two gritty little epics about the outlaw bikers, vital, sardonic, earthy, using experimental cuts and angles that soon became clichés overused by the directors of far less solid action films. The hard-driving scores, the daring uses of silence, the existential interrelationships of victims and predators gave us all that odd twist of déjà vu which is our response to a contrived reality which, through art, seems more real than life itself.'

"More?" Meyer asked.

"Don't stop now," said Annie.

"'In the two big-budget films which he directed, and which failed commercially, we see only infrequent flashes of his brilliance, of his unmistakable signature on scenes noted otherwise only for their banality of plot and situation. The truth of Kesner, the artist, was stifled by the cumbersome considerations of the money men, the little minds who believe that if a film is not an imitation of a successful film then it cannot possibly be a success.

"'We can but dream of what a triumph *Free Fall* would have been had it not been destroyed in that tragic confrontation in the heartland of Iowa. Those who were privileged to see the rushes say that it was Kesner at his peak of power and conviction, dealing with mature themes in a mature manner, in a rhapsody of form and motion. A lot of footage survived, and we understand that it is being assembled as merely a collection of sequences of visuals, of flight and color, with score by Anthony Allen and narration by Kesner's great and good friend, Josephine Laurant, who will, during her narration, deliver one of the scenes written for her by Kesner. The people behind this project, who include of course the backers of *Free Fall,* whose losses were recouped by the usual production insurance, hope to enter this memorial to the great art of Peter Gerard Kesner in the Film Festival at Cannes.'"

"Wow!" Annie said. "Was he that good? Was I dumb about him?"

Meyer smiled and folded the clipping away. "My dear, you have put your finger on the artistic conundrum we all struggle with. How, in these days of intensive communication on all levels, can you tell talent from bullshit? Everybody is as good, and as bad, as anybody wants to think they are."

Ron said, "Josie is taking the film on the road, doing the university circuit, adding remarks and a question-and-answer period. Expenses plus fifteen hundred dollars a shot. Which comes, of course, from federal grants to higher education. She says she owes it to Peter's memory."

"I don't think that movie would ever have been released," I said.

"The legend now is that it would have been an epic," Meyer said. "And there are all the funny little sidebar bits of immortality too. They've updated and released that old book ghost-written for Linda Harrigan, *Stunts and Tricks: The Autobiography of a Stuntwoman in Hollywood.* And then, of course, there is that girl from that team of balloonists, the one from Shenandoah. What was her name, Travis?"

"Diana Fossi. I never met her. She's the one who got smashed across the base of the spine with a tire iron. They've named one of the events in the big interna-

241 —

tional meet for her. The Diana Fossi Cross-Country Marathon. She'll be there in her wheelchair, to present the cup to the winning team."

"What happened to the boys who did all that?" Ron asked.

"Nothing much," I told him. "Except for the death of Mercer, the cameraman, they couldn't pin down who did what to who. They indicted a boy named Wicker for that. They haven't tried him yet, but I think he'll get a term in prison. They've negotiated probation for the others. And one town boy died weeks later of brain damage he received during the fracas, which tended to make it a little easier to get the others off."

I remembered my knee treatment and went and got the weighted canvas anklet and sat on the couch beside Annie. Meyer said, "What is interesting, at least to me, is the production of myth and legend. Look at that situation, for example. Hundreds of professional news people, law officers, investigators descended on that little city. It was a story that had everything. Dramatic deaths of celebrities, a pornography ring, a murderous riot, innocence corrupted. From what you told me, Travis, I gathered that in his scrambling around for funds to keep going, Kesner came up with a sideline. Using a trailer studio and Mercer, Linda, Jean Norman, Desmin Grizzel, and local young people, he was making pornographic video cassettes and Linda Harrigan was flying them over to Las Vegas and peddling them for cash on the line."

"That was the picture Joya Murphy-Wheeler, the balloon lady, gave me, information she'd gotten from Jean Norman, who apparently wasn't as totally zonked out all the time as the others thought. It turned out that Linda had Jeanie on Quaaludes, hash, Dexedrine, and Valium, which should have turned her brain to porridge."

"What happened to her?" Annie asked. "To Jeanie?"

"I have to backtrack," I said, "to tell you how I know. Driving to Des Moines that afternoon, I knew I had to square things with Joya. So I kept on going, on down to Ottumwa, looked her up, found her, and confessed I'd faked her out and that the real, the genuine, the true blue F B and I would no doubt track her down, probably in the person of one Forgan. She was one of the maddest women I've ever seen. She was furious. She had heard some of the news on her lunch hour. She knew there'd been trouble but didn't know how much. Yes, she'd heard of the death of Karen Hatcher and her boyfriend, and I told her how that had been the incident that ignited the whole thing. She had been shocked to hear that Kesner and Linda Harrigan were dead. She was fascinated by the story of my final balloon trip, and she shuddered when I told her what happened when the gondola hit the power lines. Finally she halfway understood what my mission had been, and why I had let her believe I was something I wasn't. We parted friends. I phoned her from here in May, the day before I went in for the knee operation, and she said that she had never been contacted at all, probably because the people she had implicated in her phone call as being the ringleaders were either dead or missing: Kesner, Harrigan, Mercer, and Grizzel. She understood that Jean Norman had been institutionalized in Omaha, near her home. Through her contacts in the balloonist groups, she had heard that they had taken several statements from her to be used in prosecuting Desmin

Grizzel, and they were confident that she was making a good enough recovery so that she would be able to testify against him in court."

"And here is the legend," Meyer said, "growing to full flower. Unbeknownst to the cinematic genius, Peter Kesner, his creature—Dirty Bob—had corrupted Mercer and the stunt lady. And the stunt lady had recruited Jean Norman. They used a portable set after hours, when Kesner and Josie and Tyler were not on location, made the tapes, and peddled them through Linda's contacts. And the word is out that the distributors of the porno tapes, under the X-Lips label, had Grizzel killed in order to save them a lot of time and trouble and possible legal action. Grizzel, with monumental idiocy, did not hide his face when he performed on those tapes. He enjoyed being on camera. Miss Norman is also identifiable, I understand. Miss Harrigan wore a silver mask. And the amateur talents they recruited in Rosedale Station are of course identifiable. So the chain of evidence is clear enough. By the way, having a recognizable Dirty Bob play the heavy made the tapes more valuable and more salable. The prosecution has picked up over a dozen of the tapes made there in Rosedale Station. The distributor, in a single public statement made before the lawyers muzzled him, claimed the tapes were acquired from an intermediary, a third party, who had represented them as being simulated rapes, which is apparently very big with what they call the hard-core audience. A very dirty business indeed. The victims contributed to their own disasters by being hungry for the glamorous life, an appetite that made them vulnerable. And then, like victims the world over, they helped rope new victims because that made them feel their own humiliation was diluted thereby."

Annie said, "My God, Meyer, where do you *get* all this stuff?"

"He buys those strange newspapers they sell at checkout counters," I told her.

"Only to recheck my grasp on reality," he said. "Reality tells me that Desmin Grizzel is alive and well."

Ron frowned. "But wouldn't they have a reason to have him killed?"

"What for?" Meyer asked. "They act as corporate entities. Incoming cash is distributed. If problems arise, collapse the corporation and move to the next floor and start a new one. It is a lot cheaper and safer and easier than arranging a murder. Pornography is all mob-connected, of course. If somebody consistently pirated the product, I suppose they would arrange a little demonstration of how unhealthy that sort of thing is. But Grizzel is a celebrity. Somewhere in the world tonight those two early motion pictures are playing, probably in three or four countries, with the Japanese or Italian or Arabic or Portuguese dubbed in. A known face is a very risky kill, as those who did away with Jimmy Hoffa would agree. From everything I have read about Desmin Grizzel, I think he is a survivor. Some children found that downed balloon in the woods, three days later, miles south of Interstate Eighty."

Ron frowned and said, "Back to topic one, Travis. Did Grizzel kill my father?"

"My gut feeling is that he did. Alone or with Curley Hanner. No strong evidence. Just little bits and pieces. Kesner aimed them at Ellis Esterland. Maybe indirectly. Maybe he just said that things would be fine if only Esterland died before Romola. We'll never know what hook they used to get Esterland up to Citrus City alone. Probably to buy something from someone for the pain. He didn't want to admit to Annie here that it was getting too bad to endure any longer. Once the murder was done, Grizzel owned a slightly larger share of Kesner. And so did Hanner. All I got out of Kesner was that hint about how maybe Grizzel had gotten rid of him. Or maybe it was the sea gulls."

"So," said Ron, "can we assume that Dirty Bob, the California biker, has disappeared back into the roaring stream of camaraderie, the helmeted knights of the road, protectors of their own?"

"Not very damn likely," I said. "He hasn't got a face you'd call forgettable. That moon face with the corona fringe of beard and the big high cheekbones and the little Mongolian eyes. He became the role model for too many imitation hard-case types."

Meyer said, "Let's consider the problem from his point of view. It might be constructive. Travis, he told you he had a beach house, motorcycles, a convertible Mercedes, a portfolio of bonds, and an attorney working on a pardon for an earlier felony. Suddenly he is on the run, and his toys are gone. But is the offense serious enough, from his point of view, to keep him on the run? Can't he hide behind Kesner and say he was following orders? Travis, after your confrontation, or whatever you want to call it, with Kesner at the Lodge, wouldn't he have had time to talk to Grizzel the next morning?"

"Of course."

"And if Grizzel had been exploiting his relationship to Kesner, using it in every way he could think of to benefit himself, and if Kesner wanted to pry him loose a little, what would he say?"

I thought it over. "I think he'd tell Grizzel that the killing of Esterland hadn't been so clean after all. That I was looking into it, and that I was curious about how Hanner had died."

"And then," Meyer said, "he was on the scene when you disposed of Kesner. His meal ticket. His hero. The man who made him a celebrity."

"But I didn't!"

"How would he know that? You dropped, the woman dropped, and Kesner went up into the power lines. And then you waved at him."

"Look. There's just a vague suspicion that he killed Esterland."

"How does he know how vague it is? How does he know he didn't make some kind of terrible mistake, that somebody wasn't watching?"

"Somebody *was* watching," Annie said. "Curley Hanner."

In the silence I began exercising the knee again. They all watched in mild autohypnosis. "He'd change his appearance," Ron suggested.

"Heavy eyebrows?" Meyer asked.

"Very. Big and black and bushy, speckled with gray. Why?"

"If he shaved his head, beard, and eyebrows, the eyes might still look familiar to people. Mirrored sunglasses could cure that. And if he changed his mode of dress completely—"

"Hide forever?" Annie asked.

"Possibly. Or maybe long enough to take care of the problem of the Norman girl. And then find you, Travis, and see what you know or don't know. Or maybe not even bother to ask."

"Oh, fine! And just how would he find me?"

"Through Lysa Dean, of course."

I stopped flexing the knee. Annie looked out at the dark night and hunched her shoulders slightly. Ron frowned at the floor.

Meyer said with hearty cheer, "We're just playing games. The ancient and honorable game of what-if."

Long after they had gone, Annie Renzetti made me turn on the light and try once again to reach Lysa Dean on the bedside phone. She nestled close to me and we both listened to the sound of ringing. I let it ring fifteen times and then hung up.

"But it doesn't make any sense," Annie said. "Those people have answering services. They have to."

"Maybe not on the private, private line. When friends call long distance, if there is no answer, she's out. It saves toll charges."

"Do you believe that?"

I reached and turned the light out. "Certainly."

"If you really did, you wouldn't sound so overconfident. Was Meyer trying to scare us?"

"He likes to make guesses about people. He's pretty good at it, but he'd be the first to tell you he strikes out a lot."

"You've known Lysa Dean a long time?"

"I helped her out of a jam a long time ago."

"Did you sleep with her when you went out there in April? That's not a jealous question, really. I don't have any claims on you. You're free to do whatever you want. You know that. I just wondered. It's such a dumb question, you don't even have to answer it. I mean, the years go by and she just seems to get lovelier."

"No, I didn't."

"Did you want to?"

"The possibility did occur to me."

"Could you have?"

"I wouldn't even want to guess."

"You know, you don't have to lie. Not with me."

"I know that, Annie love."

"Could you just hold me a little bit tighter?"

"My pleasure."

"I have the feeling something is going wrong in the world, something involving us in some terrible way."

"Nothing bad will happen."

"Why did her phone keep ringing and ringing? You said she has a live-in staff."

"It probably doesn't ring in their quarters. It's her special private line. Go to sleep, Annie."

"I'll try."

"Think about your hotel. Count the silver."

"One, two, three, four, five..."

"Silently."

"Oh."

19

That was Sunday night, of course, the twenty-first day of June. On Monday morning Annie showered and dressed early because she had to get back to her hotel chores. She stirred me awake and then went to the galley to fix the waffles and sausage. While doing so, she turned on the tiny Sony machine she had given me: AM, FM, cassette tape, and a fierce sharp little black-and-white screen. She turned the television to *Good Morning, America,* and in a few moments she came running in to get me. I was just shouldering into a robe and heard only the last part of the news item.

I tried CBS and NBC and, minutes later, got the item in its entirety—or at least the entirety granted it by those blithe morning people who twinkle and sparkle as they speak of horrors beyond belief.

"Mystery surrounds the disappearance from the drug rehabilitation center of Jean Norman, the voluptuous brunette balloonist whose testimony was crucial in the indictment of Desmin Grizzel, a.k.a. Dirty Bob, still at large after the Iowa riot on the location of *Free Fall,* where porno videotapes were being made while Kesner's lost epic was in production. She had been given the freedom of the grounds and was due to be released in the custody of her parents in another two weeks. When her parents visited her yesterday, she could not be found. Police joined in the search. Another patient saw her at approximately two P.M., talking across a low stone wall to a tall man. A fresh smear of blood on the edge of the stone at that location proved to be of the same type as Miss Norman's. The patient could not identify pictures of Grizzel as being the man she had seen by the wall."

"Meyer is a witch," Annie said. "Call Lysa Dean."

"It's four thirty in the morning out there. Later."

"Okay. Later, but then will you please call me and tell me if you talked to her?"

"I promise."

"Would you like your waffle black or charred? Don't look so abused, Trav. There's more batter. That one was supposed to be mine. I'll start yours when you come out of the shower."

I tried Lysa at three that afternoon, and she answered on the second ring.

"Hi. It's me. McGee."

"You damn thankless *bastard!* Did you forget *I* got you that 'in' with Peter Kesner? I didn't know if you got killed and buried, or you sailed off in a balloon, or what. Where the hell are you?"

"Fort Lauderdale."

"Were you in Iowa when it hit the fan?"

"I was indeed. It got a lot of coverage in the press. I didn't think you'd need a play-by-play from me. I'm grateful you thought up the idea that got me through the door."

"You weren't as grateful at the time as I wanted you to be."

"I thought I thanked you very nicely."

"Sure."

"Let me tell you why I called. Have you got a minute?"

"Three, maybe four."

"All right, then. Dirty Bob is still at large. It looks as if he got to that girl who was going to testify against him and took her off somewhere. Without going into details, he has, or thinks he has, some very pressing reasons to find me and beat the top of my head in."

"I'd even help him."

"The only way he can trace me is through you. He saw that letter from you. I think he holed up for a while, and now he is moving again. He might pay you a visit."

"So?"

"He might ask questions in a very ugly way, Lee."

"I am not afraid of that big dreary ass-grabbing motorcycle bum, darling. I have no reason to love you, or even like you, but also I have no reason to hand out information about you, so don't fret. Momma won't let big bad bully come after poor wittle McGee baby."

"Dammit, Lee, think about it. He killed Ellis Esterland, and he killed Curley Hanner, and he has probably killed Jean Norman."

"Oh," she said in a smaller voice.

"I called you because it's my fault you're in the line of fire. I'm sorry. I didn't think far enough ahead." I have lost some very great ladies because I was too slow, too stupid, and too careless. This time I was giving warning. "Can you go away for a while?"

"I'm better off here. I've got the Korean couple and a damned good security alarm system. I'll be careful."

"If he shows up, tell him where to find me. I'd like to see him again."

"You sure of that?"

"It would be a lot easier than losing you."

She started laughing, and when I finally got her to explain what was so funny, she said, "Sweetie, you can't really lose something you've never really had."

"Tell whoever patrols that area to check you out oftener than usual. Tell them you had a nut call."

"This *is* a nut call. I wouldn't be lying."

"Take me seriously, will you?"

"Honey, I've tried that twice already, and it didn't work," and still laughing, she hung up.

I phoned Annie at the Eden Beach immediately and held while they ran her down.

"Yes? Anne Renzetti speaking."

"Just hung up after a talk with Lysa."

"Wow! I'm always so glad when one of those bad feelings doesn't work out. Will she go away? I could hide her out here—well—until somebody recognized her, which would be in about eleven minutes. Bad idea. It would be fun to get to know her. I feel as if I already do know her."

"She was impressed. She's going to be careful."

"Good. I'm glad."

I locked up and wandered down the dock to Meyer's cruiser. He wasn't aboard. Then I saw him coming, evidently from the beach, trudging along, smiling to himself.

"Back a winner?" I asked.

"Oh, good afternoon! A winner? In a sense, yes. There was a gaggle of lanky young pubescent lassies on the beach, one of the early invasions of summer, all of them from Dayton, Ohio, all of them earnest, sunburnt, and inquisitive. They were huddled around a beached sea slug, decrying its exceptional ugliness, and I took a hand in the discussion, told them its life pattern, defensive equipment, normal habitat, natural enemies, and so on. And I discovered to my great pleasure that this batch was literate! They had read books. Actual books. They had all read *Lives of a Cell* and are willing to read for the rest of their lives. They'd all been exposed to the same teacher in the public school system there, and he must be a fellow of great conviction. In a nation floundering in functional illiteracy, sinking into the pre-chewed pulp of television, it heartens me to know that here and there are little groups of young-uns who know what an original idea tastes like, who know that the written word is the only possible vehicle for transmitting a complex concept from mind to mind, who constantly flex the muscles in their heads and make them stronger. They will run the world one day, Travis. And they won't have to go about breaking plate glass and skulls and burning automobiles to express themselves, to air their frustrations. Nor will these children be victimized by the blurry nonsense of the so-called social sciences. The muscular mind is a cutting tool, and contemporary education seeks to take the edge off it."

"As you have said before."

"What? Sorry about that. Lecture Eighty-six C."

"Did you hear about the Norman girl in Omaha?"

We settled into deep canvas chairs in the cockpit of the *John Maynard Keynes.* "I heard on the noon news," he said, and got up and unlocked the hatch to below-decks, went down, and came back with two icy bottles of Dos Equis, drank deeply from his, wiped his mouth on the back of a heavy and hairy hand, and said, "The body will turn up, perhaps, sooner or later."

"Lysa Dean is okay. I talked to her a little while ago. Alerted her. I think she'll keep her guard up. I told her that if he gets to her, to tell him where to find me."

In a little while I noticed how motionless he was, how he was staring into the distance. When a lady stalked by wearing a string bikini, a big pink straw hat, and high-heeled white sandals, Meyer didn't even give her the glance she had earned. She went off into the dazzle of white hot afternoon.

Finally he stirred, sighed, finished his beer. "There is certain standard information about Desmin Grizzel. Raised in Riverside, California, out on the edge of the desert, a one-parent family, with the children divided among foster homes when the mother was killed in a midnight brawl in a parking lot. Desmin went from foster home to reformatory to penitentiary, emerged into the close fellowship of the outlaw biker. A passable mechanic. A brawler. A skilled rider. And so there he was, riding toward his very limited destiny, when Peter Kesner came into his life and told Grizzel, Hanner, and their associates he wanted to use them in a motion picture. Probably they thought it some kind of joke. They became Dirty Bob and the Senator, lived the parts, made production suggestions, and so forth and

255 —

so forth. It's all in the fan magazines. So they became celebrities, cult heroes to a limited segment of America. Two movies. And the consequent talk shows, endorsements, public appearances at biker meets, races, and rallies. And some bit parts in TV series and B movies.

"Desmin Grizzel read the press releases about how, by accident, his life had been changed. He had been pulled up out of the great swamp of common folk and placed on a hilltop, where he vowed that he had seen the light, that he would never return to the wicked ways of his prior life. This is always a popular theme. I think that Desmin Grizzel began to enjoy security, if not respectability. He was closing in on forty. He had done a dirty little chore for Kesner, and he had worked Kesner for as much of Josie's money as he could grab, put it into the security of a beach house, vehicles, bonds, and the lawyer working on his pardon.

"He had made it possible for Kesner to get seed money for the new motion picture project. He had bunted his old friend Hanner over a cliff, removing an irritant and a possible danger. He was Kesner's gofer, taking orders perhaps slightly demeaning for a man who had once been a star in his own right. Then, in the matter of the tapes, he had a chance to indulge simultaneously his yearning to be on camera and also his sadistic appetites, apparently not realizing the danger involved in not hiding his identity.

"And it all went to hell. He saw Kesner die and saw you survive. He hid out somewhere, somehow, for nearly two months. Wanted. Pictured in all post offices. Federal indictment and local indictments in Iowa. Now what is his concept of his future? There is no possible way he can fit himself back into any area of security and respectability. No way at all. The myth of redemption is shattered. The fans of past years are gone. The onetime outlaw biker is once again an outlaw. Back to his origins. Society raised him up and then smacked him down, leaving him no out. He's not the sort of creature who'd turn himself in. He's a predatory animal. Big, heavy, nimble, and cruel. The fact he was tamed for a little while makes him more dangerous. He's on the move because he has somehow acquired a safe identity that gives him mobility. I would say that he probably thinks of himself in some strongly dramatic context, as a betrayed man who will take out the betrayers before the pack brings him down. The betrayers are the Norman girl, Joya Murphy-Wheeler, Lysa Dean, you, and possibly some others. He can take a lot of pleasure in the hunt, sharpened and sweetened by the knowledge that these are the last acts of his life."

"Meyer, you can't climb inside his skull."

"I know that. I can try to come close."

"He could be into a lot of heavy things that could addle his wits. He could just be thrashing around."

"True."

"But I might as well try to reach Joya."

"It shouldn't hurt," he said.

I couldn't find the number I had written down for her. I got it from information and then waited until she would be likely to be home from work. I went over what I wanted to tell her. She had seemed very forthright and direct. I remembered how she smiled when I finally experienced that strange pleasure of the balloon journey at low altitude across the land.

The voice that answered was frail and tentative. "Hello?"

"Is Joya there?"

"No. Who is calling?"

"This is Travis McGee. In Florida."

"Were you a friend?" The past tense froze my heart.

"Who are you?"

"Alpha. I'm her sister. What was it you wanted with her, Mr. McGee?"

"Is it possible to speak to her?" I knew instinctively how dumb that question was.

"No, sir. It is not possible. We had the services for her yesterday. She is... she has passed on."

"What happened to her?"

"You aren't another newspaper person, are you?"

"No. I went ballooning with your sister."

"She was crazy about that. She loved it. She always said it was worth it, but I couldn't see it. That's another thing I got to sell of hers, I guess, her share in that stupid balloon."

"You're the executor?"

"Sort of. She was divorced a long time ago and there weren't any children. She came back here to stay at the home place all alone. I mean I've got a husband and children and a life of my own. I told Joya that she shouldn't live here alone. It's on just a farm road, you know. Like two trucks a day go by."

"What happened to her?"

"Well, it happened last Thursday, the eighteenth. What she always did, except when the weather was bad, she'd get up and put on her running clothes and take a long hard run and come back and shower and eat breakfast and go to work. She kept herself in wonderful shape. Bruno always ran with her. He's part Airedale, and practically human. They never have found Bruno. When she didn't show up at work and didn't phone in, finally a girl friend of hers that works there phoned me, and I phoned Alan at the store, and we drove out there, and I used my key to get in. The burner was turned low under the coffeepot and it had boiled dry. The clothes she planned to wear to work were laid out on the bed. By then it was noon. Well, by late afternoon there must have been fifty people hunting for her, and they found her body finally in tall grass a quarter mile from the house. She had been beaten. Her poor face was a mess. Somebody had raped her and then knotted one of the pant legs of the jogging suit around her neck, very tight. The grass was all matted, like animals had been fighting there. Practically everybody in the whole area has been questioned about whether they saw strangers around. Whoever it was, they had a long time to get out of the area. It seems like such a terrible waste. I'm almost glad Momma died last year so she wasn't alive to know what happened to Joya."

"Are there any suspects?"

"I don't know. I don't think so. After the funeral yesterday, we—Alan and me—we talked to a fellow Alan went to school with. He has something to do with the law. He said it could have something to do with all that trouble over at Rosedale Station, but of course Joya left there before anything happened. Everybody thinks it was just some bum, some vagrant, some kind of drifter. There's so much crazy violence around these days. Well...I'm here trying to pack up her things. What is your name again? McGee. Oh, God, I was about to say that I'd tell Joya you called. I've got to hang up now. I'm going to cry again."

I talked to Meyer again in the evening, aboard my houseboat.

I explained to him my reservations about the professionalism of one Forgan. "From the conversation I had with Kesner after Forgan left, I know that Forgan told Kesner that Mrs. Murphy-Wheeler had put in a complaint about their making the dirty tapes on location. A citizen who complains to the authorities should be protected, unless he or she is willing to make sworn statements."

"Maybe she was. Or maybe Mr. Forgan didn't take it all that seriously. Maybe he thought he was dealing with somebody who'd been released or fired, trying to get even."

"Okay. But I was the idiot who told Grizzel about it when I sat with him and with Jean Norman later."

"If you hadn't mentioned it to him, certainly Kesner would have, Travis. And probably long before you saw Grizzel. Kesner would have wanted to warn him about Forgan and his partner looking around the area. You pick up imaginary guilt the way serge picks up lint."

"Joya was a very able and happy lady. She was outraged about how they had turned Jean Norman around. She wanted people punished. And I think it got her killed."

"But you didn't get her killed."

"Okay, Meyer. All right. I didn't."

The midnight news told us that the nude battered body of Jean Norman had been taken out of the Missouri River by a police launch after having been reported by a tug captain. It said that authorities believed there was a possible connection between the murder of Miss Norman on Sunday night and the brutal rape murder of Mrs. Murphy-Wheeler near Ottumwa the previous Thursday morning. Law enforcement units all over the Midwest were on the alert for any information as to the whereabouts of Desmin Grizzel. Bikers in nine states were being stopped and interrogated.

"And that is the one way he would not travel," Meyer said.

"I don't see how he can risk any kind of traveling, not with that well-known face."

"He's found something that works," Meyer said. "Think about Jean Norman. Would she have walked over to a wall to talk across it to Desmin Grizzel? To talk to something out of her nightmares? I'll bet she had no idea until he grabbed her and yanked her across and took her into the bushes. Would Joya, dressed for running, let Grizzel catch up with her?"

"He can't disguise his dimensions. He's the size of an offensive guard. Six two, two sixty or seventy, great big gut."

After I thought about it a while, I phoned Lysa Dean. It was a little after ten in the evening her time.

"You again?" she said. "Look, I've got guests."

"I can hear them. I won't take up much time, okay?"

"What is it?"

"Dirty Bob managed to get very close to two people who had every reason to be very wary of him."

"The woman in Omaha and the one in Iowa?"

"You've been keeping track. Good. I'm trying not to be boring about this, Lee. I don't know if there's any chance of him coming after you. I don't know if he wants to get to me that much. I don't know how much risk he's willing to accept, how crazy he is. But you know the dimensions of him."

"Big big old boy."

"Just don't put any trust at all in any stranger who comes in that size, man or woman. He can disguise everything but his size."

"I shall consider myself warned."

"I could come out there. A live-in guard."

"Well, you do tempt me, but no, thanks."

20

The Thursday newspapers carried diagrams of the floor plan of the Lysa Dean house, with those Germanic-looking crosses newspapers use to indicate where bodies are found.

A person or persons unknown had snapped the gardener's neck and flung him into the pool. The slender Korean woman who had served us the salad and tea had been chopped across the nape of the neck with a kitchen cleaver wielded with such force it was clear that she had been dead before her body hit the kitchen floor. Lysa Dean had evidently been caught a few feet from the panic button of her alarm system, in the corner of her bedroom near the bed.

It had happened, as near as could be judged, at eleven in the morning on Wednesday, the twenty-fourth. Miss Dean had not been on call that day. The dotted line showed that the intruder had been admitted to the grounds by the gardener, through the front gate. He, or they, had killed the gardener near the rear entrance to the kitchen area. He or they had then slain the maid, who had been fixing Miss Dean's breakfast of tomato juice, dry toast, and tea, and gone through the house to find Miss Dean just leaving her dressing room. There she had been chased, caught, taken to her custom bed, and brutalized. Broken fingers, chipped teeth, and bruises, which were said to have happened at least an hour before death, indicated that she had been kept alive for a considerable amount of time before she was finally smothered by being jammed face down into her pillows.

There were the inevitable references to the Manson murders, to which they bore no resemblance at all. There was editorial comment in the newspapers and on television about drugs, terrorism, pornography, the ineffectuality of the law, the vulnerability of prominent persons, the decay of morality, the decline of values.

Sidebar stories detailed her long career in cinema and television, her marriages and divorces, her awards, her life-style. Others gathered comment from people she had worked with and worked for.

"It is a sad and sickening loss. I hope whoever did this terrible thing will be brought to justice."

"She had a lively style, a quick and earthy wit. Television will be the poorer for her loss."

"Lysa Dean was an unashamedly sensuous woman who very much enjoyed her life and enjoyed being Lysa Dean."

"Everybody I know is out buying more locks and chains and alarm systems. You wouldn't believe the panic that has hit this town. It's like we're back to the Charlie Manson days all over again."

An editorial expressed bafflement at how any suspicious person or persons could have avoided detection by any of the public and private patrols. But it did say that it was a lot easier to invade the area during broad daylight than at night. Deliveries were made during the daylight hours, and unlike some of the newer secure communities, there was no central checkpoint through which all traffic had to pass.

I had a feeling of loss, but in some strange way it was diluted by the many faces of Lysa Dean. There was so much artifice involved, so much playing of games, so much posing, I could not identify the single specific person who was gone. And indeed it was that bewildering variety which had made me uncharacteristically less than eager to bed her down both times she had made her availability unmistakable. There is a curious reluctance to play that ultimate game with a composite of strangers, with all the faces of one particular Eve. She was lively, fun to be with, but I did not know her. Perhaps the closest I had come to comprehending the real Lysa Dean was when I had been in her little projection room and seen her collection of X-rated tapes and her little drawer containing the massager. Maybe at the very heart of her there was an icy and unbelievable loneliness.

I looked up the number for Ted Blaylock's Oasis. Mits answered.

"Who? Wait a sec, I got to shut the door there's so much noise out back....Okay. Who'd you say?...Oh, McGee! Hey, how is it going?"

"How is it going with you?"

"Pretty much okay, I guess. I tell you, it is very damn noisy here, with a lot of big yellow machines churning around out in back."

"What are they doing?"

"Lots of things at once. A fence and a wall and an airstrip and some kind of generator plant. They don't tell me anything hardly. We're getting a lot of business from those guys working here, though, and the motorsickle business is holding up okay. Did you get your dividend? No? I got mine. Monday. Five hundred cash, and then there was a check for salary on account of I'm sort of being a manager while they're looking for one. Somebody will probably bring you your dividend. Preach told me, he said, 'Don't declare it, kid. It's for spending.'"

"I want to know how I can get hold of Preach. I tried the number for Karma Imports in Miami and they told me they never heard of anybody named Preach or anybody named Amos Wilson. Then I tried Daviss Grudd and he said that he never gets in touch with Preach; Preach is the one who makes contact."

"Well...I have this number to call in case some kind of county or state inspectors show up out here asking lots of questions. If it wasn't any emergency, he might get sore at me."

"It's an emergency, Mits. Really."

Though reluctant, she gave me the number.

It was a Miami number. I phoned, a man answered, I asked for Preach, and he came on the line.

"I met you out at Blaylock's," I said. "You and the fellow with you talked to me out by the cabins in back."

"How far are you from a pay phone, timewise?"

"Ten minutes."

"Go look at the number, come back and phone this number, and give the pay phone number to whoever answers. Then get back there and expect a call at half past on the button. What time you got?"

"Eleven before three."

"You're two minutes fast." *Click.*

I did as instructed and went back to the pay phone affixed to a marine wall in its plastic shell.

It rang on schedule. "McGee here," I said.

"My hard-nose hero buddy. You better be very entertaining, because I am taking time off from something worth more money than you'll ever make in your life. Also, McGiggle, I am going to have somebody bouncing some little Indian piece off some walls for giving out a number."

"I conned her out of it, Preach. Don't be hard on her."

"So what is this emergency situation you have to take me out of a meeting?"

"Remember we talked about Dirty Bob and the Senator."

"They have come up in the news now and then. The Senator crashed."

"With, I think, some help. On the right kind of road, with no traffic in sight, all Dirty Bob would have to do is lean into the Senator, give him a little shoulder."

"That cat's right name was in the paper. Desmin Grizzel."

"I convinced myself he's the one that beat the old man to death. I told you about that."

"What has that got to do with the price of anything?"

"Chalk up also one pot-head girl named Jean Norman, one balloonist-type lady named Joya, and one movie-queen quiz-show-type person named Lysa Dean, along with her Korean servants."

"Busy old bastard, ain't he? They *think* he totaled

the movie lady. If he did, I take it on the unkindly side. I always thought I might get a chance to get so famous I could run out there and boff that lady a couple dozen times. But again, pal, so what?"

"It's a reasonable assumption he is going to come to Lauderdale and take care of me next."

"If he does, I suppose I will read about that in the papers too."

"You and Magoo are supposed to be the top brass of the Fantasies. You remember the pin I was wearing that day? Doesn't that give me the right to call upon the brotherhood for assistance? I am a genuine affiliated, associated sort of member."

"I am giving up all that motorcycle shit and that one-for-all-and-all-for-one shit and that childish brotherhood shit. If you need protection, call the cops."

"You are probably a little less interested in doing business with the cops than I am. But not a hell of a lot less, Preach. I don't need that kind of exposure. I need some people as near like Grizzel as I can get. Fight fire with fire."

"Forget it. Solve your own problems."

"When I tried to get hold of you, I tried Daviss Grudd. He couldn't help me. But he did say that within a short time I'll be a half owner of that business out there, and I'll be able to do anything with my stock that I want."

"If you've got any idea of trying to push me around, I'd better tell you we're willing and able and ready to do your elbows any time. You'll have to hire somebody to pick your nose."

"Who said anything about pushing you around? I really don't need any part of any motorcycle emporium and tattoo parlor, Preach."

"Even if it spins off five hundred tax-free a month?"

"I thought I might sign my interest over to the Gold Coast League of Retired Executives with the stipulation that they can't sell that half interest. If they try, they have to give it back to me."

"What kind of an outfit is that?"

"Just what it says. Retired executives from big industry who have banded together to run small business and do consulting work. They know all about corporations and overhead and voting rights and all that stuff. They run things as a hobby."

"Jesus Christ, dozens of old silver-tips crawling all over the place? That's a rotten idea."

"Not so. They'd turn it into a real profit out there."

He was silent for a time. "I certainly wouldn't want my brothers in the Fantasies to think I had turned down a legitimate plea for help from a genuine affiliated associated kind of member."

"And on the other hand, Mits might like to own the whole place."

"I think we can always get along, McGee. We're so much alike."

"What I want are two very hard people, one little wiry one and one big one with muscles. A couple of years back I would have tried to hero this thing myself. But with this one, I want to be totally sure."

"Should they be carrying?"

"If licensed, okay. If not, I can supply."

"One more time, friend. I had you checked out after our talk. You came on so hard-nose, it got my curiosity up. So I know where you live and how you live, and it is more small-time than I would have guessed. Okay, I can send you a couple of the best. So this Dismal

Gristle comes calling and has a sudden heart attack. Whether or not cops move in at that point is something I need to know before I pick the two people."

"I will go over it with them, and if they think it can be handled so quietly there will be no police, then they stay and help. Otherwise, they're free to go."

"Fair enough. You want an inconspicuous arrival."

"And soon. Slip F-Eighteen."

"The old houseboat with the sunken tub. I know."

"This isn't like you," Meyer said, after I explained it.

"I know. What I had last year was enough incredible luck to last me the rest of my life. So I am counting on not having any at all, or having it turn up all bad. Look, I have sat at table with this cat. He is something impressive."

"Like Boone Waxwell?"

"Yes. Except bigger and stronger and quicker and, I think, even more warped in the head than Waxwell was. There is a kind of surface plausibility about him that Waxwell didn't have. More shrewd, I think. Look, I went over it. They have a police guard on Josephine Laurant on the far-off chance he might have her on his crazy list. I talked to Annie Renzetti into hiding out with good friends and not leaving word at the hotel where she went, just in case he might know about her from talking to Kesner. I thought of being bait and using you as backup, but I just don't have the confidence that I could protect myself and you too."

"You think I would be just standing there maybe?"

"Don't get sore. A man who can do the unthinkable without a half-second hesitation has a lead over you and me. And more over you than over me. Don't think of it as a criticism. Nine out of ten adult males would find it impossible, thank God, to shove a knife into the belly of a fellow human, even if their own life seemed in danger."

"You're setting him up to kill him?"

"If I have to. If I can't take him, I want somebody there who will, because I do not want him loose in the world."

My assistants arrived just after dusk, an hour after Meyer had gone back to his cruiser. I checked them out before I opened up.

"Preach sent us," the small one said. "I'm Gavin. This here is Donnie."

"How did you come?"

"Car. Parked way down and walked in."

After I had closed the lounge draperies, I turned on more lights and took a better look at them. Gavin was pallid, sandy, compact as a jockey or a good flyweight. There was a flavor of Australia in his diction. He was in his thirties. His blond sideburns came down to the corners of his mouth. He wore a white guayabera, dark red slacks, Mexican sandals. Donnie was younger, tall, lazy-looking, with dark hair modeled in a wave across his forehead, with a heavy drooping mustache. He wore a work shirt, khaki shorts, and running shoes. His legs, though very tanned, looked thick and soft.

"You know what this is about?"

"Somebody wants to blow you away, Preach said. You want us to make sure it doesn't happen," Gavin said.

"Are you people armed?"

"Donnie's got nothing. I got a knife." He wore it between his shoulder blades, with the blade up for grasping, for quick grasp and quicker throw, with a full snap of the arm. It's a French fashion, deadly when the man has years of practice.

I watched them handle the handguns I gave them. I gave Gavin the Airweight Bodyguard from the bedside holster, and gave Donnie the Colt Diamondback from the medicine cabinet hidey-hole. They checked the weapons with reassuring aplomb, spinning the cylinders, dry firing, then loading. I took the nine-millimeter automatic pistol for myself, the staggered box magazine holding the full fourteen rounds.

Then I showed them what I had in mind. I made them practice the routine over and over until they could get into their hiding places quickly enough to suit me.

There is a full-length mirror affixed to the bulkhead at the end of the short corridor between the two staterooms. Quite a while ago I had a master carpenter move the bulkhead out a few inches and make a stowage locker on the other side shallower. The two-way glass mirror is hinged on one side, held in place by a catch which can be released by shoving a wire brad into an almost invisible hole in the right side of the mirror frame. A man can step in, pull the mirror door shut, fasten it with a simple turn block. As it is only twelve inches deep, he cannot turn around. He has to step in backward, and he can watch the corridor from there. Donnie fit the space with little to spare. Gavin fit reasonably well in the stowage locker in the lounge, the one with the upholstered top used for extra seating. I had emptied it out before their arrival. There was a small hole near the floor which gave him limited vision and better hearing.

"I want to make sure I understand," Gavin said. "We're backup. We're insurance. If there's big action, we bust out and take him if we have to. Or if things start to go sour for you, the code word is Preach?"

"If I have to use it, I'll yell it, and I'll be moving fast by then."

"What does this dude look like? Is there just one?"

"You've probably seen him in movies. He played the part of Dirty Bob."

Donnie spoke up in his slow deep voice. "He's nothing but a movie actor, isn't he?"

"Outlaw biker first."

"And he's been killing women," Gavin said. "I read about it. He's a bloody big sod, that one. Is he really mean?"

"Yes."

"What does he want with you, McGee?"

"He blames me for the death of a friend, the man who put him in the movies. I don't think he needs much reason. I think he is probably certifiably insane."

"When do you think he'll show up?"

"Yesterday he was in Los Angeles. He was there looking for my address. He's had thirty or more hours to get here."

"People know his face, don't they?" Donnie said.

"One time that I know about, he and his friend came across the country on motorcycles in fifty hours."

"Good time," Gavin said, "but it beats you to death."

"If it turns out that there is any way to take him alive, I'd like that."

"To give to the law?"

"Yes."

"Okay, if you keep us out of it," Donnie said. "We'll keep it in mind. But it looks safer if we kill him. How long do we go before you decide he isn't coming?"

"Until Sunday night?"

"Preach didn't tie any strings on it," Gavin said. "So it's whatever you say, mister."

"You've been...uh...involved in this sort of thing before?" I asked.

"Better you shouldn't ask," Gavin said with a sandy little smile. "We eat here, I suppose?"

"I put provisions aboard. And liquor."

"Donnie and me, we don't drink except after a job is over. Look, I didn't mean to turn you off about what you asked. I'll tell you this much. For what you've got in mind, you won't find any better south of Atlanta. Okay?"

"Glad to know it."

"You live aboard here all the time?" Gavin asked. "What do you do for a living? You retired?"

I smiled at him. "Better you shouldn't ask."

"Anyway, Preach must owe you a big one. I'm not asking. Okay? I was just making a remark."

21

The slightest pressure on the mat where people come aboard the *Flush* from the dock at the stern, where the hinged rail is flipped over and latched, rings the small warning bell—a solemn *bong,* like a discreet telephone in an advertising office.

It sounded in the early afternoon on Friday, on a day that seemed hotter than all the rest, hot enough to bring the water in the yacht basin to a slow boil, bubble the varnish on the play toys, make the metalwork too hot to touch. The sky hung low in a thick white glare. The air conditioning groaned away, eating my purse. Through the narrow gaps in the draperies I could see the tourists on the docks, milling around in slow motion, straining for a good time.

At the *bong,* I was in the galley, looking at the labels on the canned goods. Gavin and Donnie were in the lounge. They slipped quickly, quietly, neatly away to their assigned places.

The pistol was tucked into my belt, under the oversized yellow shirt, slanted on the left side, grip toward the right, handy for grasping. There are many schools, going back to the flintlock dueling-pistol days when it was thought advisable to present one's body in profile to the opponent, the right side—the side without the heart in it—nearer the opponent. The gunslinger school had its own mythology. I had long since worked it out to my own satisfaction. It was the shortest travel distance for my right hand, and as I pulled it free, I could pivot into a full-faced squat, weapon held in two hands, aiming it for full instinctive spray, like a man putting out a fire at gut height.

I touched it through the shirt to be certain it was properly positioned, went to the rear entrance to the lounge, thumbed the curtains aside, and saw Meyer's solid and reliable face a few inches beyond the door.

I unlocked the door, and just as I swung it open, the delayed warning hit me. There had been something wrong about Meyer. I backed away and he came in, moving in such a slow and uncertain way, it was as if he had forgotten how to walk. He wore a dull apologetic smile, and all the bright hot light had gone out of his little blue eyes.

The old man was right behind him, bent over, nodding, muttering to Meyer. A wattled old man with a naked polished skull, a soiled blue long-sleeved shirt, dark greasy pants, sneakers.

He urged Meyer in, slammed the door behind them with a flip of his elbow, and then, as he straightened to full height, he pushed Meyer roughly ahead of him. Meyer stumbled and nearly went down. I saw the weapon revealed, the one he had been holding against Meyer's back, four short ugly barrels of a large-caliber derringer. Grizzel stepped over to me and said, "Pull the front of that pretty yellow shirt up, Ace. Slow and easy."

With the four barrels aimed at my face, I didn't feel as if I even dared breathe. He lifted the pistol out of my belt with his left hand, squatted, and placed it on the floor, and with the edge of his foot he scuffed it into a corner without looking at it.

I glanced at Meyer. There was going to be no help there. It happens sometimes. I think it is the deep unwavering conviction that life is about to end. It is an ultimate fear, immobilizing, squalid. It crowds everything else out of the mind. There is no room for hope, no chance of being saved. I have seen it happen to some very good men, and most of them did indeed die badly and soon, and the ones who did not die were seldom the same again. Were a man to awaken from sound sleep to the dry-gourd rattle of a diamondback coiled on his chest, head big as a fist, forked tongue flickering, he would go into that dreadful numbness of the ultimate fright.

"You've changed," I said in a dry-mouthed voice.

"Sit on the floor!" Grizzel said to Meyer. Meyer sat so quickly and obediently he made a thick thudding sound. Grizzel kept his eyes on me. "Down a hundred pounds. Tried to hold at one ninety, but it wouldn't stop. Something in here, eating on me, Ace. Like fire and knives, all the time. That old fart trying to buy hash for his misery, I put him out of it, and now I got it myself. We got to find some nice quiet way to do you, Ace. Right in the middle of all these boats and folks. Maybe your best buddy in all the world can give me a little help with you."

"Why me?" I asked.

His eyes were the same. Nothing else. "Why not you? You and Joya fucked up the world for Peter K and yours truly. With Freaky Jean's help. All my life you smartass people have been on top. It's my final sworn duty to bring you down, every one of you I can get to, and I have got to a lot so far."

"Including the Senator?"

"No time for confession hour. Wish I had time to tell you about the snuff job on that movie-queen pal of yours. Would have made a great tape, Ace." He motioned toward his crotch with his free hand. "Old King Henry here hasn't lost an ounce, and he can go as good as he ever did. Should have seen Jeanie's eyes too, when she saw who the hell it was she was talking to, who this skinny old man all bent over, with the whiny voice and limp, who he really was. Strong kid. Fought nice. That's when it's best, when you got a fighter."

"You get around pretty good, pretty quick."

"Stall, stall, stall. I don't think I'm going to get any help from your dearest closest buddy here, which is what everybody calls him. Peed his pants. I travel nice, Ace. Good luggage, good clothes, first class all the way. Money came mostly from country stores, where by the time you bust the second finger on them, they tell you what shelf the money is hid on, and it is more than you can imagine. Tried a bike, but the bones of my ass are too close to the surface. These are my working clothes, Ace. Harmless old saggy fart, shuffling around. Lots of wrinkles from the weight dropping off so fast."

His glance flicked away from me and back again, over and over, so quickly it gave me no chance at all. He was looking the interior over. "What I want you should do, Ace, is let yourself down very very slow and easy. Thaaaaat's it. Hitch a little bit more toward me. Now lay back nice and slow. Good boy."

He sidled into the galley, moving with the speed of an angular bug, and emerged instantly with one of my steak knives in his left hand. "You won't hardly feel this at all, Ace."

He moved cautiously toward me. Beyond him I saw the padded cover of the stowage locker lift silently, and I saw Gavin stand up, right hand high, holding the throwing knife. I think Grizzel saw a reflection of the movement out of the corner of his eye in one of the lounge ports. And he was quick. My God, he was quick! He swiveled and fired, and the slam of the shot in that enclosed space was deafening. Gavin's grunt of effort came simultaneously with the shot. There was a silvery glint in the air, and Grizzel dropped with an eerie bony thud. He dropped loose, agawk, open eyes almost immediately dusty, without further breath or quiver, wearing the braided leather grip of the throwing knife in the crenelated socket of his throat, under the loose jowls. The slug had taken Gavin in the center of the chest, banged him back against the bulkhead, and from there he had rebounded to fall face down, heart shredded, toes still hooked over the edge of the locker.

Donnie squatted beside him and laid his fingers on Gavin's throat. "Goddamn," he whispered. "Oh, goddamn, goddamn, goddamn."

I could hear no running outside, no shouts of query, or noises of excitement. The muffled explosion had passed unnoticed.

Donnie placed my Colt carefully on the coffee table. He said, "Just hold tight, huh. I'll come back with the word."

Meyer and I were alone with the bodies. He looked up at me with the querulous expression of a child who cannot understand why it has been so punished. Tears ran down his face.

I helped him up and he looked down at Grizzel's corpse and walked woodenly to the head and closed the door quietly behind him. I heard the water running.

Donnie returned in a half hour. His eyes looked pink and irritated. In his slow and heavy voice he said, "What will happen, it will be a cleaning truck, maybe in three quarters of an hour, and the security will let them in here for a pickup, right? This carpeting is shot. Better you shouldn't try to get it cleaned. They will take it up and roll them up in it at the same time and horse them out to the truck, and you can forget it from then on. Any stains came through, they're your problem. Preach don't want no contact from you."

"What will they do with them?"

"Usually it's construction foundations where they go." He straightened and sighed. "Me, I got to tell his girl he had to go back home to Sydney, Australia, on a family emergency."

Epilogue

On an August afternoon I worked the *Busted Flush* into a bayou ringed with mangrove down near the mouth of the Snake River, below Naples. There, like a mother spider, I began building my web of lines, finding good holding ground for anchors, tying off other lines to the sturdiest mangroves, and making allowance for big tides.

A medium hurricane named Carl was due to bash Cuba by midnight, on a course that would carry its diminished muscle up through the Straits of Yucatán. We would get some of the fringe of it, and if it curved back toward the Florida west coast, we might get a hell of a lot more of it than we wanted.

We had plenty of fresh water, fuel, and provisions, and Annie was excited and stimulated by the idea of sitting it out. The afternoon was hazy white, with high tendrils of unusual-looking clouds and some burly rain clouds over the Gulf.

After she had helped me do everything I felt we could do to assure our safety, we went up onto the sun deck and sat under the canopy at the topside controls in the big captain's chairs where we could watch the weather.

Out of nowhere she said, "I still feel pretty strange about you getting yourself associated with people like that Preach."

"Who is associated?"

"How about through that Indian person, that Mits?"

"She owns the whole ball game now."

"But doesn't she give you money?"

"She tries hard."

"Doesn't it come from some kind of rotten source, like drugs?"

"Probably. Indirectly."

"Am I boring you?"

I turned and grinned at her. "Not most of the time."

"It's just that I want you to be—"

"Respectable?"

"That's not the right word. It's not as stuffy a word as that."

"Independent?"

"Closer."

"That is something I have always been, Annie, and always will be. I steer through a pretty crowded track, and once in a while I brush up against a Preach, who wants to tame me by breaking my elbows, or a Dirty Bob, who wants to punish me by killing my friends. Okay, I have a lot of moves. Earnest apology. Happy sapistry. A good straight left hand when needed. They nearly had me quelled, kid. That was before all this with Esterland."

"Will you tell me all about it sometime?"

"Probably. They had the lid almost hammered down on me. But I couldn't take a life that flat. You know.

Things have to move. Like, I lied to you about not being able to run away from the storm. We probably could have. But this is a better way."

"I know we could have. I checked the charts."

"I have a lot of trouble with bright women."

"You couldn't stand any other kind." She hesitated, biting her lip. "After the storm, are we going to hurry back to Lauderdale?"

"If you can call anything this crock can do hurrying."

"I think about Meyer."

"So do I. Look, he has to be alone for a time. Maybe it is long enough by now. I hope so. He failed his image of himself because I think he fashioned that image a little too closely to his image of me. I am more of a physical person than Meyer. He has too much imagination. That's what helps people break themselves. He didn't expect it. He's been in tighter spots. This time he saw something in the crazed, dying, evil eyes of that man. He saw his death there, and it sucked the heart right out of him. And he's ashamed, though he shouldn't be."

"Have you told him he shouldn't be?"

"Of course. I told him it can happen to anyone at any time, and I tried to tell him it had happened to me too. It almost did, once. But not quite. And I couldn't lie well enough to convince him."

"What will happen?"

"He'll want to get into something rough. He'll look for a chance to try to recover his self-respect. And it might be a very close play indeed to try to keep him from getting himself killed. He seeks that absolution, the end of shame. And that is a primitive reaction. Whatever it is, I am going to have to help hunt for the situation, and I am going to have to see that he gets away with whatever foolish move he makes."

"Then he'll be okay again?"

"Practically. Not quite. Because he knows it can happen."

A breeze came skitting into the bayou, silvering the black water. She lifted her face to it. "Hey! Feel that!" It faded away, and a mosquito sang into my ear. "Will we get a lot of wind?"

"Maybe."

"Will it turn into a constant shrieking like they say?"

"Maybe. But it is a roaring kind of shriek. Deeper than plain old shrieking."

"Could we maybe, while it's roaring or whatever, make love?"

"I will certainly see if I can arrange it, Annie. I will put some thought to it. I really will."

AUTHOR'S NOTE

Should any reader care to know more about the past, present and future of McGee, Meyer and me, he or she can drop me a note at P.O. Box HH, Venice, Florida 33595, and I will put them in touch with the proper people at the University of South Florida who are involved in such a project.

JOHN D. MACDONALD

ABOUT THE AUTHOR

JOHN D. MACDONALD is the author of more than sixty books, including the best-selling *Condominium* and eighteen other novels in the Travis McGee series. His eighteenth, *The Green Ripper,* won the American Book Award for Best Mystery of 1979.